ERIN DAWN ALLEN

THE CRYSTAL IN THE CAVE

THE SORCERESS OF STARS TRILOGY

Dedication

To every teenager
with a story-filled notebook:

Keep writing.

I promise someone will read it
someday.

APRIL-MAY 967 CE

CHAPTER 1

THE DARK-HAIRED WOMAN'S perfume smelled like lemon and cloves, but that wasn't the first thing I noticed. No, the first thing I noticed was the stormy crackle in her voice when she snapped, "Does anyone even work here?"

I dropped the towels I was folding and rushed out to the common room. "I'm sorry, my lady," I apologized. She didn't have to tell me her title. Only a lady would wear such an elegant damask cloak, and only a lady would be so grumpy about not being helped immediately.

"I need rooms," she groused. "I was under the impression this is an inn. Is someone planning to help me, or should I set up my tarp outside?" She waved one arm toward the window. A flash of lightning lit the sky, and cold rain swept against the glass.

"I'm sorry, my lady," I repeated. "May I take your cloak?" I hung the sodden garb, keeping my face neutral as I silently fumed. How could I have known to expect a guest on such a miserable day?

Beneath her cloak, the woman wore men's clothes: black breeches, a billowing black shirt, and knee-high black riding boots. Even her hair looked black. Her golden skin marked her as from somewhere in the south, like maybe Qimorath, but she didn't have an accent as far as I could tell. She was perhaps in her mid-thirties judging by the slightest of lines about her eyes, though her commanding air suggested she might be older.

I glanced at my own reflection in the mirror above the bar: simple dark brown braid, blue dress, and light skin shadowed with the faintest ghost of last summer's freckles. Even though I was tall enough for seventeen, I felt like a child next to this daunting woman.

"I'll make sure your cloak dries, my lady. Can I get you anything else? Hot cider, mulled wine, warm bread?" I knew my speech by heart, having given it since I was ten.

"We'll wait till supper. But we would take baths. Two."

"Of course. Are you with your husband, my

lady?"

She lifted one brow, and she almost looked amused. Almost. "No. We also require two rooms. I assume you have the space?" She eyed the empty common room skeptically.

"Yes, my lady. Most guests won't come our way for another week or so." I hoped she wouldn't catch my lie. It's not a lie if I don't say that "or so" could be several months, I argued silently.

I hurriedly made up two beds with fresh sheets and knocked cobwebs from the corners. Truly, I should have cleaned these rooms weeks ago, but after three years of dwindling guests, we had all started to think we might never need them again. We always kept the lesser rooms ready, the ones with bunks that slept six, but I hadn't looked in the private suites all winter. Grumbling, I lit some candles. It was nearly noon, but the clouds cast a dark gloom.

Satisfied with my quick clean, I descended the staircase, calling out, "My lady, would you...?" I paused mid-step as the front door opened and a young man walked in.

He pushed back his hood and smiled. If the first thing I noticed about the woman was her anger, the first thing I noticed about this man was his mouth. His teeth were white and straight, and his lips were full and red. Or perhaps, I thought later, I actually noticed his eyes first. They were a smoldering gray, and they danced beneath his short dark hair on his light brown skin. I tried to smooth a smile from my face.

"I've put our horses in your stables, miss," he said to me as he handed bags to the strange woman. "But I didn't want to get settled until we were sure you had rooms." She nodded once at him, and he beamed at her. I felt strangely annoyed that it wasn't at me.

"My lord, my lady, our sincerest apologies." I flinched. I hadn't even heard my mother enter. "Our hostler is away with his wife before the birth of their first child. My husband Petyr will see to your horses. My daughter Ayve and I will help you get settled. Have you prepared a room, child?"

"Yes, Alys, two," I replied, and she didn't even flinch at the knowledge that this stunning noblewoman, the first to arrive since before Joseth was born, was traveling alone with a handsome man who wasn't her husband.

"Then please allow my daughter to take you upstairs, my lord and lady."

"Just lady," the man corrected kindly. "Though the gods know I wouldn't deny a lordship's money if it were offered. I'm Stevan. Just Stevan. And this is Lady Zaitreiha. Just remember 'Eye in a tree, ah!' if you forget," he said winking at me and gesturing at her height. A warm wave washed over my body, and I allowed myself a small smile back.

"I'm Alys," my mother replied, and I was jerked back to reality when she added, "Ayve, your duties."

I pasted a blank look on my face as we climbed the stairs, but inside I seethed. Once again, I had let my parents down. It would be one thing if they showed their frustration by yelling, but all they ever did was sigh. Alys was at least the kinder of the two, but I could count on one hand the number of times I had pleased Petyr. Joseth always seemed to make them happy. Then again, he was only three.

"Here we are," I said as I led them to their doors. "Your baths will be ready soon. Is there anything else I can do for you?"

It was only in the quiet hallway that I wondered how I hadn't noticed the woman's fierce violet eyes before. I couldn't look away; my own dark green eyes felt locked in their gaze.

"No," said Lady Zaitreiha, and I blinked when the tall woman finally looked away. "Thank you, Ayve," she called softly as they entered their rooms.

The voice felt somehow familiar, as if I had heard it long before. I straightened my apron nervously and hurried off to heat some water.

***

The strange pair kept to themselves at supper, huddled at the table near the fire while my parents and I frantically tried to clean. What if more noble guests arrived? Fortunately, the front door remained firmly shut. I washed tankards behind the bar, trying my best not to stare. Lady Zaitreiha was still in men's clothes, though she had wrapped a fur stole around her shoulders.

"Build up the fire," my father hissed quietly when he saw. I dragged over a bundle of wood, ignoring them politely as I fed the flames. I was grateful that the heat would excuse my blush. I couldn't hear their conversation perfectly, but I had a strange feeling it was about me.

"Just think about it, Zai," I heard Stevan say. "We could use the extra help. Gods know I could, anyway."

Lady Zaitreiha's voice was smooth. "I want real help, and not just for a few months. Or days."

I could almost feel Stevan's grin. "You're never going to let me live down my last choice, are you?" He picked up his tankard and drank deeply. Lady Zaitreiha reached for hers, and something clattered to the floor.

"I think you dropped something, my lady." I

reached for the object. It was a small stone, cloudy white and smooth, but as I picked it up, I could have sworn it flushed a soft purple. I yelped and nearly dropped it into Lady Zaitreiha's outstretched hand.

Lady Zaitreiha watched me curiously. Stevan, oddly, seemed to be scowling. "It's alright," she murmured. She gently laid a hand on my wrist. "And thank you. I feel I should apologize for my attitude earlier. I'm a bear when my feet are wet. I hope you can forgive me."

I nodded, dazed, and dusted ashes from my skirt. My arm positively tingled where Lady Zaitreiha had touched me. I was more than relieved when Alys called for my help in the kitchen. I stayed there for the rest of the night.

CHAPTER 2

IT WAS STILL CHILLY and wet the next morning. Spring always came late to the Kreely Mountains. We were fortunate that Jeren was in the foothills of the Kreiogny side of the border, so at least the little traffic our inn got lasted until late fall. Some of the inns on the Hendassan side were snowed in by mid-September.

I was nearly dressed when Alys barged in. "Take your brother," she said before dumping Joseth in my arms and leaving. I sighed and moved him to my bed.

I vividly remembered the day the midwife had placed her hands on Alys's apron-clad belly and declared her with child. My mother had been so overjoyed that she'd prayed to the gods for three whole days to thank them. I was thirteen then, more than old enough to know how babies happened, and more than old enough to be mildly embarrassed by it.

Now I was nearing eighteen, the same age Alys was when I was born. Try as I might, I couldn't imagine having children just yet. True, I loved Joseth, even though I spent most of my days keeping him out of trouble. With his sandy hair and sky-blue eyes, he was too cute to be mad at for long. Yet having a child in my belly at only seventeen! The thought gave me enough fear to stay away from boys entirely. Not that there were many boys in Jeren who interested me, especially none so handsome as a certain gray-eyed guest...

Feeling silly, I shook my head and turned to close a drawer when I glimpsed something inside. Smiling, I withdrew the palm-sized painting of a bustling city with the faint shadow of a castle behind lush green trees. As a child, it had been my prized treasure, and I had often begged Alys to tell me the story of how she found it:

One night many years ago, in the dark of winter before I was born, a mysterious woman came to Jeren. She spoke to no one and took no food or wine, only sat at a table and gazed out the window. And though no one could make out her face beneath her hood, everyone agreed that she smelled of summer, like lavender and honey. In the morning, she had vanished without a trace except for this painting, left propped against the window at the table where she'd been sitting.

I knew the story probably wasn't true. Most likely a guest had just left it behind, and Alys had made up a story to keep me entertained. Still, a small part of me wanted to believe that extraordinary things could happen in tiny Jeren.

Then Joseth shrieked, and I was brought back to my boring, ordinary life.

* * *

The air was cold and misty, but ten guests arrived that day, shocking me and my parents beyond belief. Four more wandered in at sunrise the next morning, and another half dozen arrived before noon.

"These guests go through so much," I grumbled as I helped Petyr hitch the horses to the wagon. He was off to the market for the second time that day to replenish our supplies.

"They can take whatever they want so long as they keep giving coin," he said, ever the matter-of-fact innkeeper. "Though I do look forward to Rafe's help." He had asked our hostler to return early to help run the stables, and Rafe had fortunately agreed. Petyr climbed up and grabbed the reins. "Take care of any new guests who arrive. And help Alys." He set off at a quick trot, the horses and wheels kicking up gobs of mud.

Fortunately, no new parties arrived while Petyr was gone, and we were given a much-needed respite after lunch. Guests sat around the common room nursing their drinks and playing the latest dice game from the capital. Lady Zaitreiha and Stevan had joined a small crew of merchants by the fire. I was grateful that it wouldn't need any more wood for a while. I hadn't forgotten the lady's shocking touch.

As I wiped down the bar, Stevan sauntered my way, all dazzling grin and kind eyes. I scolded my pulse into calming itself.

"I hear you have an excellent mead," Stevan said, nodding his head at an old merchant with gray stubble. Rooster. I had been serving the man mead since before I could remember.

"We usually do, but I'm afraid we've run out. Petyr has gone to town to fetch more. He should be back soon. But perhaps you'd like a glass of whiskey to tide you over, or some soft rolls and butter?" I batted my lashes, hoping I looked the part of the coy innkeeper's daughter. I somehow just felt like a dog doing tricks.

"I do believe that's our fault," a low voice hummed. Lady Zaitreiha was finally in women's clothes, a black dress with golden swirls embroidered on the bust. There was something in the air that nearly crackled around her.

"Beg pardon, my lady?" I stammered.

"It's our fault that you've run out of mead. We may be to blame for all your surprise guests. We were at a crowded hostel a week ago, minding our own business, when one of us just happened to overhear a conversation about a charming, rustic inn near our intended destination." She shot a glance at Stevan, who raised his hands and feigned innocence.

"Is it my fault if I have excellent ears?" he protested.

"You're lucky you have ears at all after Rooster realized you were listening," Lady Zaitreiha chided. "But after some, shall we say, philosophical discussions, we agreed with Rooster that this was the perfect place for us to stay."

I shot a glance at Rooster. He raised his tankard and grinned. He had guaranteed us a prosperous season.

"You forgot the most important part of the story," Stevan added. "The part that explains why they've run out. The part where you said you'd buy everyone in earshot a glass of the inn's best mead if they had hot baths when we arrived."

Lady Zaitreiha rolled her eyes and sighed as

Stevan waggled his eyebrows. "After our last adventure, can you blame me for wanting to be clean? We visited Trask last autumn," she told me, "only they had such a rainy season that we may as well have been marching around a swamp. I swear, it took weeks to get the grit out from under my nails."

The pair reminisced about their travels while I freshened their cups. Working at the bar, I relished every new story I heard about a world beyond Jeren.

"Have you traveled much, Ayve?" Lady Zaitreiha asked suddenly.

"No, my lady."

The woman looked at me thoughtfully. "Would you like to?"

I didn't know what to say. Was this what they were talking about the other night? Was the lady about to ask me to join them? I rubbed my sweaty palms on my apron. "I think—"

The front door burst open. Petyr entered, water puddling at his feet. "Ayve. Help us unload," he instructed. Alys bustled in behind him and shooed me out from behind the bar.

"Of course, Petyr." I nodded my apologies and hurried outside.

Rafe had returned with Petyr. He pulled wooden crates down from the wagon, straw-like hair plastered to his head, as his wife Martha unhitched the horses.

"Ayve!" she cried. "I haven't seen you since the harvest festival!" Martha had only just discovered she was with child then, her stomach a slight swelling beneath her apron. Today her dress stretched so far that the hem hung well above the ground.

"Ayve and Martha, my two favorite girls!" Rafe pulled us both into a tight squeeze. I had always had a soft spot for Rafe. We had grown up together, the innkeeper's daughter and the stableman's son. I was glad he had found a wife, even if everyone had always thought it would be me in Martha's place.

We unloaded crates in the kitchen, sharing stories of our winters. It had been a long season away from my friends, and I hadn't realized how lonely I'd become.

"Will you stay here when your time comes?" I asked Martha hopefully as we worked.

"If business stays like this, most certainly. Your mother said she would fix up the shed in the woods so I could have a quieter place for birthing."

"The shed!" I had almost forgotten about it. "That was always the best place to play pirates."

Rafe opened another box. "With a good

sweeping and some airing out, it'll be the perfect place for her. Maybe our little ones can even play their own games in there one day," he added, placing a hand on Martha's.

Their child would be just a few years younger than Joseth, I realized. They might even be playmates. Traveling with a strange noblewoman would mean I wouldn't get to see either of the children grow up. Surely adventure couldn't be worth that. If Lady Zaitreiha asked again, I had my answer.

CHAPTER 3

I WAS ALMOST FINISHED stoking the fire when I realized something was different. I cracked the front door and peered at the sky. The sun was just beginning to rise, and the barest hint of orange warmed a deep blue above the trees.

"I never thought the rain would let up, either." I jumped and turned, finding Lady Zaitreiha at the bottom of the stairs. She was once again in men's clothes, wearing her tall leather boots, thick brown trousers, and a dark leather jerkin over a flowing white shirt.

"They're just clothes, Ayve," Lady Zaitreiha said gently, and my face burned when I realized I was staring. "Where I come from, gender doesn't always define clothing. It's only when I'm away from home that I remember how unusual I must look."

"Where is your home?" The question flew from my lips before I could stop myself. I clapped a hand over my mouth. "I don't know what came over me. Please, you must be ready for breakfast if you're down so early. Can I bring you something while Alys finishes cooking? Tea, perhaps?"

Lady Zaitreiha watched me quietly. "That would be nice," she finally said. She sat by the fire, long legs stretched out in front of her while she waited. I could feel her eyes on me the whole time I worked. My hands shook slightly as I poured.

"Sit with me," Lady Zaitreiha instructed as I turned to leave. She gestured at the seat beside her. I knew I couldn't refuse, not after I had so rudely blundered. I sat in the seat directly across from the lady, hoping to keep some distance between us.

"It's not wrong to ask questions where I'm from, you know," Lady Zaitreiha said. I looked up from the table and met her eyes. Their purple hue still made me uneasy. Her bold brows were furrowed, though not cruelly. "It's a very different kind of place," she continued when I didn't reply. "People come from all over to live there. And we like to get to know each other by asking questions. Granted, sometimes it's a miserable, crowded, cesspool of a city" —she wrinkled her nose— "but it's a place where curiosity is rewarded, and adventure finds those who seek it. Have you decided? Do you wish for adventure, Ayve?"

I inhaled. I thought about Joseth and my friends' child-to-be. I opened my mouth, prepared to decline.

"Yes," I heard myself whisper. My head buzzed. "Yes, I want adventure. I want it more than anything," I breathed. A dash of bravery danced in my chest. "Where are you from, Lady Zaitreiha?"

"She's from Qiameth; you can tell by this 'I'm-so-dark-and-mysterious' performance," said Stevan as he entered. "Don't take her too seriously. I've seen her laugh herself into a hiccupping fit, so rest assured she can be as human as the rest of us."

Lady Zaitreiha rolled her eyes. "Ignore him. I certainly do. Sometimes I question why I ever took him on."

"Because you like me. And need me. And my charm."

"Anyway," she said, ignoring Stevan and turning back to me, "I would say I'm from Freodon, the capital of Kreiogny. I've lived there for years now, almost as long as I was in Qiameth. We both live there, though sometimes we let our adventures carry us elsewhere."

Stevan nodded at the door as Lady Zaitreiha spoke. "Speaking of adventure," he said, handing her a bag, "it's time for us to go."

"Go?" My head whirled from the speed of the conversation. Were they really leaving already? Without me?

Lady Zaitreiha smiled. "Just for the day. This time, anyway." I swore I saw a golden spark in her eyes.

"My lady, sir, good morning!" Alys rushed in from the kitchen, wiping her hands on a towel. I immediately popped up, ashamed to be found sitting with guests. "Can I fetch you some breakfast? Hot potato hash, fresh bread, fried eggs?"

"Thank you, but we're off to the lake today. We'd take some jerky, though. We have some food in our stores, but gods know I wouldn't begrudge extra jerky."

"Yes, of course. Though if I may offer a word of caution, my lady, there can still be snow this time of year. It's a lovely stroll for young couples in summer, though not so much in spring," she added, eyeing Stevan curiously.

Stevan smiled handsomely. "We've seen worse coming through these mountains. But perhaps we could use a guide. Could we borrow your daughter for the day?" My heart sank. I could have told him not to waste his breath on my pragmatic mother.

"What's that?" Petyr wiped his boots on the mat as he came in, handing a load of firewood to me.

"We'd like to borrow Ayve for the day, please. We need a guide to the lake." I stacked the wood noisily, heart jumping into my throat.

"We'll pay, of course," Lady Zaitreiha added smoothly. "We wouldn't want to get lost, especially if there could be snow, and she must know the way better than we do." Her long legs led her to my father, and a coin purse jingled merrily. Though I couldn't see what she pressed against his palm, it had to be too much, more than I was worth, from the way my father's eyes and mouth widened into O's.

"Of course, my lady," he replied without missing a beat. He was all business, my father, and not one to turn down a deal, apparently not even if it required his daughter.

I was in shock and nearly thanked them, but my glee was tempered when I saw my father marveling over the coins still in his hand.

Well, whatever the reason, I was getting out of there for once. For adventure. I couldn't help myself and grinned. "My lady, sir, I'll meet you outside." I dashed away and pulled my sturdy leather boots from beneath my bed.

***

The trail was thick with mud, and we were soon covered up to our calves. More than once, I was jealous of the trousers Lady Zai—as she had asked to be called—had tucked into her boots. I had hitched my outer skirt into my belt, but it wasn't doing much. I'd need to do laundry for days to appease my mother. I hated laundry, even more than I hated carrying water, but it was worth it. I happily tromped through another puddle.

Lady Zai and Stevan were chatty behind me, enjoying the breeze as the path curled steadily upwards. "So, Ayve, tell us about the lake," Lady Zai called as we climbed.

"It's beautiful, my lady," I replied over my shoulder. "Pure blue and surrounded by wooded slopes and a waterfall. Young couples like to picnic there in summer." I was glad they couldn't see my face; I grew pink when I thought of why couples liked that so much.

"Do you go there often?"

"I did when I was younger," I replied. "My friend Rafe and I used to go whenever we could find the time." The games we had played were innocent, though as we grew older, I always knew he'd hoped for more. We had kissed in the woods once or twice, but I was wise enough by then to know he wasn't the one. If I hadn't been, it might be me big with child instead of Martha. I tried to imagine myself with a swollen belly washing mugs behind the bar.

A sudden thought hit me as I crossed another patch of mud. Suppose that were my life? Being big with child over and over again, washing dishes till my hands bled, until one day my children were grown and working beside me at the inn, too? For Martha, it was a dream; for me, a nightmare.

To take my mind off the thought, I decided to be bold and ask Lady Zai and Stevan questions in return. They were so unusual, they surely wouldn't mind. "How did you hear of the lake? My lady?" I added when they didn't respond right away.

Stevan was the one who answered. "It's well known in Freodon, actually," he replied. "Well, at least among academics. Sir Roland of Treoy once visited your inn, you know, just about a century ago. The historian," he added when my silence revealed my ignorance.

"Of course," I responded.

"Don't worry, it's a good sign that you haven't heard of him. It means you haven't spent your life staring at crackly old pages of boring books," he said wryly. "Roland traveled all about Freodon documenting the most mundane events in the kingdom, from the price of an egg in Galikath to the size of latrines at wayside inns. And besides commenting on your great-great grandparents' privies, he also mentioned the lake."

"You read it? In a book? You can read?" I asked, confused.

He frowned. "Why are you surprised?"

I decided to tread carefully. "I've never met a noble who let their servants read."

Stevan and Zai laughed. "What makes you think I'm her servant?"

I paused by a gnarled tree. "You're not?" I was being rude, but something told me they didn't care.

"Stevan is my work partner," Lady Zai said, her eyes crinkling, "and he is every bit my equal."

"Zai took me as her apprentice when I was a child," Stevan added. "She brought me to the city and enrolled me in classes at the royal academy. But I learned to read long before that. Everyone in Freodon reads. Don't you?"

"Sort of," I said. "Just enough to tally the books and label the food stores." I chewed my lip. "How long ago did you become her apprentice?"

"About twelve years. We've been partners for the last four, ever since I came of age."

"But sometimes I feel like his mother," Lady Zai added dryly. "Especially when he won't listen to me."

"I listen! Sometimes I just have my own ideas," he protested. A twinkle in his eyes made me think he wanted to say more, but Lady Zai pointed to the woods ahead of us.

"Left or right, Ayve? The trail goes both ways."

I was struck by a sudden idea. "Both ways lead to the lake, my lady, but if you trust me..."

I led the duo up a third, smaller path. It was nearly invisible in the undergrowth, mostly a deer trail, but it had been my favorite as a child.

Stevan was the first to notice the rumbling, rushing sound. Suddenly and without warning, the path opened onto a rocky overlook at the top of the falls. Mists rose from the water, and the sun winked on the bubbling surface below.

Lady Zai and Stevan were impressed, especially when I showed them the entrance to a small cave at the edge of the woods. It was almost hidden, but Rafe and I had found it years ago. Rafe had put his favorite wooden swords inside once. They had stayed there, nearly forgotten, until two wet winters had rotted them away. We were too old for toys by then, so neither of us had minded much.

Without a torch, we lingered at the cave's

front, unable to go much further. I pointed to the markings on the walls. They were old, though I wasn't sure how old. The edges were smoothed with time.

"Have you ever looked at them in the light?" asked Stevan as he ran his fingers in the grooves.

I shook my head. "We brought candles once, but they kept going out. The wind must funnel right in." I shuddered when I remembered how, candle after candle, each flame died almost instantly, as if it didn't want to stay lit. I'd tried to ask Rafe about it later, but he didn't seem to remember. In fact, he'd sworn he didn't remember going to the cave at all.

Lady Zai was suddenly silent, so silent that it seemed to take on a noise of its own. Stevan stood back, and Lady Zai stepped forward, her right hand open before her. Violet fire danced in her palm, illuminating the walls as she walked further in. "Follow me," she called, her voice echoing oddly. She didn't wait for a reply but moved steadily ahead.

Stevan gently linked his arm with mine. "It's dark here," he said shyly. "I don't much like the dark."

I couldn't have thought if I'd wanted to. Not only was Stevan's arm in mine, but Lady Zai was a mage. I knew mages existed, but it wasn't every day that people made fire appear in their hands. I tried to focus on Stevan's warmth at my side as we trailed after Lady Zai. I rather liked it, his warmth. I liked it much more than I liked walking deeper into the cave.

My fear faded when I saw the hundreds of markings. The carvings on the entrance were nothing in comparison. These shimmered in the violet light, almost appearing to move.

"Where?" Lady Zai was asking herself. She suddenly laughed, and her eyes glittered as she turned.

"Here," she said, extending her left hand. I hung back nervously.

Stevan gently placed a palm on the small of my back and guided me forward. "It's okay," he whispered. "You can trust us."

Hadn't I been the one to say I wanted adventure? I inhaled deeply and placed my hand in Lady Zai's.

My body sang. I could feel every nerve, every fiber, every hair on my body tingling with something so wonderful I could hardly stand it. Purple light danced on my skin, and vines of green light snaked their way up my arms and legs.

"Yes," Lady Zai breathed, and suddenly the world returned to normal as she released me. A few rocks tumbled from the cave wall to its floor, and Lady Zai grabbed something small from the ground. "Let's go," she urged, placing a hand on my shoulder. Stevan gently took hold of the other, and, feeling dazed, I allowed myself to be guided from the cave.

As we stepped into the sunlight, I felt myself grow dizzy. My knees were suddenly weak.

"Dammit, Zai, I knew she wasn't ready!"

"It's okay, Ayve, I've got you—"

The last thing I saw was Lady Zai's large purple eyes.

CHAPTER 4

I COULD HEAR CHIRPING BIRDS beneath the rumbling of the falls. I blinked and struggled to open my eyes.

"Relax. You fainted." Someone held a cool cloth to my head. The fingers were slender but firm and smelled of sweet cloves. Lady Zai. I was lying on the ground outside the cave, satchel under my head. Stevan was nearby, building a small fire. The ground was soft and the air heavy with flowers.

"Summer," I croaked. I sat up quickly, and my head spun. "It was spring when we left this morning. But this is summer weather. How long have I—?"

"It's a spell." Lady Zai gently waved a hand, and the air was suddenly cooler, the sunlight milder, the birds softer. She waved it the other way, and the illusion fell back into place. "I thought perhaps it would be nicer to wake up to than a cold, dark cave. Many people faint after their first brush with magic. I was surprised you didn't faint when you held my crystal the other night. I shouldn't have pushed you this far. I'm sorry. Lie back down; you need to rest. Your magic is tired." She gently wiped my face with the cloth.

I looked around shakily, head spinning. "You have magic." I remembered the purple fire in the cave. I had never met a mage before. Most lived in big cities. Occasionally, hedgewitches came around to train any children who showed promising signs, but it was dangerous work. Young mages were unpredictable, and their magic often got them or others injured. It was easier to send them away, so long as a family could afford it. The unluckier ones sometimes just cast their children out.

"I have magic," Lady Zai repeated. "I'm a mage at the palace."

"But you said *my* magic is tired. I don't understand. My lady." An inner voice, the one sounded a lot like Alys and Petyr, was kicking back in. I forced myself upright and at least managed to sit cross-legged as I looked at Lady Zai. Surely I'd misheard.

"Yes, your magic. You've never used it before. If I'm correct in my guess—and I usually am—I don't think you even knew you had magic."

The fire crackled gently. Stevan unrolled a few things from his knapsack and passed me his canteen. "Here, drink. It'll help." He uncorked the top. When I hesitated, he took a swig first and handed it back. I gently took a sip. The water was clear and cold. My mind instantly felt less clouded.

"Beg pardon, my lady, but I don't have magic. I can't. My family isn't magical. You have to come from magic to have magic, everyone knows that. And if my parents had magic, we wouldn't be innkeepers. We would be living in the city, rich beyond our wildest dreams, not scrubbing laundry until our hands cracked and smiling at customers until our cheeks ached. My lady."

Lady Zai shook her head. "But you do come from magic, Ayve," she corrected. "And stop with this 'lady' nonsense. Call me Zai. I am only Lady in court or when I want something." She smiled, trying to bring me in on the joke.

"But who in my family has magic? My lady," I added stubbornly.

Zai sighed and gazed at the falls. In the illusion, a misty rainbow hung above its rushing spray. "The time isn't right for me to say. But I will tell you what I know. I promise. And I keep my promises."

I looked hopefully at Stevan, but he had hung a pot over the edge of the flames and was busying himself with his pack. When he caught me staring, he shrugged. "She's telling the truth. If she says she'll tell you, she will."

"Did you know I had magic?" I asked him. I passed back the canteen, and he took another long drink before recorking it.

"Sort of," he answered. "When you held the crystal, yes. Before that, I wasn't sure."

I remembered a purple blush in Zai's small stone. It was the same color as in the cave, though the green vines of light were new.

Zai nodded. "It was a test. A way to know if someone has magic or not. Most people have at least an inkling of their skill, but you seemed fully unaware. It's a surprise because you breathe magic," Zai nearly whispered, her eyes alight with fire. "I've met very few mages with powers quite like yours. I'm surprised it's never burst out of you before. But perhaps I was a bit overeager," she admitted. "I should have used Stevan's help in the cave. I was so ready to see what you could do...

and look at you. Your magic is beautiful." She reached as if to touch my face but drew her hand back, suddenly shy.

I looked away. There was something about Zai that still made me feel uneasy. I turned my gaze to Stevan instead. "You have magic, too?"

He raised his hand, and a glorious gray shimmer crept from his fingers. "My magic was limited when I met Zai. I could start fires and clean water. Camp skills. An illusion like this," he said, gesturing to a simulated deer in the distance, "was barely a pipe dream. My family didn't want to spend the money educating me, but I wanted more. I wanted adventure. And Zai is never one to disappoint."

I glanced back at the cave. "Is that what we had in there? An adventure?"

Zai shrugged. "It was. And? What did you think?" She looked at me, her eyes revealing nothing.

"You mean being lured and used like bait for some kind of spell? Fainting only to wake up to an imaginary summer? Learning that all this time, I've secretly possessed magic? It was..." I scrambled for the right words. "It was magnificent," I burst. "I didn't know adventure could be so wonderful! I thought adventure was dodging my chores, or seeing the world, but this..." I remembered the way my body had thrummed as the vines danced on my skin. "It was, well, magical." I grinned madly.

Zai laughed. "Yes, I suppose magic is magical," she agreed. She pulled jerky from her pack and took a bite. She offered me a piece, but I was too excited to eat.

"In the cave, though, what was that?" I frowned. "What did you make happen?"

"What did we make happen, since it was your magic that took us there," Zai amended. She extended her hand. Resting in her palm was another crystal, though this one was dark purple, almost black, until the sun shone through and it lit up violet like her powers. "The ancient Ole'ad hid this thousands of years ago when they thought their ways were going extinct."

"Well, they weren't wrong, exactly," Stevan added as he stirred the pot in the fire. "They were wiped out, weren't they? Them and their gods. No one even knows what they called themselves."

"Though that hasn't stopped Stevan from reading every book he can about them," Zai grinned.

A thought scratched at my mind. "You said you read about the lake in a book. Did you know this cave was here?"

Stevan nodded.

"So if I hadn't come today, you would have gotten the crystal and been on your way? And I never would have known any of this," I mused.

Stevan looked at Zai again, and I narrowed my eyes. Today was a day for being bold, so bold I would be. "That's about the third time I've seen the two of you share that look, and it's always in conversations about me."

Zai hesitated. "Ayve, I don't want to frighten you, but I knew you were here."

"She had a vision." Stevan stood abruptly. "I'll be right back." He stalked off into the woods.

Zai watched him go, her mouth drawn into a tight frown. "Before we left," she said when he had disappeared, "I had a dream and saw you at the inn. I thought you might have what it takes to help us. But I'm wrong about these things sometimes. We've been looking for help for so long, and no one has ever worked out. I didn't want Stevan to go through that again, so I didn't tell him."

"Go through what again?" My head was swirling. This mysterious woman had dreamed about me, an ordinary girl? *Not so ordinary anymore*, some part of me whispered, but I brushed it aside.

"I've taken on a few assistants who seemed promising, but their magic never grew enough to help us like we needed. Stevan always enjoys having someone new to talk to. Gets attached, really, even if I warn him off." She shrugged apologetically. "Magic is what I do. A sorceress—even a palace-funded one—can't afford to keep someone who can't help. He actually suggested I hire you, you know," she added. "He thought you seemed promising. And once I finally told him about my dream, he was convinced. The crystal we could get any time. But you..." She eyed me thoughtfully. "Of course, that's if you want to join us at all," she said brusquely, wiping her hands on her trousers and standing as Stevan rejoined us. "And it's a lot to think about after you've just had your first real adventure. So let's eat some food, recoup, and head back to the inn for some supper." She walked off in the opposite direction, leaving me with quite a bit to think about.

* * *

As we cleaned up lunch, Zai gently lowered the illusion. I was startled to see that clouds had moved back in, and a fine fog stuck to our clothes as we followed the path back down. The woods were quiet, the animals tamed by the rain, and we were back at the inn well before dark.

"Thank you, my lady, Stevan." I could feel my father watching through the window and curtsied as gracefully as I could. "I'm glad I could be of service to you today."

Zai glanced at the window and nodded, clearly understanding the formality. "Thank you, Ayve. We had a lovely day. I do hope you'll consider my offer." Stevan nodded his agreement.

I opened the door and ushered them inside, taking their wet things and hanging them to dry near the fire. "Some hot water, please, so we may wash before dinner," Zai requested as the pair headed up the stairs.

I entered my bedroom and hurriedly shed my boots and cloak. Mud squelched on the floor beneath me. The rain was picking up. It drummed steadily against the side of the inn as I ran my fingers through wet locks, coaxing them back into a braid.

"Heavens help us, Ayve, what in the gods' names have you been doing today?" Martha rested against the doorframe. Her white apron was stained from a hard day's work.

"Adventuring," I beamed. "Lady Zai and Stevan asked me to be their guide. Oh, Martha, it was wonderful! You wouldn't believe..." I trailed off as my father's shadow darkened the room.

"Hello, Petyr," I squeaked. Water ran down my nose. I quickly wiped it away, but it was too late.

"Ayve." He stared, clearly displeased. "I

believe they paid you to be a guide, not to roll in the mud."

I licked my lips, suddenly nervous. My father was never unkind, but he was never kind, either. "The path was muddy. There wasn't much I could do. They were dressed for it, so they didn't mind."

He snorted, clearly showing what he thought of Zai's choice of clothing, but he said nothing.

"They've asked for hot water to wash before dinner."

He stared at me again, not with malice but... disappointment, I realized. It was the look he always had when he gazed at me. "Martha will take it to them. If you're already in this state, you may as well help Rafe. We've had new guests today while you were off in the woods."

"Off in the woods for money," I said pointedly, daring him to be angry.

"For money," he agreed, still looking disappointed. "But even so."

"Fine," I agreed heatedly. Martha winced in sympathy and scurried off to fetch the water. I threw my wet cloak and boots back on, my feet now cold inside wet stockings. I hurried out to the stables before I could let Petyr down even more.

* * *

The stables weren't all that bad. I wasn't much a

fan of manure, but the rain had washed away most of the smell. Besides, Rafe had the horses handled; all I had to do was keep him company. I rested comfortably on a hay bale and began to describe my day, though I conveniently left out the part about magic.

"The cave at Lovers' Lake!" he chortled. "And you were there, what, to witness their tryst? Or to join in?" he teased.

I shook my head. "They're work partners, that's all." *And they want me to work for them, too*, I thought, though I didn't dare say it out loud.

"Well, it's a good thing you had the lady with you or else her companion may have made a move." Rafe emerged from a stall, wiping sweat from his brow and leaning his pitchfork against the wall.

"Who, Stevan?" I laughed, though it oddly felt as though birds' wings were tickling the inside of my ribcage. "I don't think he's interested in me, but thank you."

Rafe plopped down next to me. "Please, I've seen how he looks at you. And I've seen you. It's not unexpected that he'd be interested." He hesitated before continuing. "Ayve. You're nearly eighteen. When are you going to find a man to marry?"

I blanched at the turn the conversation had

taken. "I don't know. I've been thinking." I had to tell someone or I might burst. "What if I don't want to?"

"What if you don't want to find a man to marry? What, you want to marry a woman instead? I hear that's all the rage in Freodon," Rafe teased.

I gently smacked his arm, though my stomach felt fluttery again. "I mean, what if I don't want to settle down? What if I want to leave Jeren?"

He was quiet. "You want to leave Jeren?"

"I don't know. It's just a thought. You have to promise not to tell anyone."

"Even Martha?"

"Especially Martha," I begged. "They've asked me to go away with them," I continued slowly. The knot in my stomach crept to my throat.

"They?" Rafe asked.

"Lady Zaitreiha. And Stevan. They work for the palace." I couldn't bring myself to call them mages. I wasn't sure how he'd respond. "They want me as their assistant."

Rafe reclined against the wall. "And you're considering it?" I knew him too well to believe the casual tone in his voice.

"No. I don't know. Maybe." I had never felt so guilty before.

Rafe was as practical as my parents. "But why?

You have a good life here. A family, the inn. Your children would take care of you. You'd have Joseth by your side. And you could hire Martha's and my little ones too," he said, gently cupping my chin. "You wouldn't leave us, would you?" His eyes were big.

"Oh, Rafe," I said, hugging him fiercely. "It's just an idea. But..."

"But?"

"But I've never wanted this," I whispered, voicing aloud the secret I'd always held. I looked at the dusty straw, blinking back tears. "I don't know if I can do it. There's so much more out there. There's a whole kingdom to see. And today was just wonderful," I gushed. "Rafe, it was everything I've ever wanted. And they can give it to me if I leave."

He didn't speak for a while, and I hoped perhaps he'd chosen to drop it. "It'd be hard to let you go," he said finally. "For me and for your parents. Labor doesn't come cheap out here. They'd need someone to take your place."

"Martha," I argued weakly.

"Who will be nursing a child soon. Guests might not take so kindly to a maid carrying a squalling babe. And all the firewood you chop, plus the help you give with cleaning, not to mention watching Joseth."

"He's nearly old enough to help," I protested. "I was just a year or so older than him when Petyr set me to cleaning rooms."

"Yes, but until then, he would hang about your mother's side, needing constant looking after. I don't know, Ayve. It's not my call to make. But I can't imagine this inn without you. And if you're honest with yourself, I don't think you can, either."

He turned on his heels and left. I waited until my tears stopped before returning inside.

CHAPTER 5

I WAS BUSY UNTIL the moment the bar closed. I was almost sad when the last patrons finally staggered off to bed, knowing I'd be able to hear my own thoughts again. I hoped I'd fall asleep quickly.

"Ayve." Petyr's voice made me jump. I put down the cup I was wiping and slung the towel over my shoulder. "Have you finished cleaning?"

I nodded.

"Good. Your mother and I need to speak with you."

They sat at the table near the fire, though the embers were just barely smoldering. I perched nervously across from them, hands clutched beneath the table. Whatever this was, it couldn't be good.

Petyr cleared his throat. "Well. Given the sudden uptick in business, Alys and I have been talking. We've decided it's time for you to be married."

"Married!" I gasped. *Rafe*, I knew. *He told.*

"Yes, married," my father repeated. "Most girls your age are betrothed by now, many even with child. We've always tried to respect your wishes and give you a choice, but—"

"Ayve, we need help with the inn." Alys, at least, had the decency to sound remorseful. "Rafe's brother is seeking a wife. We could use another hard-working man around here. And one day your children could help, too."

"Josiah?" An image of an older, slightly balding Rafe bubbled to the surface of my mind. "But he's nearly thirty! You want me to marry Josiah? And have his children?" I felt sick.

"He's twenty-five. And it's easier for men to be married older. They can still get a woman with child. But it's not as easy for a woman. Your child-rearing years are short. You must start soon." It was as if Petyr spoke of horses, not a daughter.

"Josiah is a blacksmith," Alys added softly. "He's never been married. You could make a much worse match. And Martha will be your sister.

You'll work side-by-side, your children growing up as best friends."

The wonderful, adventurous flame that had only just bloomed inside me began to sputter. Was this really how it ended, with a business transaction for marriage? "But I don't love him."

"Marriage is about security, not love," Petyr said firmly. "We gave you a chance to find love, but no one has ever captured your heart, not even Rafe. Few eligible men remain in Jeren. Josiah is a reliable choice. We need you to do this. For us. For our family."

For the inn, I knew. *For the money.*

Petyr narrowed his eyes a bit. "It's not up to daughters to decide, you know," he said, somewhat cross. "We could have arranged your marriage already, but we allowed you time. That grace is over. You don't have a choice anymore."

"But she does." I knew that soft, low voice by now. Zai's leather boots were nearly silent as she emerged from the shadows by the stairs.

"My lady, did we wake you?" My parents' bench scraped noisily as they stood. Petyr was all politeness now, and Alys curtsied. I remained seated, too afraid to take my eyes off the table lest I start crying.

Zai ignored him and sat. "It would please me to discuss your daughter's future, sir, because she *does* have a choice, and it appears it's time she makes it. Ayve, look at me."

Cool fingers grasped my chin. I lifted my head and met Zai's eyes. In the near-dark, they seemed to shimmer.

"You know my offer. And now you know theirs. Work for me, and your adventure will be ever-changing. Or marry this Josiah, and your adventure will be here with your children. Either is a worthwhile choice. But only *you* can know what you desire."

"Pardon, but it doesn't matter what she desires, my lady," my father countered. "We're her parents, and we have a right to decide what's good for our daughter."

Zai gently released my chin and sighed. "I'd hoped not to reveal my hand, but I see you leave me no choice. You raised her, yes, but she is not your daughter by birth."

Time seemed to stop. I felt each heartbeat. My body hummed again like it had in the cave. "I'm not their daughter?" The words felt strange leaving my mouth.

My parents were silent for a long time. "It was so long ago," Alys said finally, her voice heavy with grief. "I had lost so many babes already, and you seemed like a prayer answered."

An unpleasant tingling ran up my arms and

legs, gathering in my belly. "Who are my birth parents?" I whispered. "And where are they?" I couldn't believe I was asking such questions.

Alys dabbed her eyes and continued. "Your father we never met. Your mother was a guest." She raised her hands helplessly. "She disappeared. One night she was here, and the next she was gone. We found you alone in her room, crying and afraid. She was young. We thought she got frightened and assumed she'd be back. But she never returned. So you were ours, and we raised you as our daughter."

My mind whirled. I was surprised that the table was so solid. I grasped it firmly, running my fingers along the edge. It was the same old wooden table, but it suddenly lacked all meaning. It didn't belong to me anymore. Not really.

Perhaps Alys loved me. There was remorse in her voice. "But *you* never loved me," I said, turning to Petyr and voicing the thought I'd always felt guilty for having. "You wanted a child, but you didn't love me. Why?"

He didn't even look ashamed. "Because you weren't mine."

"Then why keep me?" I wondered aloud. "If I mattered so little, then why bother?" The answer came to me at once, and I laughed hollowly. "Money," I said. "You'd hoped for a reward. And when none came, why throw away free labor?"

Alys blanched. "I love you, Ayve. I've always loved you. Truly."

"But to him I was free help," I accused, pointing a finger angrily at Petyr.

"We're a practical people," he confirmed. "We have to be. We'd never survive if not. And you became a good worker."

"How did you know?" I turned to Zai. "Do you know my birth parents?" My voice quaked with anticipation.

Zai shook her head sadly. "It took only one look at you and little Joseth to know the truth."

"Then I'm going," I announced. The sudden force in my voice surprised me. "Zai, you said I had a choice, and I choose to go. This is where I grew up, but it isn't my home. I want to read books, real ones, like Stevan. And I want to learn to use magic." Petyr and Alys blinked in confusion. I rushed on before they could ask questions. "I don't want marriage. I don't want children. Not now, not when there's so much out there. Maybe not ever." My thoughts fluttered back to the cave. That could be my life. My *real* life. Not working in a tiny inn, serving guest after guest till I died.

"That's all well and good, my lady," Petyr said, bristling, "but birth parents or not, we've still raised her. And it's cost us. Ayve owes us this marriage. A marriage for sixteen years of food, and clothes, and a roof over her head."

"You have Joseth," Zai reminded them. "He may be young, but he will come of age one day, and many women will be eager to marry a man set to inherit an inn."

"That's at least a dozen more years, my lady!" Petyr protested. "You can't expect us to wait that long. We have needs *now*. The roof needs patching. Some of the windows are broken. Plus you'd be taking away our barmaid, our childcare, our laundress... How would we find someone to take her place? We'd have to hire out, and we don't have the money for that."

"Martha," I offered.

"Not when she's this far with child, Ayve." Alys shook her head. "She can barely keep up as it is, and her babe will be here soon. She's a hard worker, but she can't do her own work *and* replace you."

I remembered my conversation with Rafe and knew Alys was telling the truth. But thinking of Rafe brought the sick feeling back to my stomach.

Zai unlaced her coin purse from her belt. She reached a hand inside and rummaged noisily.

"My lady, it would take more than a few coins to cover all this," Petyr grumbled. "The roof, the windows—"

"Yes, yes, the bar and the childcare and the washing, I heard you." Zai withdrew a hand, sighed, and tossed the bag towards Petyr. It landed with a loud jangle. "That should be enough for your repairs. And you may have our horses."

Petyr started as he reached for the bag. He opened the flap and stared. "Both?" he asked finally. "Horses? My lady," he added, remembering his manners.

"Yes," Zai replied. "Trained by the best stable masters in the city. They'll serve you and your guests well so long as you treat them right."

Petyr grunted. He slowly ran his fingers through the bag's contents. Alys grasped his arm, her breathing shallow.

"Then it's settled." Zai stood abruptly. "We leave tomorrow at dawn. We'll need three days of food ready for us in the morning. Come along, Ayve. Let's pack your things." She offered a hand to me. Somehow, I managed to take it and stood dazed by her side.

"Good night, Petyr and Alys," Zai called as we started towards my room.

"Yes, my lady," came Petyr's voice from behind us. Alys said nothing, still sitting in her chair and staring at the bag of coins on the table in front of her.

* * *

Zai said little as I opened my door. It was dark. I fumbled for a candle, but it came to life on its own, the flame briefly sparking purple.

"Fire magic is one of the skills you'll learn with me," Zai said. She perched on the edge of the bed. "But first things first. Let's get your clothes. Without horses, it's whatever we can carry on our backs. We should make sure what you take is the best for what we'll face."

Zai tsk'd and hmm'd her way through my small dresser, shaking her head at nearly everything. She eventually settled on a woolen hat, two pairs of thick stockings, a wool sweater, soft mittens, spare smallclothes, and my still-dirty boots and cloak. "Most of this is for sleeping," Zai said as we rolled the clothes into a small knapsack. "The rest we'll take from my stores and Stevan's. We'll get you your own clothes in Duskett. That's the first town we'll reach."

I nodded nervously. I was familiar with the town, having been there once or twice when I was younger to help replenish supplies, but it had been years since I'd seen the place. Plus my world was still swirling from everything that had just happened.

"Rest up." Zai stood, stretching her long arms

over her head as she yawned. "Stevan will be a grump in the morning when he learns we can't sleep in. And that I've sold our horses and we're walking the whole way. Ah, well. That's life when you choose to be an assistant to a mage!" She grinned, then looked pointedly at me. "You do know that's what you've chosen, yes? Early wakeups, long days, aches and pains and hunger... Is that still what you want?"

My fingertips tickled. "I've never wanted anything as much as I've wanted this."

Zai nodded, looking pleased. "Stevan will wake you when it's time. Good night, Ayve."

I curtsied slightly. "Good night, my lady. Zai." I closed the door softly and sat on my bed. A pile of abandoned clothing perched at its foot like a dog. I lay my head on the pillow, not expecting to sleep a wink, but within moments, I began to drift, visions of purple and green flickering at the corners of my eyes.

CHAPTER 6

MY EYES SHOT OPEN and jumped to the window. The weak gray light didn't give any indication of the gigantic thunderstorm that was raging.

After another bang, I blearily focused on the door. It wasn't thunder. I staggered from bed and wrenched it open before the sound could wake the whole inn.

"Finally," Stevan grumbled. His hair was mussed, and he squinted grumpily. "We need to go."

"What time is it?" My voice felt raw.

"Nearly dawn. For an innkeeper's daughter, you sure sleep soundly."

"I didn't go to bed till late," I croaked. He grumpily thrust a bundle at me and walked away. *But I'm not an innkeeper's daughter*, I realized as he stumbled down the hall. The thought gave me courage. I squared my shoulders and fumbled for the candle, wishing I knew how to light it with magic. I tried feebly twiddling my fingers at the wick, but nothing happened except that I felt foolish. I found my tinderbox and lit it with a spark, allowing myself enough light to see the bundle's contents.

My heart soared as I realized Zai had provided me with black breeches like her own. I hugged them to my chest. Somehow, I knew I would never have to wear a skirt again, not unless I wanted to. I pulled on a large white shirt and slid into the pants delicately. They clearly belonged to Stevan; Zai's would have dragged on the ground. Even still, it took a tightly cinched belt about my waist to keep them up, and they bagged around my knees when tucked inside my boots. I laced up a leather jerkin from the pack and tied my cloak over my shoulders. Even with the large sizes, I had never felt more comfortable in my life.

There was more inside the pack, but it seemed foolish to waste time. I shoved the roll into the knapsack Zai and I had packed. Then I paused and looked around one last time. This was it, I realized. The last time I would see it. My room was small, I noted, and dull. The very opposite of where I hoped I was going.

I was about to put out the candle when something whispered to me from the back of my mind. I opened my drawer, withdrew the small painting, and tucked it inside my bag.

Zai stood by the front door, dressed and waiting with Stevan. "Give me your knapsack," he said. "We'll need to organize it properly later, when I've eaten and had something warm to drink."

"Don't worry, I'm sure we'll all be awake soon enough after a brisk sunrise walk," Zai chirped, clapping him on the shoulder. It was clear which of the two was a morning person. I wondered which I would be on the road. At the inn, I was always up early helping to care for Joseth, but that didn't mean I liked it.

Joseth. My heart fell as I saw Alys standing quietly by the door holding the boy. He turned sleepily and reached for me. I grabbed him and hugged him tight, blinking hot pinpricks from my eyes.

"I have to go away now," I whispered against his ear. His hair was soft. "For a long time. Help Alys and Petyr with the inn, okay?"

He nodded solemnly and curled into Alys's

side.

I swallowed, trying not to think that this might be the last time I ever saw him. I pushed away my feelings. It would do no good to miss him.

"Shall we?" Zai pretended not to notice my tears. She and Stevan walked out the door.

"Ayve." Alys stepped forward, nervous. "Please, whatever you think of us, know that I do love you. No matter where you come from, you are my daughter. I only want what's best for you. And if this is what's best, then you should go."

I stared at the woman who had lied to me for so long. "It is what's best. You and Petyr got your coin. It's the best price you can get for me. And it's the last time I'll be for sale. So goodbye, Alys." I stalked out the door, trying not to hear the sniffles behind me.

"Is that how you wish to leave it?" Zai leaned against the wall.

"Yes," I said a bit too stubbornly, chin jutting out in front of me.

"Okay," Zai said, and that was that. She slipped on her kit and motioned for me to do the same.

It was heavy. I struggled to strap everything to my back. Stevan helped me slide my other arm in. He cinched it tightly across my waist and hips.

And then, with no pomp or fanfare, we walked out the gate.

* * *

As I looked at the oilskin shelter I'd be sharing with Zai, I couldn't help but feel my heart leap into my throat. Spend the night *there*? Beneath a flimsy piece of tented fabric? It couldn't possibly offer any protection. Gods only knew what—or who—was bumping around in the night.

"It's spelled, you know." Zai walked out of the shadows, pointing at the shelter. "And I've just finished encircling our camp. Relax. None but the most powerful mage could even detect that we're here tonight, and I doubt any of my colleagues are out for a nighttime stroll in the Kreely Mountains," she noted dryly.

I felt dumb. Of course we would be protected with magic. Yet even with outside threats diminished, it was hard to believe that a little piece of cloth could keep anyone dry and warm. I peered at the sky suspiciously, waiting for a cloud to burst, but only stars innocently twinkled back.

"To bed," Zai ordered. "It's late, and we have two more long days ahead of us before we reach Duskett."

"Two days!" I gasped. "It took us only one day to get there when I was a child." Petyr had taken me then. We had bumped along in the carriage and come home with candied almonds, marzipans, and spices.

"That's by horse," Stevan called as he crawled beneath his own oilskin. "Which my very kind and lovely partner exchanged for a certain new assistant, if you'll remember."

"Oh, poo on you," Zai yawned. "It was an exchange you'll appreciate when you don't have to light my morning fire or fetch my breakfast anymore. Are you coming?"

I knew Zai was talking to me. I bit back a complaint and crawled into my bedroll.

"There," Zai sighed. "You'll be asleep in moments. A hard day's hike will do that to you. Sleep well, all."

But sleep didn't come. I lay curled on my side, sweating profusely into the thick blanket. I was too afraid to pull away the protective layer, even if it meant I boiled. All through the night I lay awake and listened. Every snap and rustle in the bushes was surely a bear coming to eat us, or prowling wolves waiting to pick off the first to move. I held inordinately still, sure a single rustle from my bed would lead to my untimely death. I couldn't believe I had given up the comfort and safety of the inn for this. I had found a knife in my pack at dinner, and I clutched it to my chest, praying for the night to end.

I tried to distract myself by remembering the day. It had been long. Walking with a heavy pack was hard, I had quickly learned. Zai had said they would buy me more once we reached Duskett, but how could I hold anything else when this load weighed me down already? I had trailed behind Zai and Stevan, listening to their occasional banter and trying to take in the scenery while struggling along.

I had wanted to stop for more breaks, but I was afraid to disappoint Zai. What if she decided they didn't need an assistant and just left me in the woods? Or worse, I pondered, what if she took me back? It was all I could do not to cry. Back meant Josiah and babies, but onwards meant more walking, more aches, more wide eyes in the dark as yet another bush rustled menacingly.

I must have dozed once or twice, though I always awoke with a start, clutching the knife in a panic. After what felt like ages, the sky began to lighten. I had survived, though I suddenly felt foolish. Surely the protection spells must work against animals as well as humans. My weary eyes felt heavy, and I finally fell asleep.

* * *

"Ayve. It's time to get moving. We have a long

walk ahead of us today."

I groaned. Sunlight glittered in the corners of my eyes.

"Good, you're up. Pack your bedroll and grab some breakfast. We'll hit the road again soon. No sense wasting good daylight."

Zai was far too chipper for having slept on the ground all night. *But that's it*, I thought as I forced myself to move. *Zai actually slept.* Even the longest nights at the inn never wore me down like this. I shivered slightly in the cool morning air and slowly, dutifully packed my bedroll.

After a few bites of oats—all my stomach could handle—we set off along the path. In the light of day, I felt dumber than ever about my nighttime jitters, especially when we came upon a herd of deer in a clearing. I wondered how many of the noises I had heard the night before came from hungry fawns. I quietly vowed to do better.

Despite my exhaustion, I couldn't help but end up in a good mood as we walked. We passed a bubbling stream, and a gentle mist hung over the water and reflected the green morning light. I could have sworn the air smelled of strawberries.

"You're doing well, you know," Stevan said sometime later. I looked up, blinking. "With the whole trekking thing. It takes some getting used to, especially if you've never carried everything on your back before. Is your body feeling okay?"

"My shoulders are a bit sore," I admitted, running a finger under my pack's straps. "And I slept terribly. But it's all so pretty, I hardly care. You'd think I'd know this land like the back of my hand, but besides the lake and major roads, I never really ventured out."

Stevan laughed. "If a little bit of forest impresses you, I can only imagine how you'll feel when you see Freodon!"

"Is it big, then?" I wondered if I would get tired of feeling stupid. Surely I should know something as simple as the size of the capital.

"It's big," Stevan chuckled. "Not the biggest city I've ever seen, but it's certainly overflowing with life. And that's if you can even manage to venture outside the palace, which is a maze all on its own."

"Really?" I watched a bird land on a branch. It cheeped shrilly at our passing party. "I've never seen any place bigger than Duskett," I confessed, "and even then only for a day. What if I'm not right for it?"

He shrugged. "Given what I've seen of you so far, I'm not worried. You clearly have powerful magic, and you survived your first night out in the woods. By the end of this trip, you'll be ready for anything."

We kept walking in the slowly rising morning sun. Stevan explained some of what to expect when we reached Freodon. Besides assisting Zai, I would enroll in classes at the royal academy to build my magic skills, a prospect that greatly excited me. Once my powers were up to snuff and Stevan had more time to research, we would set off somewhere to seek more hidden crystals. Daydreaming about the future helped distract me from the hard work of walking.

Around noon, Zai switched places with Stevan. I still felt shy around my new instructor. Stevan had opened up as the morning went on, joking and talking about some of the sights he'd seen on his travels through Kreiogny, but Zai was still somewhat of a mystery. She strode along effortlessly, and she carried her pack as if it weighed no more than a feather.

"Begging your pardon, my lady... Zai," I amended after we had been walking for some time. "But I couldn't help but notice: is your pack magicked? It's just you move so gracefully," I added, hoping I didn't sound too jealous.

Zai's smile reminded me of a cat's. "Sort of. Only perhaps not in the way you think. It's not magicked for ease of carrying, though there are certainly spells that could do so. The stitches are magicked for all kinds of useful things."

"Useful how?"

"Useful like waterproofing the fabric so it repels all water, useful like muting my movements so I'm less visible to passing mages. That kind of useful."

"Less visible?" I crinkled my brows. "People can't see you?" I tried to picture myself walking next to Zai's floating pack.

"More in the magic sense of visibility," Zai corrected herself. "Other mages can see me, but should they reach out with their powers to feel if I have magic of my own, they'd detect nothing, not even the spells on my pack."

"That sounds powerful."

"Indeed. Would you like to work powerful magic like that one day?"

It was a lightly posed question, but I knew that how I answered it was important. "I think so," I said finally. "But I want to know more about it first, like how it works and if there are any consequences to using it."

"That's a good approach to have." Zai sounded pleased. "All magic has consequences in some way. Spelling this pack took several days of recovery on my part, and the learning it took to get here was extensive. But if you're willing to take the time, magic like this can be quite useful."

"Is it hard to learn? It just seemed to come out

of me in the cave. Is that what it will always be like?"

Zai pushed a stray lock of hair from her forehead. "No. Well, mostly no. That was pure magic. You'll need to train yourself to channel it in specific ways. Letting it pour out of you like it did in the cave can be dangerous, causing you to feel dizzy, faint, or even become quite ill, should it go on long enough."

"When can I start lessons?" I felt breathless, and I didn't think it was from the hill we climbed.

"Not until you're used to walking, I'm afraid. Your body needs to get accustomed to physical exhaustion before we tax it with magic, too. After we depart from Duskett, perhaps. But not a moment sooner. I can tell you hardly slept last night. You'll want to be fresh before you try to wrangle your magic for the first time." Her decisive tone told me that was the end of that.

* * *

I was itching to do something. Stevan was bustling around with the fire, and Lady Zai had gone off into the woods to dig and spell a privy. My only task was to fetch water from the stream. Even the oilskins were set up when I came back. In my whole life, I had never learned how not to be busy.

Stevan waved a hand over the tinder. It

flickered to life with a tiny snap. A fine gray fog ghosted through the pile. "I need to collect some wood. I've magicked it to heat faster, so you'll need to add kindling quickly," he said, pointing to a mound of sticks. "I'll be right back. Don't let it die out."

He slid silently back into the trees, and I fed small twigs to the twisting flames.

"Good," Stevan said after what felt like no time at all. His arms were full. "Not everyone can keep a fire going, especially not one burning so hard as this."

"It was always my job at the inn," I said, mesmerized by the smoke that drifted from the flames as Stevan added larger pieces. "But I can tell this fire's magicked. Not that I can sense magic or anything, not the way I think you and Zai can. But I've fed my fair share of fires, and none have felt quite so hungry as this one." I shivered despite the growing heat. "And then there's the smoke. It's gray. Well, smoke is always gray," I amended, "only this is denser? More like a mist than smoke. Like it has weight or something."

Stevan hung a pot over the growing flames. "That's my magic you're seeing," he said as he filled the pot with water. "Most of the time, mages hide their magic. It's considered somewhat gaudy to leave your trace out in the open. But with just us here, I didn't see much of a point. Besides, you should get a chance to see these things. When I was in your place, I was dying to learn everything I could."

I nodded and watched smoke tickle the pot. The water began steaming almost instantly. "Why is your magic gray but Zai's is purple?"

Stevan snapped a twig idly in his hand. "Many mages—not all—have magic that matches their eyes. Mine are gray, for instance. Master Onan, at the palace, he has these deep blue eyes, like the sky just before dark, and his magic looks like that, too. Probably one of the most beautiful magics I've ever seen."

"So there's really such a thing as people having purple eyes?"

Stevan stirred the now-bubbling pot. "Yes. But she's an incredibly powerful mage. Something is different in people at that level. Same thing goes for black eyes, too. If you ever run across black and purple flames or eyes, my suggestion would be to run. Far and fast."

I helped Stevan dig out a bag of beans. "Does that mean my magic might be green?"

"Would you like to see?" Stevan extended a twig. I took it, unsure of what I should do. "The thing about magic is that it mostly works by wanting it, by feeling it move through you and just willing it to happen."

I hesitated. "Zai doesn't want me using magic just yet. She said so this afternoon."

"It's not using magic, technically," Stevan replied. "I'm not asking you to perform a spell. Just to feel it. Imagine your power flowing down through your fingers and into the wood."

I stared at it, feeling foolish. But if it would give me a chance to see something I hadn't even dreamed could be true...

I couldn't have said how I did it later, but it felt almost like I stopped concentrating. The best I could say is that I wanted it, and it happened. Emerald light fizzed from my fingertips, and the twig instantly burst into flame. I dropped it into the fire, giddy with excitement.

"I did it!" I crowed. "Did you see it?"

Stevan frantically poked the embers with a stick. "All magic leaves a trace," he grimaced. "Beginner magic leaves a trace she can see a mile away. I'm sorry, Ayve." My stomach slowly sank. "I thought you'd maybe be able to get it glow, if even that. Most novices take days to get to the flame stage." He jabbed the fire some more and muttered something under his breath. Smoke swirled where my twig incinerated.

"There," he said finally. "I think it's good enough. I doubt she'll be deeply probing our camp. But probably best we don't do that again."

Dinner was ready by the time Zai returned. I spooned beans gently into our wooden bowls, sprinkling in dried vegetables and bits of jerky and topping them off with a hard heel of bread. Zai frowned at the fire, but mercifully she said nothing.

Stevan found me once more before bed as I scrubbed my teeth. "We're in the clear," he said as he followed suit. "I doubt she was on the lookout for traces tonight since she thinks we're pretty safe."

I swished water around my mouth and sprayed it onto the ground like Zai had taught me. "I sure hope so," I whispered back.

That night, I slept almost the second I hit the ground, though my dreams were full of green sticks falling into purple flames.

CHAPTER 7

I WOKE REFRESHED, BUT my body ached, and I longed to crawl back beneath my blanket. I was tired, and I made the mistake of saying so around mid-morning.

"Perhaps you wouldn't be so tired if you'd listened to your teacher," Zai snipped. She said nothing more before she stalked further up the path, but my blood ran cold.

"Relax," Stevan advised. "She'll get over it. You're lucky it's taken her so long to get mad. Zai chewed me out on my first day. It may have even been my first hour. And I was barely more than a boy."

"Are you sure?"

He shrugged. "She's old enough to be your

mother, and she'll treat you like she's one sometimes, too. That's just her way of showing she cares." I gawped at him, and he laughed. "I know, she looks young. But she turned forty just last month. Some of the mages at the palace claim she must use an enchantment, though they certainly wouldn't say that to her face. Beauty magic isn't exactly a prized palace skill."

"There are different types of magic, then." I tried to relax as I dissected this knowledge.

"Basic philosophy says magic is tied to the four elements: earth, air, fire, water. Anyone can perform any type of magic, but most mages are best suited to one and only dabble in the others. A fire mage can do spells to clean water, for example, but it might take them longer or their spells might not be as powerful."

"Where does beauty magic fit into that?"

"You tell me. What are makeups made of?"

I thought long and hard. "Earth, I would think," I said. "Though to be honest, I haven't had much experience with makeup. Petyr never let me have any. He said it wasn't worth the coin, especially not when folk expected an honest face on their barkeep. But Martha had some, and I think it was mostly colored with flowers and herbs."

Stevan nodded. "It helps if beauty mages have

a little bit of fire skills so they can melt things together, but very few mages actually study it. There's just not a market for something most folks can do without needing magic at all. The truly gifted ones can completely transform appearances with it though, making someone into a whole new person."

"Like how players do on stage," I suggested.

"Yes, but better," Stevan agreed. "That's where I come from, actually. A family of players. I was born not too far from here, just over these mountains in Hendassa. We traveled often, and I met interesting people. It was in Vlaft where I met the most interesting person of all, a stunning lady in a dark velvet cloak."

"Lady Zai?"

"The one and only. She was in the audience one day, and my eyes were drawn to her the whole time. I sought her out after the show, and we left that night. I probably would've done it forever, the playing gig, if our paths hadn't crossed."

"Do you ever miss it?" I tried not to think about what answer I wanted to hear.

"Sometimes," he admitted. "But it's been so long now. I was only ten when she found me. Sometimes I'm nostalgic for my childhood, but everyone feels that way. Besides, I never would have gotten where I am today without her help. Players don't have much need for water magic—my strength," he added.

"Can you tell what someone's strength is the same way you can tell if they've been working a spell?" I held my breath, but he smiled apologetically.

"No one can, not even Zai. There are methods, though, like—"

"There you are!" Zai stood at a fork in the path, looking cross. "I've been waiting forever for you two to get here. There's a farmer and his son up ahead, so I didn't want to leave a mark." She twiddled her fingers, indicating she meant a magic mark. "We need to hurry if we want to get to Duskett before dark, and I'd like for us to be there well before then. We need to get Ayve's new clothes and pack."

Stevan shrugged as Zai pointed, and he took the lead.

* * *

The sun was mercifully still above the horizon when we arrived in Duskett. Zai instructed Stevan to get us rooms while we quickly browsed the many stalls.

I was cowed by Zai's brisk business manner and happily let her handle the shopping. When we had gathered a pile to her satisfaction, Zai pulled a coin purse from her belt. I could feel my eyes widen.

"What, did you think I'd spent *all* my money?" Zai smirked as she paid the man.

"I've just never seen anyone with two coin purses is all," I replied honestly.

It was cheaper for us to stay in the inn's communal rooms. Zai may have had a second coin purse, but her funds were limited until we returned to Freodon. I felt small surrounded by so many strangers, though none paid us any attention. I should have known as much, given the years I'd spent seeing guests ignore each other. Zai and I left our belongings with Stevan and headed for the shared baths.

The women's washroom was tiny. There was no fire in the grate, and a chill had settled in with the dark. I dreaded washing with cold water, but I knew I smelled terrible after three days of tromping through the woods.

Yet Zai smiled. "Good, we're alone," she said, waving a hand at the empty sunken tub. Water bubbled merrily, steaming slightly. "First rule of magic, Ayve, is that everything has to come from somewhere." Zai took off her boots, indicating I do the same. "Nothing can come from nothing. This water comes from somewhere. Think. Where would I find a source to draw from?"

I unlaced my boots. "The well?" I asked, thinking of the one we had passed in the town square.

"Good guess," Zai answered as she began to strip off her stockings, "but it's dangerous to meddle that closely with people's lives. What if I drained too much, risking their supply? Or what if someone were drawing water when I began to pull from it? Ah, yuck," she said, pointing to the mud stains on her toenails. "Keep thinking."

I tried again. "We went past a stream earlier," I said. "It was fresh and clear."

Zai beamed and started working on the laces of her jerkin. "Do you know its name?"

"No." I was abashed. "I never learned much of the land beyond what I needed in Jeren."

"No need to be ashamed," Zai said, stripping off her grimy shirt. "Rule number two of magic is admitting when you don't know something. It's okay not to know answers. It's not okay to make wild guesses to protect your ego. That will get you—or others—killed."

Zai slid into the bath with a happy groan. I did the same. The water was delightful on sore muscles. We talked little, though I did ask if I should wash Zai's clothes. It seemed like the kind of thing I'd been hired to do.

"Another day," Zai said. "This time, I'll take care of it when we're done. Laundry without magic isn't any fun."

My eyes widened. "You'll teach me to do laundry with magic? No more scrubbing, and beating, and rubbing and rubbing on a washboard?" I nearly melted with joy.

When we were finally clean, we emerged from the tub and wrapped ourselves in towels while Zai dunked our clothes. I had bathed in much dirtier water before, but I certainly wished there were a second tub for our garments. Yet as the clothes worked themselves around, I was startled to find the water crystal clean and steaming once more. "Rule one," I said thoughtfully. "So where does the dirt go? Or did you change out all the water?"

"You really don't know?"

I bit my lip, thinking, and shook my head.

Zai nodded. "Dirty bathwater gets dumped behind the inn. Most mages would simply remove all of the water and start again, but I'm not just any mage. I was able to remove only the grime and reheat the water."

I considered Zai's words. "Stevan said he can clean water for drinking. Is it anything like that?"

"Similar, but cleaning water for drinking can be more difficult if you're not also looking to heat it, too. That's important in the summer to keep our bodies cool." Zai rubbed her hair vigorously in her towel and began to comb it through as the clothes wrung themselves out and hung by the fire to dry.

When we were finished, before we went back to the big room, Zai held out an unlit candelabra. The room was growing dark. "Rule three," she said quietly. "You have to want it. You have to see it, feel it, *be* it. Light the candle, Ayve."

Her words somehow held more power than Stevan's had. I stretched out a hand, lifting my pointer finger. I could see it on fire, *feel* it on fire, and a green vine licked a wick delicately, setting it aflame in an instant. Zai started to offer congratulations, but my hand was still outstretched, and the other two wicks lit, too.

"Well," Zai said finally. "It seems fire magic may be a strength of yours. It's not many beginners who can handle lighting one candle, let alone three at once."

"Your words were helpful," I murmured shyly, pleased at her praise. "They helped me more than..." I flushed.

"Than Stevan's?" Zai snorted, clearly reading my mind. "Yes, I am quite a teacher. And I would thank you to leave the magic lessons to me. Stevan is a brilliant scholar, but he has not yet mastered the art of instruction. I will tolerate your first accidental experiment given your excitement to learn, but I expect that it will not happen again. Understood?"

Zai didn't seem angry anymore, but I knew she meant it. "Yes. I promise."

"Good. How are you feeling now?"

"Dizzy," I admitted. "I didn't even notice at first."

"Dinner," Zai ordered. "Then bed. We leave early tomorrow for another four days of walking. We'll continue lessons each night after making camp. It will be hard work, so you'll need your rest. Now, let's find Stevan and eat. I'm starved."

* * *

We left early the next morning. It rained most of the day, but my new cloak was so wonderful, I hardly noticed. My new knapsack better carried the weight of my supplies, and for once I was able to walk without feeling like my feet were being pulled into the ground. Still, by the end of the day, the mud and damp were starting to get to me.

The rain had finally eased enough by dinner for us to sit around a fire. Stevan poured beans into the pot and placed it in the flames. He grinned when he saw me give them a look.

"You'll get used to it," he said. "Beans every

night, over and over, except those nights we're lucky enough to catch a fish or buy a meal in town. Isn't adventure fun? Don't you love the mud in your toes, the rain on your back, and knowing that bed is just another wet tarp away?"

"If it's between a wet tarp and marriage, I know which I choose," I replied instantly. "I haven't changed my mind. I'm just going to pretend my beans are beef stew, is all."

"Mmm, beef stew!" he groaned. "With potatoes and peas?"

"Carrots, too," I teased.

"Well, while we wait on our gourmet feast," Zai said, "it's time for a magic lesson."

"What should I do?" I glanced at the fire hopefully. Perhaps I could fan the flames or maybe even learn to purify water.

"Lift this rock." Zai pointed at a small, gray stone near her foot.

My jaw nearly dropped. Surely I was capable of more! I tried not to pout and lifted a hand towards the rock. I could see it, feel it... and yet the rock didn't so much as quiver.

The corners of Stevan's mouth raised as he stirred the pot, but he said nothing. I kept my arm raised and clenched my jaw, trying again.

When Stevan finally pulled the pot out of the fire, the rock was still firmly on the ground, and I was covered in sweat.

"You've done well," Zai promised as Stevan served. "I can feel your magic increasing. It's just like any physical muscle that needs to be exercised. Clearly earth magic is less your specialty than fire. Eat. It will help you grow."

Though still grumpy, I was ravenous, and I took the bowl immediately. "Stevan said there are four types of magic," I said as we ate. I tried not to shovel too much into my mouth at once. "Can you really only be good at one?"

Zai and Stevan shared a look. "That's a question for the ages, but I'll bite," Zai said slowly. "It's true there are four elements and most mages are drawn to one. It's looking like your strength may be fire. There are specialties within those elements, like tidal mages with the navy or pyros with the army. Yet I know a great sailor who can barely clean a cup of water and a sun soldier who would burst into flames if she played with lightning. It's a balancing act, you see—tides aren't only about water; they involve the pull of the moon on the earth, too. Lightning means understanding the dance between air and fire in order to handle it deftly."

"Plus there are mages who think that animal and human magics are their own separate categories, even though tradition nests them under earth," Stevan added.

"Oh, gods, not this old argument again!" Zai complained.

"Just because you've never read Meltoothe—" Stevan objected.

"And just because you've studied one text by one discredited old coot—" Zai retorted.

They bickered about theories for a bit. I must have grown tired as they talked and zoned out, but eventually I was able to ask, "What's your strength?"

Zai smiled knowingly, and there was something almost frightening about it. "All four," she replied quietly. "Which is not to say I know everything," she amended, seeing the awed look on my face, "but my essence doesn't favor one element over another. Some mages are able to master all of them."

"It's what makes her such a good teacher," Stevan added. He scraped the last of the beans from his bowl. "She can teach anyone, no matter their element, and help them unlock their powers." He stood. "I can wash up tonight." He took our bowls and walked off into the growing dark.

"Is that what you'll do for me, then? Unlock my powers?" I asked.

Zai nodded. "Sort of. It's more like I show you

the door, but you decide if you want to go through it." She eyed me. "Stevan's pleased that he was right about you. He swore he could sense your power the moment we arrived. Though with the way you radiate it, I'd be very disappointed if he'd missed a clue like that. Might even have to pretend he was never my apprentice."

"My magic is strong, then?" I remembered the cave and how I had felt a ringing through my whole body.

"Only once have I met anyone with powers like yours. But it's getting late. It's time for reading lessons before bed."

The subject had changed so rapidly that I knew it was no use trying to ask more. I worked on my letters and words with Zai and Stevan until it was too dark to see.

CHAPTER 8

WE SETTLED INTO A ROUTINE: walk all morning, pause for a quick lunch, walk some more, set up camp, study magic, eat dinner, and then practice reading until bedtime. It was exhausting, and it was all I could do to keep up.

Just about every third day, we came across a town and restocked our food. Rooms were seldom crowded, but the few people we did come across weren't always friendly. It was funny, but I was starting to prefer sleeping beneath cold, open skies over being inside stuffy walls.

Zai remained a mystery, but I trusted my new teacher, even if she was sometimes aloof. And Stevan... I tried to convince myself that our growing glances and excuses to brush hands on the path were nothing more than coincidence. When I was tired enough, I could almost believe it.

One day, as Stevan and I were climbing down yet another slowly winding path, I realized it was getting quite a bit warmer. The air was thick with sweet, sticky pine, and the sky was a dazzling blue. Even the leaves were brilliantly green and full.

"Alright," Stevan grumbled. He stopped and dropped his pack with a thump. "It's hot down here. And unless you want to smell me for the rest of the week, I need to shed some layers."

"Where is 'here?'" I asked as Stevan began to pull off his cloak.

He shrugged. "Not far from Galikath on The River Dei. We'll follow the path west for another day or so before we finally make it to the valley, and then from there it's less than a week to the palace."

I wasn't sure what I was feeling. Surprise, perhaps? Surely not sadness that our time wandering the woods was nearly over.

Any joy I felt about the warm weather was gone by the time we made camp. The sun had grown hot, and our clothes were sticky. No one said much as we staked out our shelters.

I was worried Zai wouldn't continue lessons that night, not when we were all so tired, but before Stevan could light a fire, Zai raised a hand to stop him. "You," she barked, looking at me.

I felt my palms begin to sweat, but Stevan smiled beautifully at me. I took a deep breath and drew the fire from within, really making myself want it. Sweat stung my eyes, but I resisted the urge to wipe it away. The tinder sparked, then flamed; I blew gently until a green fire began to blaze.

Zai seemed somewhat pacified. She waved her hand, and the flames were suddenly full. "Start the meal," she ordered Stevan. "I'm headed down to the river to wash our clothes. Put on your sleeping things."

I changed quickly, happy to be free of my salt-encrusted shirt. Zai wrapped our clothes in her oilskin and lugged them to the river.

"That's as close to a favor as we'll ever get, you know," Stevan said as he placed hardtack dough on a rock. "Flaming up the fire like this."

"I was wondering. She always says it's good for us to wait. That it builds character."

Stevan laughed. "You build a lot of character working for Zai," he chuckled. "Still. It's nice of her to do laundry, too. But that's not a favor so much as we all stink."

The meal was ready when Zai came back, but she didn't have our clothes. I looked at Stevan, but he just shrugged. We ate quietly before Zai announced that she was returning to the river to finish. "I expect I'll be back late," she added. "Don't wait up."

I wondered aloud what could take so long when Zai was gone.

"She's probably doing it the old-fashioned way. I've seen her do it a few times before. She must be getting anxious. I doubt she'll be back before midnight. Let's work on your reading." He grabbed the scrolls from Zai's pack.

"Anxious?" Perhaps Zai was regretting taking me on now that she had seen how little I could do.

"This always happens when we get close to home. It's hard to return to normal after enjoying freedom like this, you know."

I didn't really know, but I had no normal to return to. Perhaps that was a good thing.

Near the end of our session, I was struggling to see the scroll in the growing darkness. "Here," I said, pointing at something on the parchment. "I can't make out this word; it's too dark. What does it say?"

"Where, here?" Stevan placed his hand over mine, pointer finger extended. I could feel the heat from his palm, and my breath caught. My body felt the same way it did in the cave, only this time I was pretty sure it wasn't because of magic.

I held still as he leaned closer. "That says Princess Aselära, Daughter of Queen Jenelle." His breath tickled my ear.

"I've never seen dots like that on a letter before."

"Queen Jenelle is from Oqira. That letter's part of the Oqiran alphabet. She and the king gave their daughter an Oqiran name to foster trust between the countries. We've had great success with eastern trades thanks to their marriage." Political texts were perhaps the most mundane things I read in my studies, but tonight with Stevan I found the scroll fascinating.

The lesson ended too early, though, when he suddenly yawned and stretched. "Perhaps it's time to stop. Even I'm having trouble making out the words, and I've read this boring report more times than I can count. Good work tonight, Ayve. You've come very far in such a short time."

A warm glow flamed in my chest. I crawled into my bedroll and listened as Stevan walked the perimeter, muttering spells as he went. He reassured me that Zai could most certainly find her way back in—she knew his trace, after all— and crawled into his own bed not far away.

It was too dark to read by, but the moon was still quite bright. I lay on my back for a while, but sleep was elusive. My thoughts wandered to a warm hand covering mine.

"Ayve?"

I jerked when Stevan began to speak. "Yes?" I hoped he couldn't hear how flustered I was. "Is everything okay?"

There was silence for a moment. "Yes," he said. "I just can't sleep."

"Me neither," I admitted.

"I guess I'm more nervous about returning to Freodon than I realized," he said, sighing quietly beneath his tarp. "It's been a while since we were on a journey. I'd forgotten how much I missed being out of the city."

"Have you traveled a lot?" I was jealous to think of all the nights he'd had sleeping beneath the stars. It seemed so unfair that I'd spent so long trapped at the inn.

"I have," he said, and I could hear him smiling at the sky as he remembered. "I was young enough when Zai found me that I was able to go to school full time, but we always found reasons to get away between sessions. And we've traveled the past four years as partners. Even before that, my family and I moved all around."

"I thought you were from Hendassa."

I heard his bedroll rustle as he nodded. "We returned there between shows. But players can only stay in one town so long before people get bored of them. We spent most of the year traveling in a big caravan of families, returning only for the winter to learn a new show."

He talked for a while. I was happy to listen. The more he spoke, the more I realized how little I knew about him.

"Ever since joining Zai, I've felt like I was living the life I was meant to have," he finished. "There was so much that I didn't know was out there. And she made sure to show it all to me. I'm glad you're here with me to learn from her, too."

It was only after an owl hooted for the third time that I realized I'd begun to drift to sleep. "Thank you," I said belatedly, not sure how much time had passed since Stevan had stopped talking. "I'm glad to be here with you, too."

Perhaps I was dreaming, but I swore I heard a soft, "Good."

CHAPTER 9

"RISE AND SHINE, MY CHILDREN!"

I squinted. The sun was higher in the sky than usual, and it was warm. Zai was poking at the fire as Stevan stumbled off into the trees. It seemed late enough that I shouldn't dally further. I clambered up and out. Our clothes hung in the clearing on a rope, still damp.

"Well, good morning. About time you two woke. It was a clear night," Zai said, pointing at the clothesline. "It's going to be a clear day, and hot, so I decided we should take a rest and let things truly dry for once. Weather magics are unpredictable, but I know enough to tell that tomorrow will be cooler, and I'd rather not sweat my way up and down the trail and ruin these nice clean clothes."

My shirt looked exceptionally white. I wanted to ask if we couldn't just dry everything with magic, but my feet ached. "I suppose you could convince me to take a rest for once!"

After breakfast, Zai instructed Stevan to clean our gear. "And scrub it right, none of this magicking it to cheat," she warned. "I want you to build some character." We shared a grin.

Zai took me deeper into the woods. I was worried at first that she was still on edge, but she seemed downright cheerful. She even chattered a bit, something I was beginning to learn Zai only did on her best days.

"I want to test your earth magic skills more," Zai announced as we walked.

"Don't we already know my earth magic isn't strong?" I was tasked with trying to move rocks for our fire ring every night. I'd only managed to get them to waist height, and any rocks bigger than my fist remained solidly on the ground.

"Remember, there are multiple ways elemental strengths manifest," Zai replied. We had reached the river, which roared mightily. Zai settled into a nook below three large trees that grew in a circle. She gestured for me to join her. "And I'm intrigued by something I remembered last night. I knew someone once, a young girl like you. She could never move a rock more than a few inches above the ground. It drove her mad. But one day she and her sister got into a fight. They were little still, but her sister was older, more powerful, and she did a stupid big sister thing and used magic to wrap her up in tree roots."

I sat beside Zai, looking at the knobby roots protruding through the ground beside us. "That sounds a little mean," I said. "Big sisters should help their siblings. Even if they are annoying."

"Yes, well, sisters can be a pain," she said flippantly, and I wondered if perhaps this story was more personal than Zai cared to admit. "Anyway," she continued, "the point is that the older sister wanted to teach the younger one a lesson, so she left her there for just a bit. But when she came back, not only was the girl free of the roots, they had formed a soft bed for her to sleep on. See, we usually test for earth magic using rocks because it's easiest to start with non-living things. Only for some mages, they connect better with their world if it's alive."

Zai pointed to tree roots poking through the soil. "Touch one," she commanded.

I reached out my hand.

"No, touch one, with your magic. Say hello to it."

I felt a little silly. Still, I knew that Zai's third rule was that I had to want it, so I closed my eyes, picturing myself shaking the gnarled tree's root like a knobby old hand.

I gasped suddenly and opened my eyes. A small root tendril had sprouted from the ground and wrapped itself around my index finger.

"Lovely," Zai whispered. If I hadn't known better, I'd say the look in Zai's eyes was hunger. "Keep going. Feel the tree. Get to know it."

The leaves fluttered overhead, and I felt an overwhelming sense of happiness. Somehow, I understood the tree was glad to meet me. I allowed myself to sit, breathing, just barely aware of the way small vines began to coil around my fingers.

"Enough." Zai's voiced snapped me back to reality, and I found myself sitting wrapped in tender green leaves. Judging by the sun and the stiffness in my back, we had been there for a while. "Shoo, now," Zai told the tree firmly. "You can't have her; she's mine." The tendrils slowly crept backwards, tickling my palm and making me laugh.

"That was wonderful," I beamed. "I felt like it was talking to me! That was nothing like fire magic."

"That's because the tree is alive in ways that

fire isn't. Fire feels alive and looks alive, but it's the opposite of life: death, consumption, destruction." She nodded twice. "I'm pleased with how this has gone. We will certainly have good work to do when we reach the palace. Well done."

I had never heard such high praise before, and I knew I should treasure it. I murmured my thanks before accepting a canteen of water. I was tired, so we sat under the tree, relaxing.

"The moon was quite full last night," Zai commented.

"Yes." I was puzzled. Were we about to discuss the stars?

"When was your last moonblood?"

I blushed furiously. "I suppose it was right before you arrived at the inn," I made myself say. Besides Alys, I had never discussed my moonblood with anyone.

Zai clucked her tongue in her no-nonsense way. "You'll need to keep an eye out for the next one to arrive, then," she said. "I realize I was a bit... remiss... in leaving you alone with Stevan last night. It's been nearly a complete moon cycle since we met you. You know how these things work, don't you, with children?"

I was mortified. "Of course, my lady! Alys taught me when I... but nothing happened!" I blurted. "Honest to gods, Stevan helped me with my reading and we went to sleep, that's all!" My cheeks flushed as I remembered the way his breath had felt against my face. *He was only close because we were reading*, a stubborn voice protested in my head.

Zai held up a hand to stop me. "I didn't mean to imply anything had happened. Stevan knows I'd crack him upside the head if he took advantage of my new assistant." She smiled wryly. "But it is my job as your teacher to make sure you are safe. There will be people in the city who aren't as well-intentioned as Stevan, and I shouldn't have forgotten my duties." There was something on her face that made me think there was more she wanted to say. "All the same," she continued, "we should get you a pregnancy charm in Galikath just to be safe. Even if all you intend with someone is talking, these things have a way of just happening."

"Okay." I thought I might cringe for the rest of my life. "But wouldn't you be able to make me one?" The thought of having to see a village healer to talk about having babies was almost too much to bear.

"While it's true there are midwifery spells, I can't say I've ever cared to learn any," Zai admitted ruefully. "I never had much interest in children or babies. It didn't seem a practical skill for me to develop. So no, I'm afraid we'll have to make a stop. Don't worry; I can distract Stevan long enough that he doesn't realize where you are. Speaking of distracting Stevan, he should almost be done cleaning our gear by now. It's nearly lunch."

I was surprised to feel my stomach grumble.

"You were communing with the tree longer than you realized," Zai said as she stood. She offered a hand. "That's the way with these trees. Takes them hundreds of years to grow, so they don't understand time in the human element and take forever just to say hello. Fire's a much faster magic in that respect."

We walked back to camp discussing magic speeds. I felt incredibly grateful for the change in topic.

* * *

It was embarrassing how tired I was after my time with the tree, but it was all I could do to keep my eyes open through lunch. I was glad when Zai suggested a short nap before afternoon lessons, and I dozed in the warm sun.

The afternoon passed quickly; we read more scrolls and discussed details of the palace. Stevan made a brief appearance in the late afternoon before returning to the river. As the sun began to set, he came back proudly holding a fish. Zai narrowed her eyes, but he shook his head in reply. "I caught it fairly," he swore. "No magic," he explained, and his smile sent my heart flipping.

"It's cheating," Zai explained as he began to clean the fish. "Using magic to hunt. Foraging is one thing—nuts, berries, mushrooms—but seeking prey with your magic is cheap. Even the most desperate mages try not to resort to it. There's value in honesty, even if you're hungry. Some would say there's value *especially* if you're hungry."

As the fish roasted, my mouth watered. It had been *ages* since we'd eaten something other than beans. I even got in the spirit myself and made a fresh batch of ash cakes. Stevan was in a good mood, dancing about the fire as he checked on the fish, joking and laughing dazzlingly.

He's flirting, I thought, smoothing my hair nervously. Or at least I was pretty sure he was. Village boys like Rafe were the only ones who had flirted with me before, and they were awkward and clumsy about it. But Stevan was all charm and white teeth. I wasn't positive, but I thought I saw Zai smiling as she rolled up the afternoon's parchments.

We ate, using the ash cakes as plates, and with no dishes to clean, we stretched out on the ground.

Well-fed and happy, we lay back and raced each other to find the first star of the night.

"I ought to study star magic when we get back," Stevan mused. The sky was a deep, rich blue. We never stayed up this late, and I felt a thrill race through my chest as I stared up at the glittering dark.

"Oh?" Zai was using her curious voice. I was beginning to learn that Zai had her most interesting thoughts when she used that voice. "You've never mentioned it before. Why the change of heart?"

I could hear Stevan shrug against the earth. "I've had time to think, I suppose. No one really knows which element they belong to. It's fascinating—some air magic seems so closely related to water magic. You know, currents, waves—all things I've come to understand. But stars seem to be their own separate thing. I can't get a reading on them. They're beautiful, and they're awe-inspiring. But they leave my magic feeling blank."

I felt dizzy at even the thought of trying to feel the stars with my magic. I decided not to chance it.

Zai hummed. "Stars are actually balls of burning gas so far away that we could never reach them in our lifetime. Not even in a thousand of our lifetimes. I read once that they could even be suns to worlds like our own. So then perhaps they really belong to fire magic, since fire mages tend to connect best with the sun, though gods know there are earth mages who can harness its powers, too. Plus there's some air element to stars since their light filters through our sky."

Stevan gave a low whistle. "Perhaps I'm biting off more than I can chew. What say you, Ayve? What do you think about the stars?"

My head was spinning again. "I can barely wrap my mind around them," I admitted. "Seems to me that's a lot of thought for something that folks should just sit back and admire."

"From the mouths of babes. Or at least assistants," Zai laughed, raising her hand in a mock toast.

"You'll find that most mages spend too much time—what was your phrase?—giving 'a lot of thought to things that folks should just sit back and admire,'" Stevan sighed. "It's one of the downfalls of spending time with such an academic-minded crowd."

"Does it ever get less dizzying?" I wondered aloud.

"Sometimes. And sometimes *you'll* be the one making others dizzy. Some might even say you do that already."

I was thankful no one could see the flush that crept up my face.

"Well, if you do pursue the stars," Zai said, changing the subject ever-so tactfully, "be careful. There are plenty of hucksters out there who claim that the relation of a star to someone's birth means something, and that's nonsense."

"There were Hendassan traders who used to say that," I remembered. "They came by once or twice a year and did star readings for a fee. Everyone was always in awe at how accurate they were."

Zai snorted. "It's not hard to make up that kind of nonsense. Still, that's not to say there isn't power in these skies. Even I can admit that the constellations seem to have a connection to the gods, which is a magic I won't even begin to dream of."

"*You?*" I popped a hand to my mouth as Stevan chuckled. I pushed myself to an elbow. "It's just I can't imagine a power that could be beyond your reach."

"It's not that it's beyond my reach," Zai said, sounding somewhat cross. She, too, propped herself up. "With study, I'm sure I could develop some mastery. I just haven't the time nor care to invest years of my life into staring at the sky when I'd rather be sleeping. Much the way I don't care for midwifery."

I tried to keep a neutral face. Fortunately, Zai began to stand.

"Well I, for one, am getting chilly, and we have an early morning ahead of us. No more days off until we get to the palace. I'm headed to bed. Good night, you two."

* * *

Sleep once again didn't want to come, though I could hear deep breathing from Zai's direction. It was still warm, and my arm was free of its blanket. The ground beneath my bedroll was soft, and I let my fingers run over the silky grass.

Something tickled my pinky finger gently. In the dark, I could just make out a small flower winding itself around my hand. Startled, I realized the ground beneath me was suddenly full of the sweetly perfumed blossoms.

"I don't remember making camp on a bed of flowers." Stevan was crouched just outside my tarp. He held a shimmering ball of gray light in his left hand and a yellow spray of flowers in the other. "I take it you had a good lesson with Zai?"

I smiled and nodded.

He held the flowers to his nose and breathed deeply. "Honeysuckle. It's not usually found this far north. At the palace, earth mages grow it in greenhouses." He inhaled again, drinking in the sweetness. "How did you know it was my favorite?"

I was startled. "I didn't. I didn't even mean to call these. They just happened."

"I'm starting to think that's the way it is with you, Ayve. Things just happen."

Stevan held out his hand, gently ushering the flowers towards me. They slowly climbed from his fingers to mine. The vines around them slowly disappeared back into the earth until it was as if they had never been there at all. Yet the bunch on my hand held firm, coiling about my fingers like a favorite pet.

"Pretty," he said as he doused his light.

I fell asleep to dreams of fingers soft as petals.

CHAPTER 10

THIS TIME, WHEN WE WALKED down the path, there was no winding back up—just down, down, down to the valley below. It was much warmer, and spring was in full bloom. The road grew wider, and every now and then we passed a farmer with a cart or country folk walking into town.

We reached Galikath by noon. It was big, nearly double the size of Duskett, maybe even triple Jeren. And the inn! I couldn't imagine how they possibly managed all of their guests.

The baths were beyond busy, so Zai paid someone to heat and carry water to private tubs in our room for us. "Worth it," she sighed as she climbed in. "I haven't felt truly clean in a month."

A month. It had been a month since we left. A month since my tiny room, since mucking out the stables. Since serving tankard after tankard of ale, since always disappointing Petyr, since understanding I was never wanted at all. A month since Alys standing by the door, Joseth in her arms, crying softly.

A feeling uncomfortably like guilt surged into my throat. I tried to force the image from my mind. They had planned to marry me off. I had escaped. I should be happy.

"There's a midwife in town you should see while we're here." Zai's eyes were closed, her head tilted back against the tub.

The feeling of guilt turned to embarrassment. "Should I? I mean, shouldn't I wait until we get to the palace? Make sure she's trustworthy?"

Zai shook her head, eyes still closed. "She used to work for the palace. She has my full confidence. Finish your bath and go."

Though it was the last thing I wanted to do, I sought out the midwife. The woman was kind, matronly, and brusque. When I explained what I was there for, she immediately asked if I had slept with any men in the last month.

"We've been traveling together, but—"

"When is your next moonblood due?"

"Any day now, it just hasn't come yet—"

The woman began to pull bottles down from the shelf. "We'll need to check first. See if you're with child before you use a charm that could hurt a babe."

"No!" I cried in alarm. "It's nothing like that, we were in separate bedrolls, we never had... did..."

"Had sex?" the midwife asked bluntly. "Made love, canoodled, threaded the needle?" The midwife laughed, though not unkindly. "If just hearing about sex makes you feel this way, mayhap you're not quite ready to use this charm just yet. But it's a good idea to have one anyway," she said, pulling a small box from the shelf, "in case you do decide to take things further than honest-to-gods sleep. Besides, you're well over the age most girls start families. I'm guessing you're headed for the city instead of a marriage?"

I nodded.

"Then I'm also guessing whatever small town you're coming from didn't teach you much about the ways of love and a woman's pleasure."

She instructed me in some of the basics before finally handing me a charm. Martha had told me some, after her wedding to Rafe, and there were things one learned from growing up at an inn, but I had never heard it spoken so confidently from a woman's perspective before.

"The charm is unneeded, you know, should

you wish to be with women," the midwife added as she began to clean up. I flushed. "I know, I'm a bit modern for some of my rural sisters, but I spent my early years working in Freodon, which is less prudish in its ways. Same love happens everywhere, only it's less talked about out here, and sometimes women don't even know they have options besides men until they're much older, poor things. Have you thought much about which you're interested in? Men? Women? Or both?"

I hesitated. *Rule two*, a voice inside whispered.

"That's fine, dearie. You don't have to know. And even if you think you do, you might find your mind changes in ten years. That's fine, too. But if you do decide to sleep with women, you should know how to be safe with them, too, because sickness can still pass between female lovers."

I left a while later wearing the charm about my neck, feeling older and wiser.

* * *

I couldn't understand why I was sad. I knew we were reaching the end of our journey, had known for two days, but somehow that knowledge had only just sunk in. Zai informed us over breakfast that we had only a few more nights of camping before we reached the city, and my heart sank further. I ran my thumb along my new charm and tried to remember that there was a time I had wanted to turn back. It was silly to be scared now.

The day's walk was slow and slogging. We had to step aside several times for large carriages to pass. By the time we made it to our intended campsite, it was full and loud. All it took was one look, and we kept walking. It was only after the sun had set that we found a quiet grove. Stevan began to light a fire, but Zai shook her head wearily. We ate cold jerky and drank water before crawling beneath our tarps and falling soundly asleep.

The next day was much the same, and I was grumpy. My chest hurt, too. I knew my moonblood was nearly upon me, and it had my nerves frazzled. I snapped at Stevan unintentionally around noon, and Zai spared him by walking with me the rest of the day. But Zai was in a bad mood, too, especially after a large cart got stuck in the path and we had to walk through thorny underbrush to get around it. We once again walked past our intended camp and skipped our hot meal in order to get some sleep.

It rained overnight, and we awoke to a damp chill. It soured my mood even further, especially when I found that my moonblood had finally arrived.

Fortunately, we managed to pick up the pace in the afternoon, and we arrived at the edge of a cliff overlooking a large town by mid-afternoon.

"Well, there it is," Zai sighed. "The end of sleeping in the woods. The end of washing clothes in streams, and of relieving oneself in a hole."

"And yet somehow I'll still miss it." Stevan stood beside her. The sun peeked out from behind a cloud.

I squinted, following their gaze, and then started. "It's the city!" I gasped. What I had taken for a town was only the buildings closest to us. Spread behind them was a colossal city with winding streets and gleaming roofs. Far in the distance, I could just make out what must be the palace, its stone walls towering over everything else.

It was all too familiar. That spire, those trees, the river snaking by... It was the exact scene I had seen a thousand times over in the painting I'd kept in my drawer. It was buried in my pack now, but it was a perfect match. Something about this felt right. I smiled at Zai, who smiled back, and we turned to make our way downhill for the last time.

* * *

The walk into the city was even more crowded

and slow. We mingled with the sluggish mob until we reached our lodgings on the outskirts.

If the Galikath inn had surprised me, this one was downright overwhelming. It was massive, at least four times the size of my childhood home, and it wasn't the only one around. I could see several others lining the street, and I was sure there must be more ahead.

"Home sweet home for the night," Zai said, pointing at a wooden sign carved with a small bird outside its front. "The Lark is the best lodging we'll find till we reach the palace. Let's hurry before all the best rooms are gone."

We had hoped to share a private room, but nearly everything was filled. "Damn tournaments," Stevan groaned as he begrudgingly paid for beds in a communal room. Still, the bunks were soft, and the baths were hot with clean towels and soap.

Before we dressed, Zai handed me a brown paper package. Inside I found a soft, emerald velvet dress with swirls embossed on the skirt and bodice.

"It's beautiful," I said, completely overwhelmed.

"I relayed your approximate size once we were close enough to spell-speak," Zai said, holding the dress up to me and nodding approvingly. "It may be a touch big, but I think it should do nicely."

"I couldn't," I protested. "It must have cost so much."

"Nonsense. You'll need something nice for dinner when we reach the palace tomorrow. There are standards I must keep here where I'm Lady Zai, and the same goes for those who work for me. It's yours. And with how well you've done in your studies on this trip, you've more than earned it."

Tears stung my eyes. Zai smiled understandingly and patted my shoulders softly. "Now get dressed. The Lark has some of the best lamb I've ever found, and I don't intend to let a bunch of young, dumb knights eat it all."

* * *

The common room was louder than my inn had ever gotten during even the wildest midwinter celebration. Though my new dress was safely packed away, Zai had also surprised me with fresh black breeches and shirt. I couldn't stop running my hands over the soft fabric as we ate.

To honor our final night, Zai ordered an earthy red wine, tender lamb, buttery potatoes, and sweet cherries with cream to round out the meal. The whole experience made me giddy, and

I felt the wine rush straight to my head.

Several people stopped by to greet Zai throughout the evening, and she eventually excused herself to sit with a beautiful woman and handsome man.

"Lady Liliane and Master Onan," Stevan informed me over the din. "Mages at the palace. You'll see more of them, especially if you take their classes."

I watched them curiously. Liliane was lovely, fair-skinned with a thick golden braid circling her head like a crown. Onan had deep brown skin with a rugged black beard and broad, strong shoulders. If I hadn't known better, I would almost say Zai was flirting with Liliane. Their conversation steadily grew more serious, and the trio leaned in together.

"They're a curious bunch, aren't they?" Stevan asked, watching me. I nodded. "Unless they're talking about the bandits in Qimorath, I bet they're dreaming up a grand plan about what to do with you next. Zai has all sorts of ideas. Those two have been at the palace almost as long as she has; she'll want to consult them before she makes any final decisions."

Sure enough, Lady Liliane looked over at me and waved. "What do you plan to do next?" I asked Stevan after I had waved back. The wine had left me feeling bold.

"I'm sure Zai will give me some instructions once we reach the palace, though I know she eventually wants me to do more research on the remaining crystals. But I wasn't kidding; I really do want to go to Qiameth and study the stars."

I took another sip of wine. Spices danced on my tongue. "Won't you miss me?" I teased.

He met my eyes without flinching. "Miss you?" If it hadn't been for the wine, I might have backpedaled and started fumbling for excuses. But to my surprise, Stevan slid his hand across the table until his fingertips nearly found mine.

A sharp laugh from a tavern maiden broke the spell. Stevan's hand shifted to reach for his goblet. Perhaps it hadn't even been real. "I'll miss walking every day, but I certainly won't miss the palace." He drank deeply.

"I see." Head spinning, I began to stand.

"Wait, don't go." I paused, half out of my chair, sitting again only when he leaned forward and truly did take my hand this time. "Please. It's not that I wouldn't—you have to understand," he stammered. "I just didn't think it would be like this."

"Like what?" My voice sounded distant in my ears.

"Like anything. You're still so young."

"Almost eighteen," I retorted. "Not much younger than you. Zai says you're twenty-two." Our knees were nearly touching.

He shook his head but didn't move his leg. "But you're barely a newborn when it comes to magic, and there are things you need to understand before..."

"Before what?" I prompted, cocking my head to one side.

He truly looked miserable and pulled his hand away. "There's so much more you don't know yet, Ayve."

I balked. "Well, yes, but I'm trying to learn, in case you hadn't noticed! Hours on end of studying, and—"

He shook his head. "No, it's the things that you don't know about—"

"I hope I'm not interrupting!" Zai sounded cheery, but ice dripped from her tall frame. She put a hand on the back of my chair. "Stevan, come with me a moment, won't you? Master Onan has a question, and I know you can answer it better than I." Not giving him a chance to reply, she pulled him from his seat and marched him over to the other table.

I sat alone, fanning myself. My head was beginning to pound with a dull ache. Stevan and Master Onan were deep in conversation, and for a second, I could almost convince myself that what he'd said had never happened. But it was no use. Even with the room spinning, I knew what he'd said. To him, I was nothing more than a child.

Head swirling, I mustered my courage and stumbled up the stairs. I frantically pulled myself from my new clothes and threw myself under the sheets. For the first time since I had left the inn, I cried myself to sleep.

CHAPTER 11

"YOU LOOK TERRIBLE."

I groaned and stuffed my bag slowly. My head was roaring. At least the room had stopped spinning.

Zai leaned back on her bunk, bag already packed, and watched. "I *could* help you, you know. I know enough about herbs to make a rudimentary hangover tonic." I eyed her hopefully. "But I won't. It's important you know your limits. It's not safe to drink so much, especially not in a new city where you don't know who to trust. You'll be surrounded by mage students, who on the whole are a jealous and competitive lot. Even with advanced skills, some tonics and poisons can be difficult to detect, and you might drink something you'd later regret. Am I making myself clear?"

I nodded miserably. "I understand. I didn't mean to drink so much, honest. It won't happen again."

"Good. Then finish packing and come along to breakfast. We have a palace to get to."

It was only as we finished the last bites that I realized Stevan still hadn't joined us.

"I've sent him on with Master Onan," Zai replied when I finally worked up the courage to ask. "There's important research that needs doing. He'll join us at dinner, I think. Palace life gets busy, so we may see less of him. Though I suppose anything is less than constantly being at each other's sides for a month."

I breathed a sigh of relief. I wasn't sure I was ready to see him yet. Perhaps I'd be up to facing him later that night. *Although this time*, I thought ruefully, *maybe without the wine*.

* * *

The palace, in my opinion, was stupidly placed. The road wound slowly uphill, circling around the whole city and spiraling to the castle grounds at the center. While I was sure it was a good defense tactic, and while it benefitted the businesses along the way, it was as dumb, I thought, as the ever-winding paths that went up and down the mountains.

Zai had hoped we could slip through the royal gates and take the less-traveled streets that led straight up to the palace, but they were clogged thanks to the influx of knights for the tournament, and Zai had no desire to get into a fight "with a bunch of brawny, brainless battle-brains," as she called them.

Despite the pace, I was fascinated by the crowds. Never in my life had I seen so many people at once, and never the wide swath of humanity represented there. In Jeren, people looked mostly the same. In Freodon, everyone was different: hair, skin, clothes, heights, languages, clothes, even accents. I tried not to gawp.

The cobblestones were dusty, and a sharp wind whipped dirt into our faces. The sky darkened ominously. Zai shouldered on through the crowd, muttering about reaching the palace before the storm hit.

We began to pass through a market section where booths lined either side of the crowded road. Even more people perused the stalls, haggling with shopkeepers and yelling at their children. Zai halted suddenly, and I walked into her pack.

She swore. "It's Madame Gerta," she said, pointing grumpily at an older woman eying a bin of figs. "I need to speak with her, and the woman is damn near famous for never leaving her rooms." She looked at the sky, clucked her tongue, and then pointed at a nearby fountain. "Wait here," she ordered. "This will only take a moment." She swept off with a swish.

The spray from the fountain was cold. I shifted slightly and turned my back to its spout.

"Would you like to see our bracelets, miss? A pretty bracelet for a pretty lady?" A girl about my age stood before me in a brown apron dress over a cream-colored shirt. With thick dirty-blonde curls, dashing apple-green eyes, and a smattering of freckles on golden skin, she was nothing short of beautiful.

"No, thank you," I stuttered. "I have no money to spend."

The girl didn't seem swayed. She opened a small box and delicately held up a dainty wooden bracelet. Small flowers were etched onto each bead.

"It's lovely," I replied, fingering it gently. "But I really don't have any money. And we'll be leaving soon—my lady will be back any minute."

The wind picked up, and a few small drops of

rain splashed the dust beside me. All at once it really began to pour, great sheets of icy rain. I gasped, and the crowd around me surged as everyone struggled to find cover.

"In here!" the girl shouted. She grabbed my hand and pulled me into a stall. It was her own, by the looks of it, a jewelry booth filled with wooden bracelets, delicate silver anklets, and elegant necklaces.

"Thank you," I said gratefully.

The girl shook her head slightly, and water bounced from her curls. "My name is Rebekah," she offered over the roaring rain.

It would be churlish not to share in return. "I'm Ayve."

Rebekah extended a hand, and I gave my own, expecting a handshake, yet she raised it to her lips and, not taking her eyes off mine, gently brushed a kiss on my knuckles. I felt a shiver run down my spine. What did this shopgirl want?

To talk, it seemed. "So where are you from, dear Ayve?"

"Is it that obvious that I'm not from here?"

Rebekah laughed, and the sound was like tinkling bells. "Well, yes, but also the big pack on your back sort of gave you away."

I reddened, and Rebekah laughed again, but it wasn't unkind. "I'm from Jeren. I'll be staying at the palace soon. With—mages." I may have been inexperienced, but I at least knew that I shouldn't mention Lady Zai to just anyone.

"Is that so? I may need to start visiting the palace more."

As quickly as it had come, the rain began to recede, and I could hear the sounds of the crowd beyond the stall again. One voice in particular stood out.

"I'm in the jewelry stall!" I shouted in reply.

Zai raced in, drenched. She eyed Rebekah, who smiled politely. "I'm glad you're safe," Zai said after a moment. "The rain should be over now. Let's be on our way."

"And the pretty lady is sure she doesn't want a pretty bracelet?" Rebekah batted her lashes and held out the bracelet one last time.

Zai rolled her eyes. "Thank you, but we have to go."

Rebekah followed us out into the open air, her eyes never leaving mine. "Welcome to the city, Ayve."

The stones were slick, though at least the stench had somewhat dissipated. The crowds had also diminished, and we finally made it to the top of the winding streets, albeit somewhat less clean that I had hoped I'd be when setting foot in the palace for the first time.

I had imagined entering through a grand marble staircase like in children's stories, but we instead entered through what appeared to be a side gate. The sun peeped out from behind clouds as we traveled through delicious courtyards with fragrant, blossoming trees. I lost track of how many times we turned. Several people called friendly hellos as we passed.

We finally, finally arrived at a towering stone wall and made our way into a cool, airy corridor. Windows lined one side, and what seemed to be magicked light globes burned steadily on the other. I realized we must be in the actual palace, not just the outer layers. We walked up and down a few more hallways until we reached a large, double oaken door. Zai placed a hand on it, muttering a word, and the lock glowed briefly purple.

"Welcome home, Ayve."

The doors opened onto a sitting room with a low mahogany table, black velvet couches, and a large hearth. The floor was made of beautiful gray stone tiles. A thick red rug covered much of the space, and a sweeping window overlooked a courtyard. Zai waved a hand, and the shutters threw themselves open to air out the room.

"These are my quarters." Zai motioned to a door to the right. "My private chambers overlook the Queen's Commons. You will sleep here, by the students' courtyard." She dropped her pack and walked into the small room straight ahead. The floor was the same stone gray with a small, braided rug beside a single bed. The sight was welcome after weeks on lumpy ground. A small desk sat in the space between the bed and door in front of the window, and there was even a dresser for my clothes.

"Well? What do you think? Better than the road?" Zai seemed to be joking, but there was a nervousness in her eyes.

I smiled. "It's wonderful," I enthused. "More than I ever could have hoped for. Thank you."

Zai nodded, clearly pleased.

I dropped my pack and ran my hand along the headboard. "Where does Stevan sleep?"

"Here, actually." I nearly choked. "Or at least he used to, but I've asked him to move up to the mages' tower to make room for you. He must have come by earlier and grabbed his stuff."

"I didn't mean to kick him out!" I blurted, but I was glad to know I wouldn't be sharing Stevan's bed with him.

"It's for the best. Gods know we need our space apart sometimes, and he needs steady access to the mages' library. Besides, you're still in the beginner stages, and I'll need you close at hand for making sure your magic doesn't run amok. And, if you forgot, I hired you as my assistant. I'll expect you to bring some of my meals, help me get dressed, keep the fires lit, and the like. You'll also take magic courses, and you'll need to be able to get to them quickly. You *are* still willing to do all of this?"

I didn't even have to think about it. "Absolutely," I replied, trying not to squeal.

* * *

After unpacking, Zai suggested a visit to the baths to wash off the dirt from the market. There was laundry to be done, too, so I checked my pockets to make sure nothing was hiding in them. Surprised when I felt something, I pulled it out and held up a wooden bead bracelet.

Zai walked in, clucking her tongue and rolling her eyes. "For goodness's sake, what a flirt that girl was."

I stared, wide-eyed.

Zai stared back. "Well, wasn't it obvious? She was flirting with you."

"Flirting? With me?"

Zai clucked her tongue. "Ayve, this is normal here." We walked out of the room, holding our laundry bags. "I was hoping the midwife would explain some things to you in Galikath."

"She did. I guess I forgot." I felt sheepish. "It's just not what it was like growing up."

"Did boys not flirt with you in Jeren?"

I shrugged. "I suppose they did sometimes."

We turned a corner and entered the baths. "And what did you do when you didn't want them to?"

"I just ignored them. Pretended I didn't know what was happening. It mostly worked. Mostly."

We handed our laundry bags to an attendant and slipped out of our clothes, adding them to our bags before grabbing towels.

"It helps to be blunter, especially in the city," Zai advised. "You'll find lots of suitors while you're here. Some wanted, some not. Most bad at reading subtleties. If you don't want someone to come onto you, you need to be direct. Did you want her to flirt with you?"

Zai sank into the bath before us, and I paused, unsure of how to answer. "I don't know," I admitted quietly as I followed her in.

Zai rocked her head side to side, thinking. "Well, the next time someone does—man or woman—be upfront if you don't want it to turn into anything. And take your time. While people might marry for business where you're from, it's love, not financial dealings, that usually makes a marriage here."

"Doesn't that get tricky?" I wanted to know as we lathered up. The baths were mostly empty, and I felt bolder asking such things when no one was around to make fun of me. "Who can inherit if two women have children?"

"It sometimes gets complicated, but what marriage doesn't? Many couples take on a surrogate or donor if they want children. It's a coveted position. Sometimes they even become a part of the family after the child is born. And some couples don't use donors or surrogates at all and adopt. In Freodon, law says once a child is taken into a family, they *are* family, blood or no."

I mulled this over as I ran a luxuriously soft bar of soap across my skin. I imagined what could have been different if that law had applied in Jeren. How differently might Petyr have treated me knowing I was his rightful daughter in the eyes of the law? Would I have found any kindness in his eyes?

Anger bubbled, but Alys's face drifted back into my mind. A sudden surge of shame roiled in my gut, and I lowered myself into the water. Perhaps, even without the law, I had always been family to Alys after all.

I tried to clear my conscience with a change of topic. "What about you, my lady? Do you ever hope to have a family of your own?" It was only after asking that I realized the question was perhaps a little personal.

Still, Zai answered, though she seemed far away as she did. "I learned early on that a marriage and children would never be for me. But the students I care for, they're the family that I need, and I love them just the same."

As one of her students, I supposed that now included me, and I felt something that might almost be a daughter's love for my teacher.

* * *

We took the afternoon easy, going on a short tour of the grounds before returning to Zai's suite. Zai promised she would resume lessons in the morning before retiring to her rooms to take a well-deserved nap. I did the same, though I tossed fitfully, too excited to close my eyes, before finally admitting defeat.

Though I wanted to go for a walk, I had a hunch how Zai would feel if I ventured out on my own, so instead I settled on climbing through my bedroom window and sitting in the courtyard. The air was pleasant, still a touch cool but warm in the sun. I found a bench and practiced my reading with a book I found on my desk. It was slow going, but it detailed the history of the ancient Ole'ad, and I found it fascinating. As the afternoon drew to a close, I climbed back inside, splashed water on my face, and went to find Zai.

"Ah, good, you're up." Zai opened her door at the same time as me. She looked marvelously rested. "We'll be eating in the royal dining hall tonight. Most nights, we'll probably dine separately, but occasionally I'll request your presence at events. Tonight happens to be the godsforsaken ball before this poxy tournament, so our presence is required. Most of my former assistants chose the mages' hall for their meals, but a few were known to enjoy the warriors' hall instead. They always claimed the youthful energy was refreshing after a tedious day in the palace, though gods know I always feel like I'm babysitting a pack of silly pups when I go in there."

I had underestimated how talkative a well-rested Zai could be.

Zai clapped her hands. "Your green dress tonight. Try to pull your hair back if you can. I'm all thumbs when it comes to styling others, but I suppose I can find an attendant if you need help. Come to my rooms when you're done."

The hem hung perfectly, and the dress hugged my body well. I wondered what Stevan would think when he saw me. The thought made me woozy. I brushed my hair and pulled the top half back in two braids. On a whim, I plucked a spray of flowers from the vase above the fire and wove it through the plaits.

The door to Zai's rooms was heavy. Her entrance area was small with just a large chair and desk, but several doors branched off to other spaces. Zai emerged from what appeared to be a bedroom, a vibrant purple dress draped around her frame. She looked radiant, loose laces and all. Shimmering jewels glittered along the bodice, and gold lace danced along the silky, sheer sleeves. The dress must have cost more money than I had ever seen in a year.

"Tie, please," Zai prompted, turning her back. I tugged the silk ribbons gently. I'd learned enough about gowns from guests to know that tightlacing wasn't a real thing, and I worked carefully to tie the dress without distorting the silhouette.

"Well done," Zai praised when I finished. "Stevan never quite got the laces right, and magic on dresses can be so tricky, lest it ruin the delicate fabric." She sat at the desk and fussed with some pots of makeup, tinting her lips, brightening her cheeks, and lining her eyes with thick black kohl. When she finished, she motioned for me to take her place.

Zai murmured her approval of my hair as she

added just the barest hint of pink to my lips and cheeks. When she finished, I recognized myself, but I felt different. Sophisticated. I felt ready.

Walking down the corridors made me feel less so. Fortunately, there was no presenting of me like they did with princesses and ladies; I simply slipped quietly into the hall with Zai. The room was loud, though not nearly as raucous as The Lark had been. We took seats at a small round table, and Zai introduced me to the guests who sat with us. They seemed to take little interest in me, for which I was immensely grateful. I sipped my non-alcoholic cider in peace while Zai caught up with the court gossip.

Master Onan and Lady Liliane were by far the most interesting. They were the youngest at the table, perhaps Zai's age or just a bit older. Master Onan had been in dark blue breeches the night before; tonight they were capped with a dashing black robe. Lady Liliane was in a golden dress of delicate silk with fine beadwork along the bodice. It matched her soft golden curls. Her laugh was soft, too, where Master Onan's was loud and rich.

Soon servers poured from the arches to begin the feast. I ate a little of this and a little of that, grimacing when Lady Liliane explained what some dishes were, laughing when Master Onan explained that the food that frightened me most was nothing but a few harmless ground walnuts.

As the meal began to wind down, and as I finally began to feel comfortable amongst the mages, I grew bolder and peered around for Stevan. He didn't seem to be at any of the tables. I did my best to keep my emotions in check.

When the dancing started, even though Zai immediately joined the throng, I felt entirely out of my element. Formal dances did not happen at the inn, and I had barely known which fork to use let alone how to follow the whirling steps of the music. Even worse, several mage students found their way to our table and asked if I would care to join them in a dance. Fortunately, Zai had prepared me for this, and I gave each a polite no. But still they kept coming.

"You think they'd learn to take a hint." I would have known that voice anywhere. Stevan stood behind me, smiling kindly. It set my heart fluttering madly. He nodded to Lady Liliane's chair, a question in his eyes. I doubted the woman, who was twirling gracefully around the dance floor, would need it any time soon, and I nodded in return. He sank into the seat with the poise of someone who'd grown up at court.

"Thank you," I said, aiming to keep my tone light. "I thought I'd never get a moment's peace again. Maybe you'll scare them off." Sure enough, the group that had gathered on the opposite wall grumbled amongst themselves but turned to find other partners throughout the room.

"Poor boys. They haven't had someone new to look at in months. I suppose they'll get used to you soon enough when you join their classes. Has Zai mentioned which she'd like you to take yet?"

"Not yet. I think that's on deck for tomorrow." I was relieved to follow Stevan's lead and act as if nothing had happened. We chatted about the dinner and my experience at the palace so far as we watched the dancers spin.

When the orchestra began a slow waltz, Stevan picked up an empty glass and swirled it in his fingers in time to the music. "Before I head out," he said lightly, "I was wondering if you'd like to finish discussing what we started last night."

I blinked. So much for pretending nothing had happened. "Okay." I took a breath, steadying myself.

"There you are! I've been looking for you all night!"

Stevan placed the glass back on the table. "Hello, Zai. You have remarkable timing. You look lovely, of course." He stood, kissing her on each cheek. "I was in the library all day, studying ancient tomes and banging my head against the wall. I should have checked in earlier; I'm sorry."

"Quite alright. I know how important that research is. Did you find it?"

He nodded. "And I'm quite tired now to boot. It was a difficult spell to translate at the best of times, let alone at the end of a month-long journey. I'd best head off to bed. I'll be in touch, Zai. Ayve." He nodded at us and took his leave, though there was something about the curious look he gave me that left me feeling off-kilter.

Zai yawned theatrically. "If he's going, then we should go, too. My colleagues are alright, but hobnobbing with nobles all night isn't quite my idea of fun. Come. I need help getting out of this dress, and you look dead on your feet. You can flirt with all of your admirers tomorrow." She grinned wickedly and winked.

"Oh, no, I'm not interested in them, honest!" I hurried to reply. *You're interested in one of them*, my inner voice corrected.

Zai laughed. "I could hardly tell. Don't worry. Outside of balls, mage students are some of the most stuck-up people in the palace. They probably won't talk to you again for at least another season, even if they're in your classes. Say goodnight, Ayve, and let's go to sleep."

* * *

Zai was mostly silent as I helped her unlace and

bid her goodnight immediately. Yet in spite of the whirlwind day—perhaps because of it—I was wide awake. I changed into a nightshirt and slid beneath the covers, but my eyes refused to close. I tossed and turned fitfully for a while, opening the lower shutters to allow in a cool breeze, but I was still much too warm. My bed was soon bathed in silvery moonlight, and I gave up on sleep. I threw a blanket around my shoulders and put on slippers, hoping a walk would do the trick.

Zai's door was shut. No light flickered from beneath. I tiptoed to the oak front door and quietly pulled the handle. Nothing happened. I tried again.

"Can I help you with something?" I wheeled to find Zai leaning on the doorframe to her rooms. Her hair fell like a curtain about her face.

I spoke carefully, knowing how quickly Zai's temper could flare. "After being in the woods for so long, it's hard to sleep in here. I thought I'd go for a walk, maybe get some air."

Zai didn't say anything for a long time. Her expression was masked with shadows, giving no clue as to what she was thinking. When she finally spoke, her tone indicated nothing. "The door stays locked at night for our protection. If you want, you can climb through your window into the students' courtyard. All windows facing it are spelled so that only each room's occupant can enter or exit. Don't stray too far. And don't stay up too late."

Somewhere behind Zai, a dark, almost sickly light seemed to flicker, but Zai slipped back inside and closed the door with a snap.

The courtyard was empty but peaceful. I lay under a tree for a while, enjoying the night air and listening to someone in a nearby room strum a lute. I wished for my oilskin. Still, I thought later when I finally slipped into a clean, fresh bed, this wasn't all that bad.

MAY–AUGUST 967 CE

CHAPTER 12

JUST LIKE I HAD for the past month, I awoke with the sun. This time, instead of dismantling a shelter, I knocked on Zai's door.

"Enter," was the reply.

Zai was sitting in the large chair, reading a small, leather-bound book and scribbling some symbols on parchment. "Crystal hunting," she said without looking up. "And good morning. I'm glad you're an early riser off the trail, too. Getting Stevan up and about in the morning was almost more than it was worth to keep him. How did you sleep?"

"Quite well," I replied, and it was true; after I finally drifted off, I had slept wonderfully. "I missed the outside, but my body was happy to have a soft mattress instead of a bedroll in the morning."

Zai nodded. "Neither is better than the other, just different. Although after a long time away from one, the other usually becomes more appealing." Zai rested the book on her lap and got right to business. "So, your duties: wake at or before the sixth morning bell. The bells are rigid here; an exact hour will pass between each. You'll light all of the fires, even if the weather seems too warm to do so, for fires are essential to your magic studies. Heat some water—just a small pot is fine; I visit the baths at night but like to freshen up in the morning. Fetch breakfast directly from the kitchen—one sausage, two eggs, a piece of buttered bread, and whatever greens they have. I'll eat here, though you are welcome to eat wherever you wish. Be ready by the eighth bell for our lessons. Understood?"

"Wake up by sixth bell; light fires; heat water; sausage, two eggs, buttered bread, and whatever greens; lessons at eighth bell." With her nod of approval, I began to build her fire.

It had been a few days since I'd last used my magic, but I was able to get the fire going quickly enough. I built up the hearth in the common room as well. I vaguely remembered where the kitchen was, but the corridors were full of bustling people. I tried to stay out of their way.

The kitchen was loud, and several cooks stirred large pots. "You're from Lady Zai, I take it." The girl who intercepted me was perhaps my age, a fair bit shorter, and had long blonde hair pinned up beneath a light blue scarf. Her curves stretched her apron in ways I deeply envied. "I assume she wants her usual?"

I blinked. "How did you—"

"Know you worked for Lady Zai? She got in yesterday, and you're the only person I don't know, so you must be her new assistant. And it's like Lady Liliane said: you have a glimmer of magic about you. Well," she snorted, "not quite a glimmer. You're full-on glowing with it. You must be pretty powerful for it to show up like that. No one I've ever known has burned so bright."

I didn't know how to respond. Fortunately, she didn't seem to be waiting for an answer. She handed me a tray and hurried over to a bubbling pot.

Zai was still immersed in her book and merely waved her thanks when I dropped off her food. I stepped back into the hallway as the seventh bell rang. I thought about finding the mages' dining hall, but the thought of seeing my previous night's suitors again made me queasy. Zai had mentioned another room, I remembered, one for warriors. I decided to chance my luck there.

The hall was further away, but it was quiet and friendly, with long benches on either side of long tables. I took a tray and got food from the kitchen staff, none of whom appeared to be mages. One kindly older man slid a few extra apple slices into my hot oats when he saw me eyeing them. The tables were full of butter, milk, and honey. On the road, we had eaten plain porridge for breakfast nearly every day. This was heaven in comparison.

I tucked into my meal and watched a few sleepy people enter. Many were close to my age or a little younger. A tan, dark-haired older boy and a golden-skinned, honey-haired girl smiled when they saw me.

"Good morning!" the girl called. "Val told us we might find Lady Zai's new assistant somewhere around here. Can we sit with you?"

"Of course!" I replied, and they slid onto the bench.

"Gatlen," the boy said. A loose curl bounced over his forehead as he shook my hand. His palm was warm and rough. "This is Kessa. And we're not dating," he added, laughing when Kessa tried to elbow him in the ribs.

"Someone made that mistake *one time* and he's never let it go," she chided. Her eyes were a bright flirty green, and if her thick hair hadn't been so smoothly slicked back in a bun, I would have sworn I was sitting with the bracelet girl from the market.

"I'm Ayve. Although I suppose you already knew that. Are you knights?"

Gatlen sighed, buttering a roll. "Eventually. This year, hopefully. We're fourth-year squires."

"Even you? A girl?" Once again, I was painfully aware of my ignorance. "Sorry. It's just nothing was like this back home. I didn't even know a girl could wear trousers, let alone be a squire. Or a knight!"

"It's alright," Kessa replied. She blew on her spoonful of oats. "Freodon throws lots of people for a loop. I'm from Qiameth, so it didn't catch me too off guard seeing how I grew up around all those oddball university folk, but poor Gatlen here is from the northern hills, and legend has it he bumbled about for an entire year before I came along to save him."

Gatlen rolled his eyes. "Yes, yes, I'm a year older than the other squires. Just because the first training master couldn't see what a genius I was and made me repeat the year—"

"Would a genius accidentally wallop themselves with their own sword, get concussed for a whole month, and need to take the summer off to recover?"

"You're nineteen, then?" I interrupted. I had the feeling interruptions were allowed with these two.

Kessa nodded. "And I'm eighteen. Just turned. We're more than ready for the knights' tests this year, so long as our knightmasters put our names forth. Now, your turn. Where are you from? How old are you? Did you really walk here from the mountains?"

I did my best to answer every question they posed. Near the end of my tale, the girl from the kitchens plopped down on the bench with a huff. "Mages, honestly, they're never satisfied," she complained, picking up her spoon and tucking in.

"Ayve, this is—"

"Val," the girl finished. "We met this morning. And right after she left, that awful Matias kept begging me to accompany him to the tournament. Thank goodness for you lot. If there's one thing you should know," the girl advised me, "it's that mages have no social skills thanks to all the time they spend inside learning arcane spells and incantations."

Gatlen and Kessa nodded their heads in agreement. "Val is the only mage we'll tolerate," Gatlen said.

"Well," I said, swallowing a bite, "I hope you'll

tolerate me, too."

They laughed and backtracked through their apologies.

We cleaned our trays as the eighth bell approached. "I apprentice with Lady Liliane," Val said as we left together. Gatlen and Kessa waved and walked off towards the squires' training grounds. "She's strongest with earth magic, specifically things that grow, so we work mostly in the kitchens and gardens. Lady Zai doesn't have a specialty, of course, but she tends to teach earth magic with crystals. Is that your specialty?"

I hesitated. "I don't think so? I'm so new to this all. Mostly Lady Zai has just had me learning the basics. I've liked fire magic so far. But I haven't touched crystals yet, just rocks, and that's been fairly abysmal."

Val eyed me curiously. "Fire magic. Fascinating. I suppose I may not have many classes with you, then. But you'll have to join us for lunch. And dinner, if you can still stand us. Naliah should be here by then, so long as she doesn't have another punishment, and Archer. You'll like them. You *will* come back, won't you?"

Stevan had been a playful new awakening, and Lady Zai protected me like a mother, but I hadn't realized how much I'd longed for friends. "Of course," I grinned. "I can't wait."

***

Zai was in a slender black dress, and a purple disc dangled from a thin cord about her neck. She asked me about breakfast and nodded through her answers, but her parent-like persona of the days before was gone, replaced by a no-nonsense teacher.

"We'll work together every day till noon," she explained. "Partly to practice controlling your magic and partly to learn spells, often through reading. Sometimes I'll require your assistance delivering notes or fetching supplies. We break for lunch at the twelfth bell. At the first afternoon bell, you'll attend academy classes. They may change each session depending on your progress, but each will last nearly one full bell. This session you'll have reading," she began, ticking the classes off on her fingers, "basics of magic, etiquette..." She frowned as I blanched. "It will be important for you to know how to interact appropriately with a wide range of people on our adventures. Yes, adventures. I haven't forgotten why I took you on. But you have a lot of work to do first. It's important that you build your skills before we go off roaming the countryside again.

"After etiquette, you're permitted to choose one elemental class of your choice. Each is led by a master mage, so you needn't worry about the quality of the instruction when making your pick. These classes change each quarter depending on who is in the palace, so if you don't like the area you've selected or want to expand your horizons further, you can change your mind for summer. I'll write you a list of their locations before lunch. After that, come straight back here, and we'll determine what your evenings look like together. Any questions?"

I struggled to reply. How could I know what I didn't know? "Am I officially enrolled as an academy student, then?" I asked finally. "Am I on a path to become a royal mage? A sorceress?"

"No," Zai said gently. For a brief moment, she sounded like a mother again. "The afternoon classes are available to any young people employed at the palace, but sorcery students take courses in the morning when you'll be working with me. Those classes are much more tedious and take nearly twelve years of study to complete. Most students here begin very young, some as early as six or seven, and never any over thirteen. Students must also be apprenticed to a mage, which is expensive. Furthermore, those who wish to receive their seal," she said, tapping her purple, necklace, "must pass all of their tests."

"There are tests?"

"Of course. Magic is dangerous, and the monarchs can't allow just anyone to walk around claiming status. But the path you're on will prepare you for anything you might come across in your adventures and more, so I wouldn't worry. Now, if that's all of your questions, we'll need to start your lessons. Shall we...?" She paused and frowned at the air. "Have you lit all of the fires?"

"Yes, this morning, I—"

"No. I asked if you lit *all* of the fires." Zai walked to my door and pushed it open. She turned around, nostrils flared. "Was I unclear this morning? When I said you must light all of the fires? Did the hearth in your room somehow not count?"

"No, I—"

"No, my *lady*," Zai growled back. "In our lessons, I expect you to follow proper court etiquette. It may make or break our cover one day. And I expect you to follow all instructions I give *exactly*, or else there could be disastrous consequences as we uncover more advanced spells. Understood?"

"Yes, my lady." My head hurt with the sudden change.

Zai flicked a hand towards my room, and I heard the fire go up in the grate with an angry *fwoosh*.

There was no time to dwell on angry Lady Zai because the rest of the morning was exhausting. I learned not just to light fires but to *keep* them lit without having to add more wood. Over and over, Zai made me set a fire and attempt to keep it going as she doused it with a flick of her wrist. It was disheartening, the way it was so easy for her to undo my work, as if a fire were never in the grate at all.

We eventually took a break, if you could call reading complicated spell books a break. It was dull work; I had to slowly read a spell aloud several times before I could understand it, and not a single one worked for me yet.

But when the twelfth bell rang, Zai was somehow not disappointed. Her teacher persona seemed to melt away as she steeped a mug of tea. "You did quite well today, Ayve," she commended.

"Thank you, my lady."

"Ah, no, we're back to Zai. It's your lunch now, which means I'm cutting into it. Go eat. Replenish your energies. You'll need them, especially for Madame Gerta." She shooed me from the room.

* * *

It was dizzying, having to keep these two Zais in mind, but when I explained this to my new friends at lunch, they reassured me that this was perfectly normal.

"Lady Liliane is so kind and sweet in the public eye, but I swear she's cross with me all the time behind closed doors," Val comforted me. "It's nothing personal; it's just who they are. Part of being a royal mage is being able to act as different people depending on the circumstances. I really think they ought to offer a class in it, since it's so expected of us. Don't tell that to any of them, though, or they'll chew your head off."

"She would know, seeing as Lady Liliane assigned her two evenings of punishment the last time she complained," Gatlen commented.

"It's not fair, you all having masters. Being a page is dumb. I could be a good squire if they'd just let me move on already." Naliah was the physical opposite of Val: tall, lean, with deep brown skin and cropped dark hair, and yet somehow she was even more spunky and outgoing than the older girl. I had still been shy at twelve, so I would have found it hard to believe Naliah was so young if she hadn't constantly been complaining about it.

"Just you wait. Being at their beck and call, always having to do what they want," Kessa grumbled. "But I'm sure Lady Zai will be just fine," she added hurriedly. "Don't let it get to you too much, Ayve. You'll adjust soon enough. Right,

Archer?"

The red-headed boy nodded, though his face was rather grim. At fourteen, he had only just begun his time as a squire, but his silence implied he was already anticipating his knighthood.

Promising to meet them for dinner, I hurried off to afternoon lessons. My feelings had been soothed at lunch, but I was embarrassed once again as I realized my classes were full of children much younger than me, perhaps ten or eleven at best. And to think I had asked Zai if I was officially enrolled as a mage!

The scholar who served as our teacher made no mention of my age but simply set me to the task of reading with them. Though I felt out of place, the texts were fascinating. On our journey, Zai had me practice on historical accounts, and the morning had been full of long, frustrating spells. But the scholar had us reading make-believe stories. I found myself immersed in a wild tale of a magic bean stalk, and class flew by.

Several of the children in my group continued to the basics of magic course with me. The teacher, Master Varrick, was kind and friendly. He was young, perhaps only a few years older than Stevan, but the children loved him and crowded around him before the class began.

"Welcome, Ayve," he said, shaking my hand

over the heads of several excited ten-year-olds. His eyes were light blue and reminded me of the sky after rain. "We're working on setting fires today. Have you any experience?"

"Yes, sir. Lady Zai had me practice over and over again on our way here. Today she worked with me on sustaining fires without new fuel."

"Wonderful!" He clapped his hands. "Then you can help me with these rascals today."

He set me to the task of helping some of the younger children practice. To my surprise, Naliah was mixed into the bunch.

"Some people don't show signs of magic till late," she shrugged as she squinted at her kindling. "Sir Rodrick, the page-master, noticed some sparks in me last autumn. I don't have it strong, but I got enough to belong here. There's nothing wrong with magic showing up late; it's just something that happens."

I reflected on my own journey and felt a little better.

Etiquette was horribly boring. Perhaps it was simply that nothing could compare to trying to help children light fires with their unwieldy magic, but I fought back yawns the entire time. Madame Gerta was well over seventy and clearly pined for the days of yore. Unimpressed with my limited country knowledge, she tasked me with memorizing the difference between noble titles by assigning a dull and tedious page of reading. I had never been so happy to hear a bell as I was at the end of class.

Yet when it rang, I had no idea where to go. I guiltily realized I had left Zai's list of classes back on my desk. I bumbled about the palace, trying to find my way back, but the grounds were far too large, and I felt hopelessly lost.

"Ayve!" a voice squealed. "Are you joining Lady Liliane's class? Can I be so lucky?" Val stood at the door to a small glass greenhouse.

"Uh, yes. Plants, right?"

"Yes, plants of the Kreely Mountains. I was hoping you might choose this one since we're learning about your home!"

Home. It was odd how that word had lost its meaning.

"Let's hurry. Yesterday the stupid boys got all the good shears, and I had to wait forever to cut my trimmings." Val tugged my hand and pulled me inside.

The greenhouse was obviously enchanted as we were instantly transported into the heat of a deep summer. I rolled back my sleeves and fanned myself in the thick, warm air. Somewhere, a waterfall rushed, and the ground before us climbed steeply, rising higher than the roof could allow.

Lady Liliane was buttery sunshine. "Welcome," she called, and her one word was like music. She led the small class on a walk up to the waterfall. The students traipsed behind her like eager puppies, and I was reminded of my first adventure to the cave. Although, I thought to myself, I imagined I could find a proper latrine here if I needed it!

Val chattered non-stop on the way up. "These classes are meant to inspire our creativity," she explained. "Part of being a good mage is thinking outside the ordinary, so the instructors really try to challenge us. Sometimes it's magical challenges, but more often it's mental. Those are the worst; I hate logic puzzles. But it'll be worth it one day when I command a kitchen of my own."

"That's your dream, then?"

"Oh, yes, one day, though I'm sure I'll have to work my way up first by—" She was cut off as we reached the top of a ledge. Lady Liliane motioned for everyone to gather about her. She explained a little about the qualities of the soil, none of which I understood, but Val nodded fervently beside me the whole time.

"Your task today is to draw forth what belongs," Lady Liliane said mysteriously. I glanced about at the other mages, sure they must be as confused as I was, but they all hummed agreement and spread out amongst the foliage. Val was already squinting and muttering to herself, one hand on the tree beside her.

I knew it was no use. I hadn't a clue in the world what Lady Liliane meant. I strolled to the other side of the bluff, hoping it looked like I knew what I was doing.

Sunlight tickled my face, and I wasn't sure if it was real or magicked. Either way, it was pleasant. I allowed myself to sit in the shade under the pretense that I was talking to the soil like the other mages and leaned back against a large rock. I felt at peace, if a little warm, and blotted my face with my sleeve.

As I pulled my arm away from my face, a curious sensation danced along my shoulder. It felt almost like the honeysuckle, though less firm. I smiled when I saw a small pom of pink flowers resting on my arm. A rather large bush with sprays of flowers was growing behind the rock. I had somehow missed it when I sat down. I reached up a finger to touch it. Bizarrely, I was sure it laughed.

"Oh, well done! Look what Ayve has uncovered!" Lady Liliane came pattering up the path. "It is indeed lilacs that grow here, Ayve. I believe Lady Zai mentioned you're from the

Kreely Mountains. Did you know they were native to this soil?"

I shook my head, eyes wide, as a cluster of students gathered around. "I've seen these flowers—lilacs—a few times but didn't know they were what you were looking for."

A few mage students looked miffed. "But how did you call them to you?" one demanded. He looked rather cross.

Lady Liliane looked at me, anticipating an answer. I stopped and thought before I could say "I don't know." Zai would expect me to take the time and think before just giving up. "I suppose it's more that they came to me," I realized. "There wasn't much I had to do when they were so eager to be discovered."

Lady Liliane snipped a small cluster from the plant and added it to her satchel. "It seems Lady Zai was more than right about you. I know she talked up your fire magic, but you have a real gift in this field, too. I look forward to seeing what you'll be able to do as you build your skills."

It was clear the other students were bitter, but perhaps they would finally leave me alone. Val at least looked pleased. "I'm friends with the smartest girl in class!" she chirped as we brought more lilacs to life. "I knew I was right about you! Kessa and Gatlen will be so jealous."

CHAPTER 13

BY THE TIME I made it back to Zai's quarters, I was exhausted. Val had made me promise to join everyone again for dinner at the seventh bell, but I wasn't sure I would make it. My eyelids drooped, and the beginnings of a headache twinged behind my brows. I was hopeful that Zai had nothing more planned for the night as I pushed open the door.

"Well!" There was an odd moment like time had paused, where I couldn't quite tell which Zai to expect, but the crinkled corners of her eyes gave her away. "You look dead on your feet, which is the sign of a good first day. How was it? And do sit while you share, lest you fall asleep standing up."

I gratefully sank onto a couch. I left out some details about the greenhouse, but I did share whose class I was taking.

"You chose well. Lady Liliane is a dear friend, and she'll take good care of you." Zai looked pleased. "I suppose it's about time I lead a session again," she mused. "It must be at least half a year since I've taught. I should talk to the king about a crystal class this summer."

I stifled a yawn. "Do apprentices and assistants always take their mentor's courses?" I wondered aloud. "Val was in Lady Liliane's."

"Some do, some don't. In my opinion, it's good to have a variety. All mages have gaps in their learning, and the more instructors you have, the more likely you are to fill those gaps. I would be honored if you took my session, of course, but you are certainly not obligated." She hesitated. "Perhaps you might like to see some of what crystal work entails. If you're not too tired, that is." She looked hopeful, like a child waiting for a sweet.

"Of course," I said through another yawn. "I'd love to."

We entered one of Zai's smaller rooms. It was dark; the windows were covered in thick curtains, and only a few candles burned on a desk.

Zai pulled a small black cloth from a drawer. "I'm still researching this one," she said in a hushed tone. The room seemed to absorb sound. "This crystal has been known to me for most of my adult life, yet I have only just touched its surface."

I held my breath, eager, but when the cloth unfolded, I found the ugliest, roughest crystal I could imagine. It was brownish gray with no shine and could have passed for a plain old rock were it not for the silver wire wrapped around it. Yet even the silver was tarnished and dull.

"It's beautiful, isn't it?" Zai asked, misreading my silence. "Reach for it. Sense it. See what you can find."

I dutifully called for a thread of green and coaxed it towards the crystal, but it didn't seem to want to leave my hand. Eventually I managed to wrap it in a green fog, but I couldn't feel anything. It just felt like a plain old rock. "I'm sorry," I apologized softly. Sweat began to bead on my forehead, and my eyes felt heavy again.

Zai wrapped the crystal back in its cloth and returned it to the drawer. "Another day," she said as we left the room.

Back in the open air, I felt mildly better, though my head still hurt. "Do I have any other duties tonight?"

Zai thought for a moment. "I can see you will apply yourself. Some assistants I've asked to work for me at night since they didn't take classes during the day, but that's not you. You will have no obligations most evenings besides completing any of the work your teachers assigned and quenching the fires before you retire. If I have any events, I will require your help dressing and preparing. Otherwise, the time is yours. You should find dinner at the seventh evening bell and finish up any remaining work after. You may visit the courtyard or baths, but I would prefer you not wander the castle yet until you have your bearings."

While I might have felt frustrated with restrictions a day ago, I now understood just how big the castle was, and I wasn't eager to go traipsing its grounds again on my own. Besides, I couldn't imagine ever wanting to do anything at night but sleep.

"If you wish to rest before dinner, you have well over an hour." Zai seemed to be reading my mind. "I do not think our paths will cross again tonight, so if you have any final questions, now would be the time to ask them."

"None, Zai, thank you." I started towards my bedroom.

"One more thing, Ayve. The door to these

suites locks promptly at the tenth bell. If you decide to roam and are not back by that time, you will face consequences. Your first job is to learn, and you cannot learn if you are not well-rested. I will consider adjusting your curfew in the future if you keep up with your studies. Is that understood?"

Thinking about being well-rested made me feel complacent. "Yes, of course," I agreed. "Thank you."

I hardly even remembered falling asleep.

* * *

I awoke from my nap as the dinner bell began to ring, headache nearly gone. My fire was still smoldering. I quenched it, knowing I would need to do the others post-dinner, and reveled when I realized my magic strength seemed to have returned while I napped. I washed my face and hurried to eat.

Everyone was there again, though it felt like ages since we last sat down. Naliah was still spry with energy and chattered away, though Gatlen, Kessa, and Archer were much quieter. Apparently, I learned, they hadn't finished work for one of their classes, so they'd received an extra hour of scrubbing mail.

"But Archer, you don't take that class," Naliah

pointed out.

"I just enjoy the company," he blushed, and I couldn't help but notice the way he glanced at Kessa.

Val mostly grumbled about some of the boys. "I think they're punishing me for rejecting them," she pouted. "Thank goodness I don't have to work the kitchens tomorrow. So Ayve," she said, turning and raising a brow, "besides getting yelled at, what did you *do* this morning? You weren't in any of the mage classes, but Lady Liliane said you're working for Zai."

"I'm her assistant, not apprentice, so I only do the afternoon courses." I swallowed my hunk of bread. "Mornings are for lessons with Zai to prepare for future trips. Reading, spells, magic practice—the usual things, I guess."

Gatlen's mouth actually hung open. "Four bells' worth of private lessons with Lady Zai?"

I stared back. "Yes. Why?"

"That's downright unheard of!" Val exclaimed. "No one ever does that much, assistant *or* apprentice. And definitely not with Lady Zai."

"Even Stevan?" I asked.

"Especially Stevan!" they chorused.

"He and Lady Zai were notorious for butting heads," Kessa commented. "Four bells together and one of them would have exploded, probably at the hand of the other."

"Have any of you heard where he is?" I tried to keep my tone light. "I'd love to ask him about his lessons with her, only I haven't seen him all day."

"He's in Qiameth, I think." Val lowered her fork. "Didn't Lady Zai tell you? It's all she and Master Onan could talk about last night. Some musty old spell needs researching. And Stevan wanted to study the stars or something. I overheard it all when I was telling that awful Matias I didn't want to dance with him again. He won't be back for a while, at least not till after summer session."

The disappointment in my face was too hard to hide. "Oh, don't fret, he'll be here again before you know it," Val reassured me, patting my shoulder. "He was always off on missions like this when he apprenticed for her. How in the gods' name he ever passed his final mage tests at eighteen when he was so often away from his classes—"

"Wait, passed?" I sputtered. "Stevan? Has his mage's seal?"

Gatlen shook his head. "He's Master Stevan, didn't you know? The only apprentice Lady Zai ever took."

"See, this is why I always liked him." Val

pointed her fork animatedly as she talked. "Doesn't go around bragging about his title like some of these jumped-up sorcery students around here. Yes, Master Stevan. He passed his final test just about four years ago."

"He's one of the youngest full mages this century," Archer added. "No one was surprised when he asked to take the exams early. He learned loads under Lady Zai, and his talent was renowned."

"Yes, Archer's written a poem about it." Naliah blew a raspberry at him. "He likes all that romantic stuff. Me, I want smash-'em-up-slap-'em-silly stories, thanks."

The group rambled about Archer's extensive works of poetry as I tried to let the news sit with me. I couldn't believe I had traveled with such a young and powerful mage that whole time without ever knowing who he really was. What else was Stevan—*Master* Stevan—hiding?

CHAPTER 14

ON THE FIFTH DAY, my head was *screaming*. Just getting out of bed was enough to make me want to vomit. I gritted my teeth and forced myself to go about my morning duties. Zai didn't seem to notice anything amiss, but I skipped my own breakfast and rested a little longer in the hopes that I would feel better. Once in bed, I couldn't do anything but focus on the throbbing.

"Is everything alright?" Zai finally asked when the first hour of lessons had passed. "You're unusually quiet, even for someone who's reading the most boring of Master Erkin's texts."

"Just a headache is all. My lady." I pressed a finger into the corner of my eye.

"A cup of willow bark tea, then." Zai rustled through some cabinets near the door. "Healers can zap headaches right away, but the more that's done, the more you run the danger of them returning more often, and worse. No assistant of mine will be held back by self-inflicted headaches. Only ever willow bark tea. Am I clear?"

I wanted to reply, *knew* I needed to reply, but the words couldn't find my tongue. Or could they? Had I spoken them and simply forgotten?

A sudden stench made me retch, and I found myself lying on my back on the thick red carpet.

"Stupid, stupid," Zai was saying somewhere overhead.

"I'm sorry," I tried to apologize as I sat up.

"Not you, *me*," Zai growled. "Stay down; you've fainted."

"Oh," I replied dumbly.

Zai made me lie on the ground for a while, giving me sips of water and eventually allowing me to sit up. Carefully, slowly, I moved to the couch.

"Ayve, listen to me carefully. I need you to tell me exactly how you work the spell each day to light our fires."

Thinking was still difficult, but I did my best. "I do what you taught, my lady. I draw heat with my magic and ignite the wood. And I loop a thread about them to ensure they burn all day."

"Is there something you do at the end?" Zai questioned, more urgently. "To close them out?"

Thick fog swirled in my mind. "I don't think so."

Zai cursed. "This is my fault. You fainted because I never taught you a closing spell. Here—" She reached for my wrist, and I felt a force rush through me like a cold wave crashing to shore. My head instantly cleared, and my eyes opened wide.

"What *was* that?" I gasped.

"I used my magic to make your spell end. It is highly dangerous, and I expect you to never let anyone else do it to you lest they hurt you in the process. Your magic was constantly feeding the fires, slowly leaching your power, because I never taught you a closing spell so that the replenishing spell would take from itself instead of drawing from you."

"Oh." I hadn't even realized that this was a thing.

"Have you had headaches every day?" A kettle began to whistle.

"A bit, yes. Nothing terrible. Not like today."

Zai returned with a cup of steaming tea. "Drink. We're done with lessons for the day. You need to rest."

I sipped the tea. Where Alys's willow tea had

always been bitter, this was sweet and earthy.

"Buckwheat honey," Zai noted, seeing my face. "Ayve, I take you for granted. You're a quick learner, so I forget sometimes that I need to start small. I need you to tell me when you're not well or if something doesn't feel right. It won't matter how fast you learn if you burn yourself out first."

"I'm sorry."

"I'm the one who's sorry. My excitement to see how fast you could learn could have seriously hurt you. It is not a lesson I will forget any time soon."

"How much time do I have to learn things before we need to leave for an adventure?" I asked. Now that my head was clear, and now that I knew Zai was feeling a little guilty, I had a brief window to ask questions more freely. "I like things here, truly, even with how little I've seen so far, but oddly enough, I miss the woods." I didn't want to admit that I dreamed about sleeping beneath the stars every night.

Zai scratched her nose. "A year, perhaps? I hope we can have some smaller treks over session breaks, little tasks here and there, but this crystal research is taxing me more than I'd care to admit. I need resources that can only be found here. And *you* need time to learn. At best we'd leave early spring. I think you'll be ready before that, of course. You're learning everything even faster than I expected. I knew you would, but calling flowers to you on your first day in the greenhouse? Yes, I spoke to Lady Liliane," she laughed, seeing my face, "and I am pleased at both your talent and your modesty. It's likely you'll be ready by the new year. But again, I need time, and I shouldn't push you in unsafe ways. Besides, even with Stevan's research from Qiameth, there's so much we still don't know."

"What was he like as a student? Was he a fast learner like me? Stevan—I mean, Master Stevan."

Zai pursed her lips. "He did his best to hide his title from you. He thought traveling with one city mage had you on edge enough as it was. Yes, he was fast, though he was always too quick to jump in without thinking." She seemed reluctant to talk but continued. "He was younger than you when we met, hardly more than a child. Just old enough that enrolling in school was barely still in reach, just young enough that he didn't have the sense not to set his mind on becoming a royal mage anyway. No student I'd known had ever been so determined, and when he began to blaze through class after class, I didn't doubt him."

"He was that talented, then?"

Zai shrugged. "Talented? Yes, I suppose, though stubborn is probably a better word for it.

He was adept in water-purifying spells, which was surprising given he'd never had a tutor. But he struggled some with the other elements, and he would never admit when he was wrong. Still, he passed his final tests four years early, and he's clearly one of the most gifted sorcerers of his time, so something must have gone right in his learning."

"Perhaps it was because he had you as his teacher."

Zai smiled, but she looked sad. "Well, thank you. A master must know when to accept compliments."

"Will he be back soon? From Qiameth?"

Something had shifted in Zai, and I could tell I was running out of time. "Perhaps. It depends on how long it takes him to learn what we need to know."

"What is it we need to know? You keep mentioning crystals. Are they connected to the one you showed me?"

Zai pursed her lips. "It's not yet the time for me to tell you. Forgive me, Ayve, but you are still so young in both your magic and your years. When the time is right, you'll know." Whatever door had been open was now closed. "If you're feeling better, we might as well resume lessons after all. It's high time I showed you how to set a closing spell."

***

The days took on a pattern as I settled into my new routine. Earth class was my favorite, partly for what we studied and partly for the time I got to spend with Val. The girl quickly became my closest confidant, and I learned before the first month was out that Val was madly in love with Gatlen, who seemed oblivious to all women everywhere.

Naliah began to feel almost like a little sister. We often met in the courtyard at night, and soon, as the weather grew warmer, the whole crew started to join. Despite Naliah's insistence that romance was for saps, I couldn't help but notice the quiet look she sometimes got when Archer played love songs on his lute.

We began to study there at night to escape the stuffy heat of the day. I rarely had any actual work assigned, but I rather enjoyed perusing thick storybooks. The reading scholar had given me a list of recommendations, so I spent most of my free hours lost in their tales. My friends didn't seem so lucky; they nearly always had bells upon bells of work and grumbled enviously at my fun. Sometimes, to pacify them on the extra hard nights, I would call soft beds of clover from the earth for them to lie on.

One evening, as summer solstice drew closer, Archer gently strummed while everyone lazed around. There was little work to do; the knights' practical exam was coming soon for Gatlen and Kessa, and Archer's knightmaster had lessened his load in anticipation of the solstice festivities. Only Naliah was in a sour mood, sulking in the grass.

"I think I might just become one of the Queen's Ladies," she boasted. "Leave behind all this knighthood foolishness."

"Oh, the page exams aren't that bad," Kessa scolded. "Nothing like what Gatlen and I are about to face. Sir Rodrick is just trying to scare you. You'll be fine. And you still have a year to go before you have to take them anyway."

"Exactly!" Naliah replied. "What a waste of my youth! The Queen's Ladies takes girls as young as thirteen. That means I could start before the year is over. Instead of being smacked up and down the training yard, I could be riding horses with the princess, fencing with the royal weapons master—"

"And wearing pretty dresses to all the royal balls," Archer pointed out. "I thought you hated dresses."

"Of course I do! But I would take dresses over more punishments any day."

"What about you, Ayve? Val?" Archer asked. "Would you want to become one of the Queen's Ladies? Fierce yet beautiful, ferocious yet refined?"

I shook my head. "No thanks. If Madame Gerta's class is any indication, chickens know more about proper etiquette than I do."

Val groaned. "Madame Gerta! What an old bat. I hated her class. If I had to practice my curtseys to foreign diplomats one more time, I would have thrown myself out a window. You can keep your Queen's Ladies, Archer. I'm happier with some dirt on my face and a trowel in my hands—so long as I can clean up at the end of the day," Val added, and she batted her lashes prettily.

"You like the Queen's Ladies?" I asked Archer.

Gatlen snorted. "He likes *all* the pretty ladies. Go on, Archer, play us the song you wrote for that seamstress you saw in the market once."

Perhaps it was the setting sun, but Archer's face seemed redder than normal. "I wrote that when I was but a child," he protested. "I've moved on. But if you want to hear a tale about great beauty, who am I to disagree?" He started up a new tune. I had to admit it wasn't half bad; if his knighthood didn't go the way he wanted, perhaps he could have a career as a bard.

His song was rudely interrupted by loud caws.

A murder of crows appeared in the purple sky and swarmed the courtyard, landing on every branch and statue. Everyone went quiet.

A strange prickly sensation picked at my skin. I reached for the birds, but they were gone before I could coax a thread from my tired mind, swirling away in a cacophony of feathers.

Naliah was spooked. "Death birds," Naliah shuddered. "They only bring bad omens." Archer traced the sign against evil over his chest.

"Just crows," Kessa argued, and Gatlen nodded in agreement. "And if they did bring a bad omen, it wasn't to us. We're just a ragtag pack of students, not a band of heroes. What could they want with any of us?"

Still, we all agreed it was time for bed after that.

CHAPTER 15

SUMMER SETTLED AROUND the palace like a lazy river. The grounds were resplendent with bright, thickly perfumed flowers, and warm, humid air draped itself over every surface. There was a week-long solstice festival filled with wine, dancing, and merriment followed by a full week off from classes. I readied Zai for the festival banquets, though the work meant I had to miss the city celebrations. Zai hadn't permitted me to attend them anyway, and I was secretly glad to have a built-in excuse to avoid the hectic crowds. Besides, my friends were busy. Gatlen and Kessa had passed their knight trials, and both were gone for the season to patrol the northern borders.

They promised they'd be home before winter set in, but I was nervous for them all the same.

"Don't fret too much," Naliah said when I shared my worries. "They'll probably just stare off into the distance for hours each day reporting on how some leaves blew in a tree." As a page, she was stuck at the palace for the summer session.

Archer was still at the palace, too, though he moped in the shadows most days. He spent his nights in the courtyard writing miserable ballads, and one solstice night he finally confessed to me that he loved Kessa. I sympathized and patted his arm, but it was hard to be around someone who only wanted to sigh and brood.

Val was around, but "you may as well think of me as gone," she apologized wearily over dinner. "Summer is busy in the gardens, and Lady Liliane has decided I need to build my kitchen skills by staffing them for the whole festival, plus when it's over she's sending me into the city once a week to tend the community gardens on top of all my classes. She's right to give me the work, of course," she said bitterly, spearing a green bean with her fork, "but that doesn't mean I'm not dead tired. I almost can't wait till summer is over."

Though there were no academy lessons in the week after solstice, Zai and I still spent mornings together. We had begun to work on more complicated tasks like warding water against sickness, setting up protection circles, and sending out distress calls. I realized Zai was teaching me useful camp skills, and a vision of adventure danced before my eyes.

Sure enough, the weekend before classes resumed, we packed up and trundled off to the northern woods to put my new skills to use. It was different, of course, knowing the safety and bustle of the castle were so close by. Still, I set the protective circle around the camp, started the fire, and even sanitized our water... all things Stevan used to do, I realized as we ate. I missed him still, though perhaps a little less clearly than before. I wondered if he was returning to the city for the summer sessions. Feeling bold as we sat around the fire later that night, I decided to ask Zai.

"No, he won't be back till at least autumn," Zai said. "He's still at Qiameth for the time being."

"Is he researching the crystals some more?" I asked casually.

Zai's face was oddly neutral. "No, he found that information a while ago. He's doing his own learning now. He may be my partner out on the road, but he's his own free mage the rest of the time."

I was doing a terrible job of hiding my feelings.

Zai hesitated. "I hope I'm not overstepping my bounds as your teacher here. This feels meddling, almost, to share this with you. But I thought you ought to know. Stevan may have stayed in Qiameth because... Well, he was here last week for the solstice festival. Just for three days or so. But when I saw him at the mages' tavern, he was with a woman he met in Qiameth," she said somewhat apologetically. "I could be wrong. But I don't want you getting your hopes up."

The feeling in my chest, though awful, was not one of heartache. "Ah, well." I tried to sound chipper. "I should have known. He just about said as much before he left."

Zai moved as if to touch my arm but rubbed her own shoulder instead. "Don't let Stevan ruin things for you. There are plenty of eligible suitors at the palace if you're interested."

I tried to wrap my mind around dating and shook my head. "I have enough going on as it is," I replied. "Maybe one day I'll feel less tired when I fall into bed each night, but for now I'd rather focus on my studies. Besides, I want more adventure," I said, gesturing to the forest around us. "And I only get that if I learn how to do all of these spells. I won't let anything distract me from that goal."

The satisfaction in Zai's voice was hard to

miss. "And I will do whatever I can to help you get there."

* * *

On the first morning of summer classes, Zai increased the strength she used to combat my defensive techniques. I felt foolish for thinking I had actually been stopping her all this time. Four bells into our day, I had only succeeded once in keeping my door shut against Zai's attacks. Still, as always, Zai seemed pleased with my progress.

Lunch was quiet. Naliah was less talkative than normal, though I chalked it up to the extra hour of weapons practice the pages now had. Archer had spent the weekend patrolling with his knightmaster, Sir Orfrund, and had gained a horrible tan that clashed brilliantly with his hair.

The first class after lunch was reading as always. There was no real teacher for the summer, I discovered, just a scholar's apprentice, so he took us to the library to find a book of our choice. I was delighted. I had borrowed many books from Zai, but I had never yet visited the actual library. It had seemed too intimidating from a distance. Yet up close I found it so cozy and full that it was all I could do not to weep. I browsed the shelves until I landed on a massive book, longer than any I'd ever read before, with chapters and delicate illustrations.

I was about to settle into a corner to read when I spied a small, faded brown leather book on a chair. It was so unremarkable that I couldn't help but pick it up. It reminded me of a tome I had seen in Zai's rooms, though this one was written in a language I wasn't familiar with.

"Begging your pardon, miss," a disheveled scholar apologized. "I haven't had a chance to clean this section yet. I can put that away if you wish." He extended his hands.

"What language is this?" The letters were so oddly familiar.

"Ancient Ole'adan."

"I didn't realize they wrote books," I said curiously, turning it in my hands and remembering the marks in the cave. I had read enough of their history from the book in my room to know they had died out long before most cultures had written records, and stories of the curious people were full of unresolved mysteries.

"Most people think they didn't, but I would argue otherwise. I'm writing my thesis on it, in fact," he said, flushing proudly. "Contrary to popular belief, they *did* have a written language. But they rarely wrote books since they roamed great distances through forests. They took only what they could carry on their backs, and books would have gotten in the way. Most of what remains is their etchings on cave walls. Nearly all of their remaining written works were recorded by researchers at later dates.

"This volume in particular is one of the few I actually believe they wrote near the end of their time," he added, seeing the curiosity on my face. He seemed delighted to talk to someone who was interested. "The Book of Açirin. It tells of magic's origins through intricate spells, or at least what the Ole'ad claimed were its origins. Some of the explanations are too fantastical to be true. Yet it's the oldest written account on magic we have, at least to date. Most mages attempt to translate this book into the common tongue at some point in their career in an attempt to learn some of the Ole'adan language."

"How does anyone translate it if it's so old?"

He pulled a book from a nearby shelf. It was another small volume, though this one much newer-looking with a gold title stamped on the spine. "An Oqiran scholar wrote this version several centuries after the Ole'ad vanished," he explained. "She put the original on one side and the translation on the other. Accounts are vague, but it appears she may have interviewed one of the last remaining Ole'ad descendants to learn what some of the words said. Still, it has several inaccuracies, and no translation can ever be perfect," he lamented. "Mages start by using this version to build word recognition and understand a bit of the grammar. Very few master the language, but most are able to recite a page or two by the time they earn their seals." He hesitated. "Are you an academy student? Did you want to check out a copy?" He looked hopeful.

"I work for Lady Zai," I answered, hoping that it wasn't really a lie if I didn't answer his original question. "And yes, please."

* * *

My bag was much heavier when I finally reached my basics of magic class. Master Varrick was still the teacher, but for the summer, it was only me, Naliah, and a handful of other children who weren't yet ready for the next level. Varrick almost immediately informed me that if I spent the summer ensuring I was proficient in the foundations, he believed I could pass the test for the intermediate session by autumn. Naliah bit her lip but said nothing.

"You know, I should probably brush up on my spellwork every night," I said lightly as we packed up. "Would you be willing to practice with me, Naliah?"

Naliah looked relieved. "Yes, please. I want to

brush up, too. If you can pass, then so can I! I don't want to get left behind with the babies." We set a plan to meet nightly before dinner.

In etiquette, I practiced curtseying for a quarter bell because my right knee was still half an inch too high for a Hendassan duchess.

Finally, for my summer choice session, I chose Zai's crystal class. Every seat in the room was filled.

Zai—*Lady* Zai, of course—provided each table with an array of crystals. "Feel them," she instructed the class, and each student immediately frowned at the stones in front of them as they reached deep with their magic. I rather thought everyone looked constipated, but I let my own magic wander as well. Unlike the grubby crystal in Zai's quarters, these I could sense immediately. They were pretty and sparkly, some pale and some as bright as Suuldun parrots.

My group was mostly boys my own age. With a start, I realized some had asked me to dance a month ago. But it was like Zai said: at best, they were indifferent. Only one dared talk to me, and he spoke cruelly, telling me I wasn't a real mage and should stop hogging a space in the class.

I smirked at him. "Unless I'm much mistaken, you're not a real mage, either, just an apprentice. But perhaps you should let Lady Zai know if that's how you truly feel."

The boy ignored me after that. And despite their advanced years of study, no one in the class could figure out what the crystals were for. The most I could tell by the end of the first session was that each rock hummed at a different frequency, but even that took me longer than everyone else to discover. As usual, Zai didn't seem upset at her students' seeming lack of progress but dismissed us for the day, pleased.

I stayed behind to help Zai clean up. "What did you think?" she asked as we carefully wrapped the crystals.

"They felt different. I wish I could pinpoint why. And I know you won't tell me, so it's no use asking," I sighed dramatically. With lessons over, I knew I could be freer with my tone.

Zai laughed. "What kind of teacher would I be if I didn't make you do the thinking? But lean into that difference. That's all I can tell you." We were nearly done, and Zai placed the bundle into her bag. "Would you like to try my crystal again?" she asked, and I instantly knew which one she meant. "It's been a while since you've attempted it, and it might help you understand these ones more." I felt less tired than I had in spring, and I did have time to spare until magic practice with Naliah, so I readily agreed.

Back in Zai's room, the thick velvet curtains were still drawn. I sat on a stool, staring at the shabby little rock before me, but where I could feel hums from the colorful crystals in class, this one still gave off nothing, not even a tiny quiver.

"Perhaps you should break now, Ayve." Zai's voice sounded oddly distorted. "It's been nearly half a bell. And I do believe you said you're meeting your friend."

I pulled myself from the crystal and looked about the room, feeling disoriented. "I must have lost track of time," I said. My mind felt fuzzy.

"Did you feel anything?" Zai carefully bundled her precious crystal back in its wrappings.

I shook my head. "Nothing. It makes me wonder..."

"Yes?"

"It makes me wonder how very special it must be that I can't reach it. And how very *not* special those others might be if even a novice like me could feel them."

I always knew Zai was truly happy when the smile reached her eyes. "Think on that," she said, and she shooed me into the sunlight.

* * *

Naliah was already in the courtyard, and we practiced our magic basics until dinner. The sky had started to cloud over, and the day had been long, so I didn't worry when neither of us spoke much.

When the bell rang, we went to dinner. Archer was exhausted from his first full day of combat practice, and he excused himself early. A relaxing bath sounded like a good way to end the day to me. I yawned and stretched. "Care to join?" I asked.

Naliah bit her lip and shook her head. I was startled to see tears in her eyes.

"Naliah?" I asked, concerned. Naliah shook her head again, so I gently tugged her arm and pulled her back to the courtyard.

It had begun to drizzle slightly. We found a spot under an apple tree and sat.

"Talk," I ordered, though not unkindly.

Naliah shrugged stubbornly and dug a hand through the grass. "I interviewed today. For the Queen's Ladies." She paused. "I got in."

I applauded her excitedly. "That's wonderful!" I exclaimed. "Isn't it?" I added, seeing the look on my friend's face. "I thought it was exactly what you wanted."

Naliah's lip quivered, and then suddenly she was crying. "Gatlen and Kessa are gone," she wept, tears splashing down her cheeks. "And they might never come back. Lots of knights don't. And if they do, they'll be big older knights and they won't care about a puny page like me. And *you*, I thought you would at least stay with me for a while, but you're advancing so fast and will be in intermediate classes soon! Besides, Val says you're going away in the spring, so what's the point? Why should I stay here when all my friends are leaving me anyway?"

I swept Naliah into a tight hug and let her cry it out. Once she began to calm, I held her to my side and stroked her hair. "Spring is a long way away," I told her. "I don't think Zai plans for us to be gone forever. And Gatlen and Kessa would never forget about you. They're not like those other big dumb knights. They're stationed together, so they'll protect each other. Even if they do come back with blown up egos, you still have Archer and Val to help you bring them back down."

Naliah sniffed. "Sir Orfrund threatened to take Archer away for the winter to toughen him up; all the pages heard him say it. And Val is nice, but she's not my friend the way you are. Everything comes easy to her, and she's so busy that she doesn't always hear me. Not a lot of people hear me. They don't think I could know anything at twelve. But I do. I know a lot. And I know that it's not fair."

I nodded. "I remember twelve," I said. "Back

when I was at the inn, my parents"—I hesitated, then continued—"my parents always told me what to do and never listened to anything I had to say. My friend Rafe was my age," I added, and I was surprised to feel a lump in my throat. "He used to tell me that we should listen to our elders because they knew what was best for us, but I would argue back that they should at least *ask* what we wanted."

"And what did you want?" Naliah dried her eyes with her sleeve.

"A life," I admitted. "But they saw only the work they wanted done around the inn, and every day I felt more like their maid than their child." I decided not to mention that I *wasn't* their child, not the way Naliah thought. "That was the year Rafe and I stopped playing together in the woods. That was also the year he kissed me," I giggled, and Naliah's eyes widened as she demanded the story.

We spent the rest of the evening swapping tales about our lives. Naliah had lived in Freodon her whole life, and my country upbringing was as fascinating for her as a childhood spent on city streets was to me. She was significantly more cheerful as we said goodbye.

The moonlight sparkled on damp leaves as I slipped through my window, and the tenth bell began to ring.

CHAPTER 16

I FINALLY MANAGED to get a bath the next morning after my chores. The door to Zai's rooms had been locked when I got up, which was odd, but we had been practicing my ability to start a fire from a distance, so I assumed it was part of my training. I left Zai's breakfast tray outside her door and headed off to my own meal feeling refreshed.

Naliah was in better spirits, though Val looked worn. The summer gardens were flourishing, but that meant extra time spent out in the hot sun. I patted Val's arm sympathetically as she grumbled into her tea.

The tray was gone when I returned, but Zai's

door was still locked. I frowned and sat on the couch, leafing through the Book of Açirin while I waited. When the eighth bell chimed, Zai's door still didn't open. I alternated between reading and practicing the warding spell on my own door.

Nearly a full bell later, the door finally opened, and I immediately knew it wasn't going to be pretty. Zai looked livid—*Lady* Zai, I amended, for I knew I was about to be on the receiving end of the mage's foul temper.

"Good morning." Nothing about the way she spoke was good. I ceased my spellwork. "Did I ask you to stop?" Zai snapped angrily. I took a deep breath and began to weave the spell again.

"Weak." Zai slashed a hand through the air, and I instantly felt the spell dissolve. "Do it again."

I worked the spell over and over, but each time, Zai tore it down as if it were nothing more than a cobweb. I tried every trick I knew, but Zai was vicious. I bit my lip in frustration and wove the spell again.

I finally managed something nearly passable. I felt a sigh of relief escape my lips before Zai snarled a strange word. A loud clap echoed, and my door nearly rattled off its hinges. My spell didn't stand a chance.

"Please, this is too hard!" I finally begged. "I'm trying my best, but your attacks are too strong!"

"You must learn to protect yourself. It's clear you don't think you need my protection anymore, though your shoddy spellwork certainly doesn't prove it."

I was confused until Zai marched to my room and touched the tip of one long finger to the frame. The door instantly glowed red.

"You broke curfew," she said quietly, angrily.

"No!" I rushed. "I thought I made it in as the bell was ringing, honest! I was in the courtyard with Naliah! I didn't realize. I'm sorry!"

Zai removed her finger, and the glow began to fade. I was hopeful this was a symbolic sign. "You need to be careful, Ayve." Zai was still angry, but the fury that radiated from was lessening. She perched on the edge of the other couch, rigid.

"I *was* careful, honest. It was just me and Naliah. It was raining, so no one else was there. And I thought no one can follow me in."

Zai pursed her lips. Finally, she said, "Since the time we arrived, there have been at least three threats made against you."

I pressed my hands to my cheeks. "Threats?" I had no idea how to respond.

"One said they would do you harm unless I paid a handsome fee. One claimed you're nothing more than a common serving wench who I've used to hide stolen magics. Pure lunacy, of course, but that kind of thing could tarnish your name. And one has set spies after you and would use your powers to grow their own."

I was stunned. I lowered myself onto the cushion by Zai. "Shouldn't we report them to the King's Justice? That's what you do with crimes. And then there's a trial, to see if they're guilty or not." The King's Justice only came to Jeren once a year, but despite the spectacle their arrival could cause, the trials were always quite serious, ruled by truthstones that wouldn't let anyone lie in their presence. Many a lover found themselves hiding for a few days until the justices left town.

"Ayve, these threats are made by powerful mages. Truthstones do nothing to those who can outwit them." She ran a hand impatiently through her long black hair. "People have caught wind of how strong you are. Some aren't happy about it. Others know that you are young still, and that your affections could be swayed and used to lift them higher."

We sat in silence. Now that the danger of Zai yelling was past, I was truly frightened. "Who are they?" I asked at last. "The ones who threatened me."

Zai shrugged coolly. "I dealt with one. She won't be a problem anymore. The others..." She sighed heavily. "Mages have a way of disguising their traces. I've inklings, but no proof. It's best we're cautious until I know more. *If* I ever know more. And that caution includes being inside before your curfew."

Zai ended lessons for the morning. Neither of us was in the mood to do much more learning after that. And despite my nearly timely arrival, Zai reminded me there were punishments for breaking rules, no matter how minor, so she banned me from the courtyard for a week. She closed the door to my room, telling me she would see me at crystal lessons that afternoon.

I wondered who could have made the threats. Besides the few students who'd snubbed me, everyone I'd met had been so friendly. And gods knew those boys weren't powerful enough to hide themselves from Zai. I was certain Zai knew more than she was saying, and I wished she would tell me. I wasn't a child! But the dressing-down had certainly left me feeling small, and I wasn't brave enough to pursue the matter further.

I tried to read the Book of Açirin again, but it was no use. I gazed out my window and reached with my magic for the trees in the courtyard, listening to their leaves sing.

* * *

Naliah was downright peppy, saying she'd had the

best morning of page training she could ever remember. All thoughts of leaving seemed to have vanished from her mind. I tried to be happy for her, though after my strange morning, it was hard to stay cheerful.

Val noticed, of course. "Spill," she demanded.

I was reluctant but briefly described what had happened. I left out the parts about threats, not wanting to scare anyone, and I tried not to make Naliah feel guilty since it wasn't, after all, her fault. Still, she was apologetic for holding me in the courtyard so long.

"It's fine," I shrugged. "I just can't believe how mad Zai was. She's gotten angry with me a few times before, and I always thought that was as bad as it could get. But now I can't go out in the courtyard for a whole week. One tiny blip and such a big punishment."

"That's the way it is with Sir Orfrund," Archer commiserated. "Last week I fell asleep in the baths and didn't get back till after midnight. He had me scrubbing floors the whole next day."

Val snorted. "At least Sir Orfrund doesn't write to your mother if you don't do your chores on time. Then not only do I have to weed the garden and listens to lectures from Liliane, but I'm also stuck attending temple and praying to change my ways to become a 'proper lady.'"

It was Naliah's turn, and she simply shrugged. "I'm in trouble so often, I've forgotten what it's like not to have extra punishments!" she quipped.

* * *

Zai's stormy temper had dissipated by the time her class began, and she mostly left me alone. One or two older mages had made progress; they still didn't know what the crystals did but had uncovered that each was connected to one of the four elements. Zai seemed extraordinarily pleased with the young man who had figured it out first, and I wondered if she wished *he* were her assistant instead.

When the final bell rang, I hoped to sneak out without being noticed, but Zai instructed me to stay and help clean. We packed the crystals silently and carried them back to our quarters.

"Remember, you're not to go into the courtyard tonight." Zai spoke lightly as we placed the final bag back in the cupboard, and I could tell she was in a better mood. A sudden inspiration struck me.

"If I can't go out, would I be allowed to bring my friends *into* my room?" I asked politely. "You would approve them first, of course," I continued, before Zai could deny my request, "and we would keep the door open, but at least this way you would know I'm safe, and on rainy nights"—a rumble of thunder growled menacingly—"we would have somewhere dry to study, too."

Zai pursed her lips. "I'll think about it," she said finally.

I was overjoyed. Perhaps there was hope. "Thank you," I said, bowing before I returned to my room.

I sat on my bed and wrapped my arms around my legs. More than ever, Zai had reminded me of what I'd always imagined a mother to be, and all I had wanted to do in that moment was hug her. Though Alys had not been much for hugs, Joseth had, and I longed for a comforting touch again.

Biting back tears, I fetched a piece of paper and tediously wrote a short letter, drawing a cartoon for Joseth at the end. I left the letter on my desk, thinking that I'd ask someone how to send mail at dinner.

On my way out the door, Zai called for me to stop.

"Do you need me to help with something tonight?"

I hadn't noticed before, but Zai had dark circles under her eyes. She looked tired, like she hadn't slept well in a week. Even on our worst nights in the woods, I'd never seen Zai look like this.

"You may bring your friends tonight for approval. They must arrive by the eighth bell. I have much work to do and do not have time to wait for tardy teenagers. Am I clear?"

I hoped my "yes" captured the full extent of my gratitude.

* * *

Naliah and Archer hovered in the hallway. Without Val, who was working the evening shift in the city kitchens, they were scared.

"Hurry," I urged them, "or if you show up after the bell, she really *will* be angry."

Zai was in her rooms and came out when we knocked. She was in a simple black dress with the purple pendant featuring prominently against it. The overall effect was positively intimidating. "Naliah, Archer," she said cordially, offering them each a handshake. I had the feeling it was more than a handshake judging by the wide-eyed look each had before she released her grip. "I've heard excellent things about your musical abilities," she told Archer, "and your spunk in the fighting yards," she added, nodding at Naliah. Both quietly spoke their thanks.

"Your friends are permitted to stay," Zai said. "But they must leave well before the tenth bell rings, and no dawdling. Sir Rodrick and Sir

Orfrund have their own curfews, and no one will be late because of my assistant."

"Yes, my lady," they agreed.

Zai nodded once. "Ayve, I need you to finish readying me. Your friends may wait in your room."

Behind Zai's door, I helped lace her boots and brush Zai's long hair until it shone. Zai lined her lids and painted her lips a dark plum. The effect was staggering; with the dark circles beneath her eyes, Zai was hauntingly beautiful.

Another thunderstorm had begun. Zai grabbed a rich purple cloak from the wall and ran a hand over it, whispering softly. She passed the cloak to me. "Do you know what my spell did?"

I waved my own hand over the fabric. About to respond "waterproofing," I stopped and *felt* with my magic to make sure of it. Yes, it was waterproofed, but there was something else that I wasn't sure of. I cocked my head to the side and looked at Zai.

"Well done not rushing to conclusions," she praised. It seemed the morning was forgiven. "I've added a dampening spell. I would like to move about the city tonight without attracting attention—not to be invisible, but to pass by rather unnoticed. And you may see that I would attract rather a lot of attention dolled up like this," she added dryly. "I'm off to meet someone, and I will be back late. Do not expect to see me until the morning. But," she reminded me, "my spell will notify me if so much as a toe pokes through your window."

Zai threw the cloak about her shoulders. It suddenly took a great effort for me to look at her; my gaze seemed to slide right off and onto the wall instead.

"I noticed a letter on your desk tonight," Zai mentioned casually, though I could barely focus on where the voice was coming from. "I sent it for you. In the future, you can leave any letters in the common room basket for the servants to take to the mailroom."

It was only after a few long seconds that I realized Zai was gone. It seemed the spell had worked after all. I returned to my room where Naliah and I practiced magic while Archer read. As the storm raged, we doused the fire and lit a few candles. Overall, I thought later as I tucked myself in, it was a nice night.

* * *

When my week indoors was finally over, I was grateful that Naliah and Archer were approved to visit my room. It had grown stiflingly hot, and the thick stone walls offered a respite from the heat.

Zai was out nearly every night, so we took to lounging in Zai's common room instead of cramming into my bedroom.

I had learned a neat trick through my morning's reading lessons with Zai, and the fire gave off a cool breeze instead of heat. Naliah clapped delightedly when she felt the effect. Archer watched me thoughtfully. "You've picked up reading fast," he commented finally.

I shrugged. "I knew some words before I got here. We had to keep track of supplies and inventory, after all. Spells aren't too much harder."

"That's about what I knew, too. But what it's taken you a few months to learn took me nearly three years."

I felt the surprise on my face. "I hadn't realized this wasn't normal. I wonder if it's my magic that's helping me along."

"Of course it is." Naliah draped herself over an ottoman. "I heard Master Varrick telling Master Onan that—"

"Wait, when did you eavesdrop on Master Varrick?" Archer questioned.

Naliah huffed. "I was in the stables. I wasn't exactly *eavesdropping*. I just happened to be in the hay loft."

Archer shot her a look.

"Fine, I just happened to be in the hay loft because I was tired of having to muck out the stables for yet another silly infraction that really shouldn't matter, and the two of them rode in together. Master Varrick was talking about Ayve. He said she was his quickest pupil, and Master Onan said she had power almost unlike any he'd ever seen before. He said he was curious to see where it would take her and hoped Lady Zai wouldn't hold Ayve back out of jealousy the same way she tried to do with... I can't remember the name now. He passed his test before I got here."

Heart skipping a beat, I asked, "Stevan?"

"Yes! That's it. Then Master Varrick asked what happened to Stevan, and Master Onan said that he had a fight with Lady Zai over something to do with some crystal and went off to study in Qiameth for a while. And then I didn't hear any more because stupid Liesl ratted me out, and now I have to do fifty extra pushups every day for 'shirking my duty' or some nonsense."

Oblivious to my confusion, Naliah chattered happily for the rest of the night. Yet after they were gone, I sat on my bed in the dark, mind racing too fast to sleep. What could they have fought about? Why hadn't Zai mentioned it to me? Perhaps she was sad, I mused, or maybe just angry. And she did know my feelings about him, so maybe she didn't want to upset me.

I wasn't sure it was the right thing to do, but I wrote a letter to Stevan by candlelight. I took it to the basket above the mantel when I was done so I wouldn't lose my nerve.

CHAPTER 17

IT WAS THE HOTTEST SUMMER I had ever known. Tempers soured, and fights broke out in the halls between pages each day as the heat rose. Even sweet Val was grumpy; the hours in the garden left her hair limp with sweat, and she came in more often than not with a red nose and cheeks in spite of the sun lotion she applied religiously.

Most afternoons, during reading lessons, I escaped by visiting the library's basement. It was dark, but I didn't mind if it kept the heat from seeping into my skin. Even the lightest linen trousers and skirts only did so much, but down there, the cool stone walls lent a damp chill to the air.

It was on one of those visits that Master Varrick wandered in and said hello. Seeing him outside of a classroom, I remembered that he was still quite young for a teacher. He seemed more like a friend than instructor as he pulled up a chair. "I was hoping to catch you before class to share the good news. You and Naliah were approved for taking the basics test before the session ends."

"That's wonderful!" My smile blossomed. "Naliah will be pleased. She's been working so hard to get ready in time."

Master Varrick nodded. "She certainly found herself a good tutor. You're one of the fastest learners I've ever had. I'll sorely miss your help with the younger children, but you will certainly enjoy moving on with your learning." He stood to leave, and his eyes alit on my work. "That wouldn't happen to be the infamous Book of Açirin, would it?"

I nodded.

"May I see? I haven't picked up a copy since my days in university."

I passed the book over. "I don't understand much of the Ole'adan language yet. I hope to, one day."

His eyes wandered over the pages. "Yes, most of us do. Nearly everyone gives up eventually, though a few end up in Qiameth studying arcane magics." He handed the book back to me. "Well? What do you think? Have you been able to translate anything?"

I hesitated, not sure I wanted to show anyone my shaky work, not even friendly Master Varrick, but I passed over my notebook. He thumbed through the pages and whistled. "Some are a little rough, but you've done an admirable job so far."

"Thank you." I took the notebook back and returned it to my bag. "Did you translate much of it?" I asked.

"Only parts. I teach basics of magic for a reason," he chuckled. "I like the simplicity of modern spells. I never saw much need to meddle with the past. The only Ole'adan I ever translated was required for my classes, and I usually chose poetry, not history."

On a whim, I opened the book again and pointed to a page. "Would you want to help me with one translation before you go? I've been stuck on this one for a while. Maybe you know something that could help." I smoothed the page. "This one mentions roots, I think, but I don't really understand why. I thought this was a spell for power based on the title, but it doesn't seem to talk about that at all, only about digging deep and roots in the soil."

Varrick eagerly leaned forward in his chair.

"Ah, you've reached one of the biggest debates of this book. Some of the spells seem to be one thing on the surface but may hold deeper meaning underneath. Rural mages have used similar spells to ensure that crops take hold for centuries, but others swear that if harnessed correctly, the knowledge here could help mages draw power from something the same way roots draw power from the soil."

"You mean mages could draw power from the earth?"

He shook his head in neither a yes nor a no motion. "Sort of. The best theory I've heard is this is actually a primitive way to root one's powers in earthen vessels, but it is unclear what those vessels are supposed to be. Some say the spell refers to the soil itself, some say a vase of dirt, and still others say there would need to be multiple objects, like talismans or crystals. But no matter how good the translation or which vessels have been tried, no mage has yet been able to use it for so much as ensuring a healthy crop of farts. Of course..."

I leaned in closer. "Of course?"

Master Varrick glanced over his shoulder towards the door. "I'm not sure I should go on. And yet you're so keen after just a few weeks..." He let the idea linger before venturing on. "Of course, there are those who take it one step further, who say the roots must be anchored in *other mages*. This is blasphemous, naturally; anchoring yourself in another mage's powers is tantamount to stealing someone's soul."

"Really?" My voice came out hushed, nearly a whisper.

"Oh, yes. Taking power from another, especially without their consent? Magic is our very essence. Even non-mages have their own essences if you look close enough. To tap into that source and use it to enhance your own strength? Most would say that's evil. It would corrupt your own magic, surely, to filter another mage's power through your own, so it has been suggested that a sorcerer would need some sort of purifying device before attempting it."

"What kind of purifying device?"

He frowned. "I'm not sure, honestly. There are many you'll come across soon in your studies: herbs, counterspells, even crystals. But which one is most effective for stealing magic is beyond me," he said, "and I would prefer to keep it that way. I leave such research for the students in Qiameth. As a matter of fact, you might even know one who you could ask about all of this."

"*I* know a student in Qiameth?"

"From what he said over summer solstice, Master Stevan studied purifying crystals this past spring."

"You know Stevan?" It was amazing how a simple name could still make my heart leap.

"Indeed. He was in one of the first classes I ever assisted with when I began teaching here. He's only a few years younger than me and was far too advanced for the class, of course. He tested out within a week."

"Have you spoken to him recently?" I remembered my letter to him on the mantel.

"No, unfortunately. And I can see you haven't either, but don't take it personally," he advised. "Most of the towers in Qiameth are dark and full of books. Mages there hardly know what time it is let alone what day or sometimes even year. I believe the research is meant to help Lady Zai with her own studies, though. Do you know much about what she's working on these days?"

For the first time, I realized that I didn't. "No," I apologized. "We spend so much time together, but I've never dared to ask. She works with crystals, and we test this really old one sometimes, but I'm not familiar with the details."

"Really? What do you do when you test this old crystal?" His tone was light, but something about the sudden tension in his shoulders was surprising.

"Master Varrick!" With impeccable timing,

Lady Zai strode through the door. She and Master Varrick chatted for a bit, seeming to forget I was there, and although she was friendly, I couldn't help but notice her smile didn't reach her eyes.

Varrick bid us goodbye before long. Zai looked after him as he left, waiting for the click of his heels to fade from the hall. "I'll need your help this afternoon," she instructed when the sound had finally gone. "I'm sure you're disappointed to know you'll have to skip etiquette. Meet me in our quarters at third bell."

* * *

"Lay them down here. No, keep them out of the shade; they work better in the sun."

The help Zai needed, it turned out, was arranging the crystals before her class began. A light wind had eased the afternoon heat, and Zai had found a clearing in the palace woods with gentle energies "that might enhance the crystals' magics," she had explained. None of the students had yet discovered what they were for, and though I didn't hold out hope that I'd be the one to crack the mystery, I was grateful not to waste a nice afternoon inside. The heat had subsided somewhat, and I let the breeze glide through my clothes gratefully.

When we finished laying the crystals on

squares of black cloth, Zai stood and dusted her palms. "I'm off to fetch the class," she announced. "There's a sign on the door, but gods know none of them will read it. There's no need to walk all the way back with me; you can enjoy the sunshine here."

Several birds trilled overhead. Somewhere in the distance, a bee buzzed sleepily. It was the first time, I reflected, that I had been alone, truly *alone*, in the wilderness since we had made it to the palace. I knew there was little to fear; after all, there were guards at the gates to the woods, and thick walls surrounded the other sides. Still, I was glad for the space, and I was glad Zai trusted me on my own. It was nice to have time to myself.

Memories of our walk to Freodon flooded my mind. Had it really only been a few months since then? Everything had changed so much, even my magic. I reached out with it, greeting the trees and laughing as I felt a squirrel skittering through their branches. It surprised me how much more I noticed. The world felt so friendly. Back on our walk, everything had felt foreign, but my magic was a source of solace now, and it was comforting to feel the world around me.

Comforting. I frowned, thinking about something. I looked at the green crystal closest to me. It was an earth crystal, just as those other mage students had discovered—but something about it was *wrong*. It wasn't earthy in the same way as the trees or even the squirrel. Something about it felt... human.

I reached for the other crystals. Water, air, fire—they had the same odd feeling, too. Something about them felt less like their elements and more like the way I felt after sitting in the dining hall too long.

I closed my eyes and allowed my magic to wash over them again. Zai had said magic left a trace. I thought, hard, and suddenly I could *see* the crystals in my mind. There they were, four little rocks on black velvet—but each was glowing brightly purple.

"They're not crystals!" I blurted out, opening my eyes.

The class stared back, Zai at their lead. How long I had been probing, I didn't know, but the class had reached the clearing and was gathered around me, most looking surly. And there on the ground were the crystals I had probed, each glowing steadily purple.

Zai positively beamed. "Share, Ayve. What have you discovered?"

I was too excited to care that the others were mad. "They're not crystals at all. They're magic! It's elemental magic somehow encapsulated in the shape of crystals."

"Well done. These are elemental charms, not crystals. They function much the same, though they're less powerful. They're meant to help surrounding villages get through times of need: drought, famine, earthquakes, flooding. Talismans, technically, though the common folk think of them as crystals, and they're much needed in the kingdom. Anyone can work them, even if they haven't a speck of magic in their blood. And now that we know what they are, we can begin discovering how to make them—once you are able to do as Ayve has done, of course," she said crisply, whipping around to face the other students.

Zai set everyone to probing at the crystals, and now that the secret was unearthed, many were quickly able to produce the same purple glow. She tasked me with helping those who struggled to understand the nuances of exploring the crystals. I explained how I felt the wrongness, and most were eventually able to create a glow. Yet it was clear whenever Zai wandered further away that everyone was annoyed. As the class packed up near the end of the session, I heard one voice distinctly state that he could have done what I did if he'd been in the teacher's bed, too.

* * *

"Ayve, if you're not going to eat that roll, will you chuck it at me? I'm starved."

I blinked at Naliah, who was pouting at my plate. I passed the roll to her and pushed my food away.

"Alright, what's the matter? You look like Archer when that stomach sickness went around." Val had finished dinner and was idly twirling her hair around her fingers.

I wasn't sure I should share, but my rage was beginning to spill over. I told the story, distraught by the end.

Val shrugged. "Whoever it was is obviously just jealous. I bet it's Matias. He's always mad that he's not any good. His parents are famous healers, but he can barely light a candle. Honestly, I wouldn't worry too much."

"It's just," I seethed, "Zai is like a mother to me. That he could dare imply—!"

Val grinned wickedly. "You know, if you really want to prove that nothing's going on, you could always find someone around the palace to have fun with. There are plenty of eligible suitors!" She waggled her eyebrows suggestively.

Naliah rolled her eyes. "Love is a waste of time," she complained as she buttered another roll.

Val rolled her eyes back. "Wait till you're just a little older."

Naliah stuck out her tongue. "I'll be thirteen this weekend, thank you very much, and I bet I'll still think love is stupid then."

Val clapped her hands together. "A birthday! Well, we need a party to celebrate. Ayve, you'll come, won't you?"

"I—"

"Fantastic. We'll have it in Liliane's chambers, and we'll invite Zai so she can't possibly protest. Oh, I just love parties!"

We headed back to my room after dinner as usual. Val was the least afraid of Zai; she had been around her for years thanks to her apprenticeship with Liliane. Naliah clung to my side as Val worked her charms.

"A party?"

"Yes, my lady. Naliah will be thirteen, and we want to properly welcome her to womanhood. We'll be in Lady Liliane's chambers this Saturday night, and we'd love for you to attend." I thought the curtsey at the end was a bit much, but it seemed to be what Zai expected.

"Of course," she replied. "I wouldn't miss it!" She smiled kindly at Naliah, who tried not to flinch. "I have some business to attend to first, but I'll come as soon as I can."

Naliah and I were rightly impressed as we entered my room and said so. Val brushed off our compliments. "The fastest way to get a yes is to make it something Lady Zai can attend, too. That way it's like chaperoning, only more fun. I've spent my whole life around nobles and mages; I know how to work their strings."

Zai had approved my friends to exit through my window, so we clambered out and sat under the apple tree and basked in its heavy scent. "Shouldn't you ask Lady Liliane?" I wondered much later, when we were beginning to feel drowsy in the balmy night air. Naliah was already asleep beside me.

"I'm sure she'll say yes. Besides, if I tell her Zai is coming, she'll have no reason to say no." She sounded quite smug.

"I think there's something I don't know," I said finally. It would do no good trying to dance around an issue with Val.

"But don't you? After all, the whole palace knows about Ladies Zai and Liliane."

I was confused. "Isn't Lady Liliane with Master Onan?" I asked.

"Yes, and?"

Archer had arrived before the last bell rang, and he looked at me. "Some people choose two lovers," he said simply. "It's not common, and it's more frowned upon in some places than in others, but it happens. Love doesn't always let you choose who you find."

I looked at my friend—my squire, poet, musician friend—and wondered some things about him. And perhaps myself.

* * *

Although the servants did light cleaning throughout the week, Zai preferred to do most of the tidying up herself. We spent the first hour or so every Saturday doing some old-fashioned organizing, no magic allowed. Zai always happily sighed about how it built character; I always secretly thought it reminded me of home. More and more, though, I was starting to realize that this *was* home.

While dusting the mantle, I casually asked if any letters had come for me.

"No, none," Zai apologized.

I tried to hide my disappointment. I wasn't sure how long it would take to deliver mail, though I supposed it would be a while. After all, it took a whole month for me to walk to the palace from Jeren, and Qiameth was at least two weeks away by boat. And with rumors of unrest in Qimorath, maybe the mail had been delayed.

I spent the rest of the day on homework and

reading. As evening approached, I began to ready myself for the party.

Zai stopped by as I finished lacing myself into a soft blue gown. "Well, don't you look lovely!" she admired. "I'll be by shortly; I've business to attend to first. But I thought perhaps, if you'd like, you could stay out an extra hour tonight, until the eleventh bell."

"Truly?" I couldn't believe my luck. "Thank you!" My grin stretched from ear to ear.

Lady Liliane's chambers were lighter and airier than Zai's. I helped Val set up a few brightly colored magical streamers before the others arrived. It was a silly spell that Val taught me, but I had never used silly magic before, and I adored it. I had the feeling Lady Liliane was a bit more into those things than Lady Zai; her quarters were much more purposefully decorated than Zai's practical space. We floated translucent pearly bubbles over the sitting area, and Val covered the tables with gaudy turquoise and orange cloths. The room was truly, radiantly Naliah.

The party was in full swing when Archer finally arrived with the guest of honor. There were several other pages and squires, but I was relieved to note that no mages besides Val had come. Most people sat around talking and snacking, though Archer occasionally played a song.

Naliah, despite her previous protests, was having fun. She tumbled on the carpet with some page friends I had never met, and I got the sense that Naliah was a much better warrior than she made herself out to be.

Zai arrived a little later, flustering everyone as they all attempted to stand and bow. Lady Liliane greeted Zai with a chaste kiss on the cheek, and the two retreated to Liliane's rooms. Later, after Naliah and her page friends had giggled their way through a game of Queen's Dare, the pair emerged, looking flushed and a little guilty.

"We're going for a stroll; don't wait up," Lady Liliane called over her shoulder as they left, and Val pointedly raised her brows at me. I still hadn't quite made up my mind about what to do with this new knowledge.

With the adults gone, Val took out a stoppered bottle and passed it amongst the older attendees.

"Oh, no, I really shouldn't," I demurred at first, but it had been ages, and it didn't take much convincing.

"Made with palace blackberries," Val grinned when I hummed my approval. "Kessa and I picked them last summer. I've been waiting to taste this for *ages*."

Naliah was a whirlwind of delight, laughing

and joking and playing with her friends. It was nice, I reflected, to see her like this. Perhaps we ought to start inviting some of her yearmates out to the courtyard at night. She might not be so worried about abandoning her knighthood if more evenings could be like this.

The bottle went fast, but Val crooked a finger at me and lured me to a bay window by the courtyard. She pulled a second bottle from the cushions with a flourish, and we shared it together. I was beginning to feel delightfully giddy when our silly conversation took an even sillier turn.

"Well, obviously everyone knows who *I* like," Val tittered. "I've been pining for Gatlen since the day we met." She sighed. "It's an unrequited love, I know. The whole palace can tell that I'm madly in love with him, and yet the man doesn't have a clue I exist some days. I just hope he hasn't met anyone on his travels. You know how those knights are, all alone on the highway, performing great deeds rescuing damsels in distress and what have you."

"I thought those were just tales," I said, licking the sweet wine from my lips. "Most of the knights who made it to our inn were rather ordinary, though they certainly did attract a large audience. And I thought knights are free to like whoever they want in Freodon. Maybe they'd be happier rescuing begging bachelors than distressed damsels."

"So that leaves *you*," Val continued, ignoring my commentary. "You *must* like someone. But I'll be damned if anyone knows who. And there must be someone because sometimes when Archer plays, you get that look on your face that Naliah gets when the bread runs out, and the gods know you're not in love with Archer. So who?"

She continued to pester me for a while, and I tried to protest, but the wine had loosened my tongue.

"Stevan?!" Val squealed when I finally confessed. I described the night camping with the flowers and the unfortunate conversation when we first arrived.

"It's so tragically romantic," she swooned as I finished. "I can't believe you've never kissed!"

"And never will," I added glumly. "He's gone off to Qiameth for who knows how long, and Zai says she's seen him with some woman."

"Poor Ayve. No kiss for you. Wait, you have been kissed before, haven't you?!" She looked horrified for a moment and glanced about the room as if to find a subject to help me remedy this.

I laughed and told her all about my first bumbling kiss with Rafe.

Val sighed again. "Well, we'll just have to find someone else for you. Don't worry; the palace is huge. I'm sure we can find you someone. Unless you already have someone in mind?" Her eyes glinted mischievously

I took a large swig from the bottle to prepare myself for what I knew I would say next. Easier to blame it on the wine, I figured. "Actually," I said casually, "there was someone I met once. On my way into the palace. By the jewelry sellers."

"Old Merchant Croft?" Val wrinkled her nose.

"No, but she may have worked for him, I suppose."

Val's eyes widened, and she grinned. "Don't tell me: blonde curly hair, gorgeous green eyes?"

I nodded. My face was hot, and my chest felt tight.

"But that's Kessa's sister!"

I looked up, my fear replaced by shock. "Kessa? Has a sister?" I'd had the thought before, but I'd brushed it away.

Val laughed. "Rebekah! They're twins, though not identical. Rebekah used to work in the palace, but now she's down at the market working" —she leaned closer— "*as a spy*," she finished dramatically. "Ooh, this is too lovely! Well, we'll just have to find a time for you to get down to her stall again soon."

"If Zai ever lets me," I said. "Tonight's the first time she's let me out of her sight for so long.

Maybe she's finally beginning to trust me."

I kept waiting for Val to say something, to acknowledge what I had just admitted to, but like everything else in Freodon, this seemed to be taken for granted, and it was as if I had done nothing more than mention the weather. I supposed this would make it easier to handle my knowledge of Ladies Zai and Liliane at any rate.

* * *

At breakfast the next day, Naliah was still raving about her party.

"So," Val asked, "now that you're thirteen, do you still think love is stupid?"

"Definitely," Naliah affirmed.

"Oh, really? Is that why you were flirting with Keiran all night?" Val teased.

Naliah pouted and tossed a muffin at her. Val laughed and ducked. Sir Rodrick, who happened to be passing by, was less than pleased. He scolded Naliah, assigning her kitchen duty after dinner for the rest of the week.

"See, thirteen is exactly the same," Naliah sighed. "Love is still dumb, and I still can't stay out of trouble!"

SEPTEMBER-DECEMBER
967 CE

CHAPTER 18

THE REST OF THE SUMMER was perfect. Classes were fun. My friends were happy. Even my interactions with Zai were smooth. As soon as more students learned to detect Zai's magic in the crystals, we began learning to craft our own, though I didn't get very far. I quietly thought this was a good thing since it helped the other students soften towards me a bit. They seemed to have forgotten I was still a beginner, lightning-fast learning speed or not, but by season's end, they were friendly, if not exactly friends.

Naliah and I began inviting some of her yearmates out to the courtyard at night. Even the infamous Keiran joined, though Naliah had given up on flirting with him. All sorts of work happened there: practice fights, math figures, even dancing, which Naliah was determined to learn. A few mage students even joined a couple of times each week, practicing spells and philosophizing under the trees.

"You know, this is the most I've seen that old courtyard used in years," Zai commented one Saturday night as I helped her get ready for some lord's ball. She threaded golden hoops through her ears as I pinned back her hair. "Besides Val's little group, most of the mages and warriors didn't really interact before you got here. You've done good work this summer."

A cool breeze drifted in through the window. "It's going to rain," I said, not sure how to respond to the compliment. "I'll ready your cloak."

Zai watched me move in the mirror. "It will be sad, come autumn, when the courtyard isn't as lively anymore," she noted. "The chill and the dark will be here all too soon." I was glum for a moment, thinking about the little family I'd have to give up, when Zai surprised me. "You can meet in the library instead, I think," she said crisply, taking the cloak from me and throwing it around her shoulders.

"The library?"

Zai nodded, raising the hood. "I have faith in

your defense skills. And in your friends. We'll make a charm in your morning studies soon, one that will warn you of anyone who wishes to do you harm. So long as you keep it with you every night, I see no reason you shouldn't continue to meet with your friends. And it's that or I have a hundred children running about my chambers," Zai snorted.

***

In the autumn session, Naliah and I would finally begin intermediate magic, and palace gossip was all aflutter when it was revealed that the water class I'd signed up for was to be led by none other than Master Onan. I was curious to get to know Lady Liliane's other partner, especially after learning about her and Zai this summer. I still wasn't sure how it all worked, having two different lovers, and though I'd never dare ask Master Onan to his face, I saw this as a good opportunity to learn by proxy.

I would have to wait, though, as there was a week off between sessions, this time for the harvest festival. Though not quite as big of an affair as the summer solstice, it was supposed to be fun, and Val was free this time.

"I still don't think Zai is going to let me go into the city," I said doubtfully.

"She will," Val replied determinedly. "If she's ready to let you study in the library, she'll be ready to let you celebrate, too. You'll see."

Now it was Naliah who would not be around. It was the annual page camping trip to prove they could survive for a week on their own. The training masters stayed nearby should disaster strike, but the students were left in charge. A season ago, Naliah would have been fretting about a week without us, but now that she had better friends amongst her yearmates, she was happy to go. I was jealous; I wished *I* could be out in the woods, though as the wind picked up one evening, I was grateful to go back inside and warm myself in front of the fire.

The harvest festival kicked off with jugglers, singers, and a rich dessert of spiced apple turnovers. Inside the palace courtyard, tents had been erected with vendors for the nobles and palace folk. I enjoyed browsing the pretty wares, but Val wanted more than anything to go down to the public markets, which she claimed were a lot more fun.

"Absolutely not," Zai refused when I finally worked up the nerve to ask her. "There is plenty to enjoy up here. There's nothing at the markets but crowds and outrageous prices. You can get the same within the palace walls without any added dangers. I trust your defense skills, but there are too many unknowns down there."

Though Val pouted the rest of the night, I didn't mind. Perhaps Zai would be ready by winter solstice.

* * *

The final day of the festival was lovely. Zai gave me the entire day off to do absolutely nothing. It was the perfect weather for relaxing; the sky was a brilliant blue with a smattering of soft white clouds. The apple tree in the courtyard was flourishing, and Val promised to use some of the fallen fruit to brew cider. We spent the day at the palace festival playing games and winning small prizes.

Some of the mage students we passed stopped and made friendly small talk. I assumed they were only talking to me because I was with Val, so I was caught off guard when they asked what elemental class I had chosen for fall session.

"Water," I said, blinking in surprise.

"Really!" one boy replied. He had been in Liliane's session, but I had never gotten to know him well. "I've heard remarkable things about your time with Lady Zai for crystals, so I'm curious: why change?"

This may have been the longest he had ever

spoken to me. "I enjoyed my earth classes," I replied, "but I figured I should expand my skills as much as possible. I'm still new to this, so I don't really know where my strengths lie yet. Lady Zai agreed it would be good for me to test my powers and get to know them more. And not only is it with Master Onan, but rumor has it a powerful water mage is assisting him. It sounds like too good an opportunity to miss."

"Rumor also has it the assistant is a *handsome* water mage," Val teased. She had been after me for weeks once she heard that.

"Well, we'll miss you in the earth classes, but you're right to want to study with Master Onan. If anyone can help you develop your water strength, it's him." The group exchanged a few more pleasantries and said their goodbyes.

"It's interesting," I observed. "All summer long, no one wanted anything to do with me, but suddenly it's like none of that ever happened."

"They're not threatened now that you're venturing outside of their favored element," Val explained. "They just had to realize that you're not trying to best them. Don't worry; I'm sure the water students are quaking in their boots!"

A while later, after winning a silk scarf, we ran across Master Varrick. He looked strange out of his mage's robes in rough brown trousers and a sage shirt. He sat near the fountain in the courtyard, warming himself in the sun.

"Hello!" he called. It was clear talking to a teacher in her free time wasn't at the top of Val's list, but I didn't mind Master Varrick, and it wouldn't hurt to be polite for a while.

"Hello!" I called back, gently dragging Val along. The fountain spray was refreshing in the warm sun.

"Are you enjoying your day at the festival?" he asked.

"Yes, very much. I wasn't able to get out much for the summer solstice, so it's nice to see what all the fuss is about."

"Oh? Were you out of town?"

I didn't want to besmirch Zai's name. "Lady Zai thought it was best that I wait until my defense abilities were stronger."

"And are they now? Stronger?"

I smiled. I knew a mage's request when I heard one. Raising my arms, I reached into my well of power. A gentle wind whipped, and a shimmering green bubble enveloped us. Val rolled her eyes and tapped her foot.

"Wonderful!" Master Varrick applauded, and I erased the spell with a wave of my hand. "That was quite remarkable, especially for someone who just tested out of basics. Was that Hodin's Spell?"

"Yes, with a flair of Allishele's Protection," I said. Val slowly started edging away towards a group of our peers. I gave up on her and sat on the warm stone beside Master Varrick.

"Impressive. My class must have been so boring for you."

My eyes widened. "Gods, no! So much of what I learned is from you! And I could never be bored helping the younger ones. They're so...?"

"Energetic?" Master Varrick suggested.

"Annoying," I lamented, and Master Varrick laughed.

"Well," he continued when his chuckles died down, "I'll certainly miss having your help with them. But if you're already splicing Allishele's into Hodin's, you're more than ready for intermediate magic. What elemental class are you taking this quarter, by the way? I'm offering my first ever—veiling spells with air magic." He looked hopeful.

"River spells, actually," I admitted. "Master Onan is leading the session, and I've heard wonderful things about him. But I'm trying to explore more elements outside my comfort zone before we leave, so perhaps I can join yours next time."

"Getting ready to leave already?" His eyes were on the crowd around us, but I could sense his every attention was on me. "It seems like you only just got here. Where will you go?"

It felt silly, not telling him everything. After all, he was my teacher. But if Zai knew I had been sharing her plans... "I'm not sure," I said. It wasn't a lie, either. "Perhaps we'll make a stop back at Jeren." Now I was definitely lying, but what harm could it do? I turned my face to the sun and tried to warm myself from within.

"Well, you'll have to keep me posted. If you're not leaving before the spring equinox, I'd love to have you in my class again." Varrick stood and stretched. "It was good talking with you, Ayve. I hope to see you around."

Moments after he left, Val swooped back in. "Finally!" she exclaimed. "I can't believe you're wasting the last day of the festival talking to a teacher! Honest, you're just as bad as Archer sometimes. Let's go; Matias says there's dragon's beard at the tent by the stables. I'm buying!" She grabbed my hand and rushed us away.

* * *

The pages returned right on schedule. Naliah came tumbling into the dining room all atwitter. Her limbs had always been gangly, but in the last week, she seemed to have grown a few inches, and when she plopped onto the bench beside Archer, it scooted across the stones with a loud screech.

"They're back!" she cried.

"The pages? Yes, we noticed," Val said, wrinkling her nose at the state of Naliah's clothing.

Naliah gave Val a *look* and sighed. "Gatlen and Kessa," she said, exasperated.

"Gatlen's here?" Val automatically sat up straighter, smoothing her hair and looking around.

"Not *here* here, but back in the city. They've taken up residence in the knights' quarters down in the city proper for the fall. We ran into them on our way back. They're planning to join the harvest festival activities down there tonight." Naliah pouted. "They asked me to go, but pages have to clean gear and wash up tonight. I'm not even supposed to be here until I've done my chores. I stink."

"Yes, you do," Val said dryly.

Naliah glared even harder. "If I weren't so nice, maybe I wouldn't tell you that they asked if you three would join them tonight. And I am begging you to please, please, *please* go! Have the fun that I can't and tell me all about it!"

"You know, if you cleaned your gear right now, you could still go later tonight," Archer helpfully pointed out.

Naliah looked slightly sheepish. "I'm going to the festival up here. I'm not allowed outside the palace walls after... well, let's just say it wasn't my fault, but we made a pact on our trip not to rat anyone out, so we've all agreed to stay up here tonight."

"We?"

"Me and the others. Yondou, Tsuly, Giza, and Keiran."

I was so proud of Naliah for having friends that I could almost pretend I wasn't disappointed. "Val, you'll have to tell me all about it," I said, faking a cheerful smile. "I've pushed my luck with Lady Zai for one week as far as it will go. Tell them I say hi and to come to dinner soon."

Val's protests were weak and died off almost instantly.

"I can go," Archer said, a little too quickly. "It'd be nice to see Kessa. And Gatlen." Like Naliah, Archer had grown over the summer, and his voice had deepened. He stroked his scruff of beard thoughtfully.

"You could come with me and my friends," Naliah offered helpfully.

"That's okay," I declined kindly. "I don't want to intrude. But maybe I'll see you there if I make it back out." Secretly, I thought, perhaps I would just stay in my room and read by the fire. I missed my friends, but I wouldn't mind a little rest before the new quarter began.

* * *

I helped Zai put on her finishing touches for the final harvest ball. In her lacy black dress with a dark lip and eye, she was stunningly witchy.

"I expect I'll be home late," Zai said as I tied a black beaded mask around her face. "I may even visit some acquaintances"—I pictured Lady Liliane and Master Onan—"and not come home at all. I needn't remind you, I hope, that curfew still stands, though perhaps you'd enjoy it being extended till midnight?"

"Thank you, my lady," I agreed, "but I have no plans to go out. Val and some of them are heading down into the city tonight, and Naliah and her friends are going to the festival up here, but to tell the truth, I'm exhausted." I yawned, realizing for the first time that I meant it. "I'm looking forward to a quiet night in."

"Well, as quiet as can be when the blasted pyro mages will be setting off fire flowers," Zai grumbled. "Though it's a pretty show, and you should be able to catch some of it from your window if you wish."

"I suppose," I said, though I was hopeful I would be sound asleep before they started.

"Still." Zai rooted around a drawer and pulled out a small yellow crystal on a leather cord. "Take this. Just in case. It's a protection talisman, though not very strong, and will warn you if anyone wishes to do you harm."

"Thank you, my lady." I held out my hand to accept the crystal, but Zai motioned for me to turn around and knotted the cord at the nape of my neck. "I thought I would learn to make my own this session."

"You will." Zai let go, and the crystal rested softly against my chest. "But they take time to make, and I'd rather you have a weak one than none at all. I confiscated this one from a student years ago when she tried to pass it off as hers in a lesson." Zai snorted. "As if her magic would suddenly change from blue to yellow. It's from the shopkeeper on Hinkett Street, sure as I'm standing here. He's a good man, though, and I trust his suppliers."

Zai stepped in front of me and raised one long, slender finger. "May I?" She gently touched a nail to the crystal. It instantly alit, reminding me of starlight. "Still good," she said, seemingly satisfied, and the light began to fade. "If you see it flare up at all tonight, get out. This thing doesn't have a very discriminating range, and it could mean there's someone two feet or two *miles* from you."

"Yes, my lady. But I'd certainly hope there's

no one who wants to hurt me while I'm in my bed."

Zai smiled, her eyes a mystery behind her mask. "Just in case," she reaffirmed. "And remember, not one second past midnight, or I will know." She turned from the room, cloak swishing and boots clicking.

If I had been confused about Zai's behavior, I certainly didn't have to wait long to understand. There, lounging on my bed, tossing an apple up and down, was Stevan.

"What, no hello?" he asked as I stood in the door, mouth agape. He caught the apple, and it thumped softly against his palm. "Good to see you, too," he said when I still didn't say anything.

"I thought Zai had these rooms spelled," was my stunned response. "So that only I could enter through the window." I had shut it earlier, but it was wide open now, allowing a sweet, cool draft to rush in.

He shrugged. "I used to live here, remember? I suppose Zai never removed me from the wards. And she knows I'm in town. If I'm not mistaken, she gave you extra safeguards tonight and cautioned you to be back before midnight."

I clutched the talisman, cursing myself for not hiding it beneath my dress. "You heard," I accused as I pulled the window shut with a loud snap.

"Perhaps," he admitted. He bit into the apple. "But I also know Zai. She wouldn't expect her assistant to stay in on the last night of the festival. She got a little too used to a certain former apprentice being a bit of a party animal," he smirked.

"Does this mean you're back now?" I ignored his other comments and perched cautiously on the edge of my desk chair. I wasn't sure what our relationship was anymore.

He sat up, clearly sensing my unease. "Yes. I finished my research in Qiameth. I'm back for the fall session, if not longer."

"Will you move back in?" I wasn't sure I was ready to give up my room. Not after things had been so good.

He rubbed his chin thoughtfully. "Maybe. It depends on what Zai says. She has a spare room in her suite." I thought of the final door I had never seen behind. "I'd prefer to have a place of my own, though. And I wouldn't dare dream of kicking you out. You're her assistant, so this room is yours by right."

"Where are you staying now?" This conversation felt absurd. Four months apart, and all I could ask about was living arrangements?

"I have friends down in the city. I only just got back this morning, and there's no room at the inns.

I haven't seen Zai yet; last we spoke was through the fire. But like I said, she knows I'm here. She'd be a poor former mentor if she couldn't sense me the moment I set foot in this room."

He finished the apple and rose as he tossed the core into the fire, waving a hand so that it instantly burned and filled the air with a sweet spice. "I'm heading down to The Crow," he said. "I believe some of your friends might already be there. It's a tavern," he explained, "one of the more popular with students as they don't tend to care what ages when they serve. Want to come?" He opened the window again and straddled the frame, extending one hand.

I hesitated. If I didn't go, I might never get to talk to him again. And yet... "I can't. I can be out till midnight, but I can't go beyond the palace walls."

He tutted. "I happen to know Zai will be out all night, and I happen to know that she'll be at a masquerade within palace walls, so she can't *possibly* know who's coming and going through the main gates. I also may happen to know how to override her spell, so that should a resident of this room, say, want to come back past midnight, they could."

The tension in my chest was unbearable. "Ok," I agreed at last. "But couldn't we just walk out the front door?"

He smiled widely. "We could, but who doesn't like a little adventure?" Laughter echoed from somewhere in the courtyard beyond, and dying leaves danced across the stones. I slipped my hand into his and followed him through the window, my nerves blazing with fire. All thoughts of exhaustion were swept from my head as I focused on his warm, calloused palm.

Once we were through, he waved his arm at the windows and shutters, which closed softly behind us. He hugged me firmly. "It's good to see you," he said, and guided me into the night.

* * *

Although I held my breath as we walked through the gates, no magical purple force swooped down and stopped us as I had feared. I was still nervous, though, and chattered anxiously about the spring and summer as we wound our way down the cobblestone path.

"I'm glad Val's crew took you in!" Stevan exclaimed when he heard about my friends. "They're a nice lot. I don't know Naliah all that well, but I hear she's got pluck," he added, which made me snort.

"What have you been up to?" I finally dared to ask as we continued our descent.

"Studying, mostly. Believe it or not, studying star magic."

I thought back to our conversation that night in the woods. "Is it truly related to air magic, then?"

It was dark, and the torches flickered on the street, but I knew he was pleased that I had remembered. "Yes, fascinatingly so, though I will admit Zai was right about its relation to fire and the other elements, too. There's so much more than I could ever hope to learn, but at least I know more than I used to. I imagine this new knowledge will come in handy." He sounded almost smug.

"Handy? How?" I demanded.

"That's not for me to say. Not yet, at least. Turn here." He abruptly stepped to the side, pulling me down an alley. It was even darker there, and as we twisted and turned down rough stone stairwells, we passed several groups drinking ale and carousing. Further back in the shadows, I could just see the outline of a couple kissing. Without meaning to, I found myself watching them hungrily.

"We're here," Stevan said not too long after, and we walked through the open door of a large tavern. The air was hot, and the roar from the mob was nearly deafening. I stuck my fingers in my ears as we picked our way through the crowded room. Stevan pointed to a table in the back where Gatlen, Kessa, and Val sat drinking and chatting. I was pleased to see that Val was snuggled up quite closely to Gatlen. Judging by the empty pitchers, they were already a few tankards in, and they roared a tumultuous greeting when we approached.

"You made it!" Val squealed as she hugged me wildly. When she pulled away, her eyes were sparkling, and it was clear she had ideas about what the night might hold.

Stevan fetched another pitcher for the table, and we all raised a hearty cheer. "Ah, that's good!" he groaned. "All they have down in Qiameth is fruit wines and ales so weak they might as well be water. Give me good old barley wine any day!"

"Try the piss wines of the hills for three months," Gatlen complained. "At least Qiameth knows how to flavor things."

I downed my drink quickly. It was a dark brew, and nutty. Since the disastrous night when we'd arrived in Freodon, I'd only had the rare drink at dinner events and that one night of blackberry wine with Val. I said as much to the group when Kessa asked for my opinion on it.

"Then be careful," Kessa laughed. "This stuff's strong. But delicious." She licked foam from her upper lip.

Time melted as Gatlen and Kessa regaled the table with tales from their journey. "That's a mighty big word for something so small," Gatlen protested when Val begged to hear more stories. "After all, we spent most of our time helping villagers plow fields and chop wood for the winter."

"Of course, there *was* that band of outlaws you helped bring in," Kessa pointed out, and Val squealed and demanded the tale. Gatlen rolled his eyes but smiled, clearly enjoying the attention.

When the pitcher was gone, another seemed to appear as if by magic. A pleasant buzzing hummed throughout my body. I remembered, quite suddenly, that Petyr hadn't wanted me to drink ale growing up. "It isn't cost-effective," he'd told me once when he caught me and Rafe sneaking it from the storeroom. We had drunk ourselves silly and accidentally locked ourselves in. We'd had to bang on the doors until Martha found us. "If you're going to steal our wares, at least steal something stronger so that you have to take less."

The memory left me angry. I didn't want to remember the past, especially after it had stayed so well buried all summer. I hurriedly downed another drink.

"What's wrong?" Stevan asked quietly.

I shook my head. "Nothing. Just remembering,

that's all. The last time I had ale. With Rafe. I haven't thought about Jeren in a while."

Stevan allowed one finger to trace the back of my hand. My breath hitched. "I'm glad you didn't marry his older brother, you know," he said quietly.

My arm tickled pleasantly until I could think of nothing else. "I'd almost forgotten about that," I admitted. "I'm glad, too."

He slid an arm across the back of my chair, and I leaned closer. His body felt hot in the already close space.

I was sure the others must have talked some more after that, but if they did, I didn't hear a word. I vaguely remembered some bawdy songs and a troop of players. In spite of all the noise and commotion, my world had narrowed to one warm, solid form at my side.

Someone eventually bought hand pies for the table, though I tried to pass.

"You should eat," Stevan chided, placing one in front of both of us. "Else you'll be dizzy later."

"I'm dizzy now," I giggled in reply.

"Then you should really eat one, my beautiful," said a voice on my other side.

I turned. Why would I be surprised that tonight, of all nights, was when we would meet again?

"Rebekah!" Kessa cried. She jumped up from the table and hugged her sister excitedly. Though Kessa's hair was straighter and her nose was somewhat wider, the resemblance was remarkable.

Rebekah grabbed a chair and dragged it over. She rested a hand gently on my shoulder as she lowered herself, and I was pretty sure sparks flew where we had touched.

"Rebekah," she said, introducing herself to Stevan.

"Stevan," he said, and they shook hands. His leg grew tense against my own.

"Ok, so now that I *finally* have you both in the same place," Val said, "can you *please* tell me why Kessa has straight hair if you're twins?"

Rebekah didn't laugh like Kessa did, but their eyes crinkled the same. "We're fraternal," Kessa said, "which I'm pretty sure you know, seeing how you've asked me that a thousand times already."

"Yes, but that still doesn't really explain it," Val protested. "Not something big like that."

"We spent a lot of time apart as kids," Rebekah offered. "Kessa came north with our father, but I stayed in Qiameth longer with our mother. The styles are so different here. All about being sleek, contained. Things are much wilder in the south," she said, and I could have sworn she winked.

"I don't think so," Stevan disagreed. His voice was strained. "I just spent the summer there. Everyone was rather uptight and repressed, I thought."

Rebekah tutted. "Spending a summer with mages is not spending a summer in Qiameth. Come with me sometime. I will show you the real city and all of its wanton ways." This time, she *definitely* winked.

I wasn't sure what was happening, but it was odd to be caught in the middle of it. I drained another tankard, lifting it over my head to get the final dregs.

"Ah!" A hand delicately touched my wrist. "You still have it. Good. I was hoping."

I lowered my arm quickly, looking at the wooden bracelet Rebekah fingered so gently. "I just threw it on today," I muttered. "It seemed nice... for the festival... Val and I went," I finished lamely. "I didn't know I'd be going out tonight," I added, widening my eyes in a silent plea to Stevan.

"I think we need another pitcher. And perhaps some more food? On me." He began to scoot, and I tipped sideways to allow him out. I fell back onto the hard seat, watching him walk away into the crowd. Was he mad?

Rebekah sighed. "Well, I suppose this is a good time to go to the privy."

Kessa raised her eyebrows at her sister. "Rebekah," she warned.

"Kessa," she teased in reply, and then she was gone.

Kessa rolled her eyes. "Apparently being a palace spy doesn't provide enough fun. She might not even come back now that she's played her game. Anyway, tell me about everyone else," she said, leaning towards me. Gatlen was deep in conversation with Val, if you could call staring dopily into each other's eyes a deep conversation.

"They're good," I said. My tongue felt thick, and I wished I had some water. "Naliah is as exceptional as ever. I think she's finally happy now that she has some page friends."

"Good," Kessa sighed. "Poor girl was miserable when she started here. I was worried we'd lose her to the Queen's Ladies. She seemed well when we saw her this morning, but Naliah's moods can change fast, so I didn't want to presume. And Archer?" Her tone was casual, but there must have been something in the air.

"Fine," I shrugged. "I'm surprised he's not here yet. He's still writing songs. He spent most of the summer moping, but I think he's better now. In fact, he might even be seeing someone."

That was a lie, but the "Oh?" it produced from Kessa was worth it to confirm my hunch.

Another knight stopped by the table, and I allowed myself to slip out of the conversation. Stevan still hadn't returned, and Rebekah did indeed seem to have disappeared, so I took the opportunity to visit the privy myself. I hadn't realized how drunk I'd become. The dance floor was crowded, and a handsome man took my hand and twirled me as I passed. I laughed and stumbled down the hallway towards the small room, which was mercifully empty. After, I checked my appearance in the polished metal mirror. My face was flushed, and my hair was mussed, but I'd never seen myself look so happy. I grinned and winked at myself flirtily.

I was still grinning when I stepped back into the hall and was swept suddenly into a tight hug from behind. "Stevan," I laughed, but my laughter stopped when blonde curls draped over my shoulders. I turned, and Rebekah held my hands above my head and pinned me to the wall, kissing me.

I was flummoxed. What was I supposed to say? "I..." was all I could muster when Rebekah finally broke away.

"You? Yes, indeed," Rebekah said impishly. Even in the dark, her green eyes glimmered.

"Oh, I see," someone muttered.

I looked away and met Stevan's gray eyes

glaring back at me from the end of the hallway. "Wait, Stevan—"

But he was gone before I could say anything. I drunkenly dithered, unsure of what to do, and Rebekah placed a gentle kiss on my forehead. "Poor dear," she sighed. "It seems you have quite a choice to make." And she, too, wandered away.

I wasn't sure how long I stood there. I couldn't pick between them. Not like this. I gathered my courage and ventured back into the crowd, making straight for the door. I left, picking my way back up the cobblestone street, realizing I had no idea of how I'd gotten there in the first place, hoping against hope that I'd make it back to the palace. I wasn't even sure what time it was; I hadn't been able to hear the bells inside the boisterous space.

Somehow, I found myself back through the gates and climbing through my window. I immediately rolled into a restless, drunken sleep.

CHAPTER 19

THE WATER PITCHER was just barely out of reach, but that was far enough to make me groan. My head roared its displeasure as I forced myself to sit up and grab the handles. I wished I could magic it over to myself, but I was so hungover, I was positive I would miss and smash it against the wall. With great effort, I poured a cup and forced myself to drink. After repeating a few times and woozily visiting the privy, I climbed back into bed and threw a pillow over my head.

Perhaps I dozed, but it wasn't restful. Eventually, I threw the covers from my sweaty body, groaning as I rose. It was raining, and damp air on damp skin left me shivering. I piled on warmer clothes and pulled back my hair. It was early still, and I had no duties on Sundays, but sometimes Zai had tea and scones. I freshened up as best I could and opened my door.

I very nearly slammed it shut when I found Zai greeting Stevan in the common room. Heart pounding, I threw on a dressing gown and forced myself to join them.

"Good morning, sleepyhead!" Zai gracefully perched on the couch. Stevan sat on the armchair closest to the fire. If he was hungover, he certainly didn't show it.

"Good morning," I mumbled. "Hello, Stevan. It's good to see you," I added, knowing it would look odd if I said nothing after a season apart.

"Hello, Ayve. It's been a while. How has the palace been treating you?" He played along, at least. That made it easier.

"Well, thank you. I've enjoyed my classes. And working for Zai has been wonderful."

Zai scoffed and pulled a scone from the tray on the table. "Wonderful is the word she uses to describe new challenges," she explained. "I believe she's used the same word to describe Madame Gerta's class before. But how are *you*?" she exclaimed. "It's been forever since we've really spoken. I take it things went well in Qiameth?"

I poured myself a cup of tea while they talked,

hoping I wouldn't vomit.

"Well, that all sounds lovely," Zai said finally, clasping her hands together. "I'm glad Master Sida took such good care of you. She's young, but she knows her way around the stars."

"She? Women can have the title of Master?" I instantly regretted my question; I'd now slipped back into Zai's focus.

"Yes, of course," Zai said, reaching for another scone. "I went by Master when I first got here. Most mages do. It was only when the King bestowed lands on me that I became Lady. Surely someone explained that to you?"

I shook my head. I was dizzy, and now I felt dumb, too. "I just assumed all sorceresses were called ladies. Like Lady Liliane."

Zai shook her head. "Only those who have noble titles. 'Master' doesn't denote gender, just ability. Well, that certainly tells me we need to introduce you to more mages," she said, dusting crumbs from her hands. "I'll need to think about who you should meet this next quarter. Speaking of," she said, turning to Stevan, "what are your plans? I've heard rumors, which you know is not my preferred method for learning about my former apprentice," she said matter-of-factly.

Stevan smiled faintly. "No, I should have told you. I'm sorry. Master Sida just kept me so busy."

"Oh?" Zai asked, and she raised one dark eyebrow.

I might have been imagining it, but Stevan's cheeks seemed to flush. "She was very demanding when it came to research. It wasn't enough that I study the stars but the oceans, too. I can't tell you how many hours I spent comparing the currents of the air to the currents of the water. I still don't understand much about either of them, but I know more now than I did before."

"I see." Zai didn't sound convinced. "We'll have to talk more soon." I tried to pretend I didn't see Zai's eyes slide my way. "Once we can find time to really sit down together. Morning scones are no place for serious magic talk."

"Yes," Stevan agreed, looking relieved. "It's funny, but the mages in Qiameth don't see anything wrong with talking about magic at all hours of the day. There'd be times I went for a bath and got cornered for a full bell."

Zai smiled, and her eyes crinkled in amusement. "Yes, Qiamethans are notorious for that. It's everyone there, not just mages. They think *we're* quite rude in Freodon, with all these unspoken rules about when and where things can happen. But given that I'm a former Qiamethan myself, I can be rude and ask: where do you plan to stay? Will you require a room here again?"

Stevan shook his head. "I stopped by the quartermaster's on my way here. The mages' tower is full through winter, but there are plenty of rooms free in the knights' lodging. Sounds like a good many will be gone for the winter since the situation still hasn't improved in Qimorath. Palace servants are moving my belongings there now. In fact, I should probably head out; the room must be nearly ready. I need to get settled before the term begins tomorrow."

"Of course." She walked him to the door. "Ayve and I will continue morning sessions this quarter," she said before he parted. "You're welcome to join us any time."

"Thank you," Stevan said, and I noticed his response neither accepted nor declined. "I'll see you soon. Goodbye, Ayve," he called, and I at least managed a guttural "mm" as he walked away.

Zai sat back down. "Looks like you got up just in time! I was beginning to wonder if I should wake you before you slept all day. I presume you made it out last night after all. How was it?" She took a long drink from her tea.

I felt myself begin to sweat again. Was Zai trying to catch me? Had I come home after midnight? "It was alright," I finally shrugged, picking up a book from the table. "A little crowded, if you ask me. But still fun."

Zai placed her tea back down. "I take it things didn't go all that well with Stevan, though."

My heart nearly shot through my chest.

Zai held up a hand. "I don't need to know the details of where you saw him, or how long you were gone. As far as I know, when I left, you walked into your room to find Stevan on your bed, where I knew he'd be, and you went to the palace festival together. But something clearly happened. I've never seen you two more formal with each other. And you look like you're going to be sick."

That was all it took. Zai managed to get a small wastebasket beneath my head as I leaned over and retched violently. When I was done, Zai brought me a small glass of water and a cool washcloth for my head.

"I'm sorry," I apologized, hot tears spilling from my eyes. "I'll go back to my room."

"Nonsense, you'll stay here," Zai chided. "Move too soon and you'll be doing that all over again. Lie down, and I'll fetch a blanket."

I shivered and gratefully accepted the warm quilt Zai brought. She sat on the armchair nearby, reading quietly. I closed my eyes for a while, but tears continued leaking steadily into my hair.

Zai sighed quietly and closed her book. "I had hoped you would be over him by now."

I sniffed. "So did I. But then I... and he... it got

complicated."

"Relationships always do. You know, when he went away to study, I had half a mind to order him back. I knew he was running. That's what he does. He was very much a ladies' man during his time as my apprentice, but the second any of them got close, he moved on. And if what I heard from my sources in Qiameth is true, he's still very much the same. I'd thought…" She shook her head and stood. "But look at me, meddling in places I don't belong."

I smiled weakly. "Right now, I'm rather glad for your meddling," I whispered. "Thank you for taking care of me."

Zai stroked my forehead briefly. Then the touch was suddenly gone, leaving me to wonder if I had imagined it. "Rest up," Zai told me as she went back to her rooms. "Don't try to move until you've slept a little. You'll feel better soon."

"I already do," I replied softly as the door closed.

* * *

Despite resting nearly all of Sunday, I was still up at my usual hour on Monday. The new term was beginning whether I was ready or not. I'd recently discovered that I had become so quick at lighting fires and fetching Zai's breakfast that I actually had time for a true soak in the baths, so I headed there after waking. A few other mage students, some who I recognized from my classes, were there too, and we chatted briefly.

Breakfast was the same as usual, though Gatlen and Kessa were out on patrol. Val pouted a bit, but even she was too excited about new courses to mope for long. While my peers rushed off to their first classes of the day, I returned to Zai's rooms. I felt a twinge of jealousy that I wouldn't be joining them, but I was rather looking forward to my new lessons with Zai.

Lessons, apparently, now involved long walks on the outer curtain walls. It was chilly, and a misty sideways rain slowly soaked through our clothes.

"Here," Zai would say every now and then, stopping, and I would feel with my magic to see who had worked a spell somewhere. It had been so easy on the talismans during the summer, but in the dark rain it was nearly impossible, especially with so many spells drifting up from the classrooms below. I managed, once, to find a cleansing spell that Zai had worked, but Zai warned me not to get too excited.

"You know my magic," she cautioned. "It's always easier to spot traces of people you know, but you need to be able to do it for everyone. Say you're out in the field one day, and you discover a trap laid by an enemy mage. You need to learn to recognize their magic in case you run across them later. Perhaps they're truly a foreign spy working for another kingdom, and it is only because you know their magic that you can catch them."

"Is it likely that I'll be catching spies one day?" I asked, doubtful.

Zai shrugged. "Mages take on all sorts of tasks they never thought they would. City magic is flashy, but it doesn't always pay. Odd jobs and side tasks are one way to stay afloat."

"But I'm not going to *be* a mage," I countered, "not really. Not a full one. Not unless I take the tests." I tried not to sound hopeful. It wouldn't do to let anyone, not even Zai, know that sometimes, late at night, I imagined myself standing before the panel, wowing everyone as I passed. *"The fastest anyone ever learned,"* they would whisper, *"even faster than Stevan."*

"No," Zai replied, bursting my bubble, "you're right. I don't think the tests would be right for you. It's not worth the hours of study they would take. But you'll be a sorceress's assistant for as long as you'll have me, and even if you choose to leave, there is always work for magically trained people. Plenty of students don't take the tests and find employment through the kingdom. Countryfolk have all sorts of words for that: hedgewitches, conjurers, enchanters... Assuming you'd want to leave Freodon, of course."

We moved along. I clutched my cloak tighter to me, though it did little to keep me warm. I wasn't sure I could picture leaving the city. Not yet, anyway. And despite what Zai said, a small part of me still wanted to take the exams. I decided to ignore it for now. "If I can detect someone's magic, would I know who they are before I ever met them? Like their name? Or would I just know their essence?"

Zai slowed her stroll and pointed to another spot she wanted me to test. "Essence. That's a good word for it. It's a very advanced skill to know names from traces alone. Very few can do it, and even then accuracy is limited. We mostly just get to know, as you call it, essences. But yes, it is possible."

I knew the answer before I even asked the question. "And are you one of those very few?"

"I am. It's a form of divination, I suppose, a tricky art at best, but with the right conditions, I can conjure up an image of sorts of the creator in my head. It's like remembering someone before you've met them, if that makes sense."

It didn't, but I needed to concentrate on the task at hand. I spent a frustrating rest of the morning trying and failing again and again.

* * *

Gatlen and Kessa were at lunch, though both were grumpy after having worked the soggy morning shift.

"*And* we're working the evening shift, too," Kessa grumbled. "Go to work in the dark, come home in the dark, and none of it for jobs that a knight ought to be doing. This is a soldier's duty."

"A knight signs on for whatever task is asked of them when they take their vows," Naliah pointed out helpfully. She was peppy, not having earned any extra punishments during her morning classes for the first time in history.

"I'll remind you that you said that when *you're* a knight," Kessa returned, sticking out her tongue. "I know it's sorely needed work, but it's hard to be content when there's so much going on in Qimorath."

"What's going on in Qimorath?" Val asked as she slid onto the bench next to Gatlen. He wrapped an arm around her shoulders, but I was pleased they at least drew the line there in the dining hall. I wasn't sure I could handle snuggly kisses over lunch.

"Bandits," Kessa said grimly. "It happens every summer when the heat rises and the sandstorms blow, but the crops were poor this year, and folks are hungry. Raids usually stop by autumn, but it seems one of the groups has found something of a commander, some exiled military leader from Suuldus. They keep striking at towns, stealing supplies and killing people. Qimorathans expect some level of conflict, but nothing organized like this. They've even gotten close to Qiameth, and the usual tactics aren't working to make them stop. I'd love nothing more than to ride south and defend my family, but the monarchs are reluctant to involve us in foreign affairs, and it'd be breaking my oath to go."

I gripped her shoulder in solace.

Kessa nodded her thanks and picked up her knife, forcing herself to eat. "I know it won't help to worry myself sick. And it's good that the work here keeps me busy, even if it's cold, soggy work." She used her foot to poke at Gatlen, who was busy making googly eyes at Val. "You need to eat, too, good *sir*," she prodded. "Love won't fill your belly when you're breaking up pub fights tonight."

Val giggled at the word love, but from the looks she and Gatlen gave each other, I thought Kessa might be right.

Naliah lightened the moment by snatching the parchment scrap Archer had been writing on. Her eyes widened as she read. "Archer!" she chided. "He's written a poem about them! And a rather raunchy one, too," she laughed as she handed it back.

"Archer, if you know what's good for you, you'll give that to me—" Gatlen began.

"Oh, Archer, don't!" Val protested.

"Let me see!" Kessa prodded.

Though I wanted nothing more than to talk to Val about the weekend, the rest of lunch was spent bantering over the secret poem, which Archer finally agreed to share later—though he only agreed, I noted, when Gatlen and Val left to return their trays.

In the last few minutes before the afternoon bell rang, I was finally able to corner Val and beg her to please, *please* talk.

"Of course!" Val said, eyebrows raised in alarm at my urgency. "It's not like Gatlen will be around to distract me, anyway. He and I won't have a night alone until I'm forty at this rate."

CHAPTER 20

IF THE MORNING had been full of literal rain and damp, the afternoon was its metaphorical counterpart. I had been moved up a reading level, and we were instantly tasked with analyzing accounts by two different historians about the same battle. It was tedious, and I struggled. We would have a discussion tomorrow, the scholar said, and we would be given marks for how well we participated. When the bell rang, I wasn't even halfway done. I begrudgingly admitted that perhaps I should have spent my summer doing more than reading stories and esoteric spells. I guiltily realized I hadn't even done much work on translating the Book of Açirin. It was due back at the library, and I stopped there on the way to my next class.

The final bell was ringing as I slipped into the intermediate magic room. The desks were arranged in a horseshoe, and I slid into the last open one next to Naliah.

"Good, we're all here. Let's begin."

My mouth fell open. In addition to Master Elys, the intermediate magic teacher, perched on the desk was none other than "Master Stevan," he announced. "Pleased to meet you. I'm Master Elys's teaching assistant this session, and don't go thinking that just because I'm new to teaching that I'm a fool. I was in your place not too long ago, and I know I can't make you do anything you don't want to do. But I also know that the tests are *hard*, and if you have any interest in passing, you'd do well to listen to and learn from us. And each other. Because that's the most important thing you need to understand—that you can learn more from working with your fellow mages than you can from trying to do it on your own."

Master Elys, a kindly woman of about fifty, nodded at his words. "Let's put that theory to the test, shall we? I'd like you to form groups of four and tackle the spell on page seven of your texts."

Naliah and I instantly partnered up, and two of the girls from the baths that morning joined us.

The spell was challenging, though doable, and I could see why we needed to be in groups. While one person led the spell, the others needed to perform a protective shield, blocking out errant magics. With so many students in the room, it was difficult to concentrate, and it was one of Naliah's yearmates who first suggested all teams perform the spell at the same time while staying silent.

"Well done," Stevan praised the boy after.

"It's that kind of teamwork that will make a difference for a mage," Master Elys agreed. "Many aspire to be the aloof sorcerer who only needs themself, but few can succeed on that path. I'd like you all to write a response for the rest of class, due back tomorrow if you haven't finished, about how teamwork could be applied to the spell on page ten."

We spent the rest of the class sharing our theories. A few still tried to work alone, I noted, but most relented and talked to at least one other person.

Every time Stevan wandered near my group, I tensed, but he treated me no differently than the other students. He listened to Naliah's question and even looked at me when he answered, giving no indication of anything different. I wasn't sure if I was grateful or not.

"That was fun," Naliah said as we packed up at

the end. "But it's going to take forever to finish tonight. Want to meet in the library?"

I thought wistfully of my time with Val. Surely we could still find time to sneak away. "Please," I said gratefully, and our groupmates agreed to meet us there, too.

Etiquette, of course, was with Madame Gerta. While I had grown in every other subject, this class seemed to thwart me. Perhaps there were no other sections, I reasoned, although the older students *must* be somewhere. Maybe it was time to ask Val.

We spent the first half of class rereading the same dry, dusty passage I had read nearly a dozen times before about the proper way to enter a royal ball. When Madame Gerta caught me gazing out the window, she rapped her stick on my desk and demanded to know if Sir Gadrup's writings were boring.

"Beg pardon, Madame Gerta," I began, feeling brave, "but I was wondering when I might be able to take the test? And pass on to the next level?"

I endured a lecture of remarkable ferocity for such an old woman after that. "Questioning my teaching!" she raged, and "Demonstrating an utter *lack* of etiquette whilst asking for an undue promotion!" I did my best to maintain a straight face as I was assigned extra passages to read that night, thinking that allowing myself a groan might very well earn me a suspension. Fortunately, the tirade was cut short when a messenger came by.

"Good afternoon, Madame Gerta," the messenger said, bowing to the exact right depth required for a madame. "Master Onan sends his well wishes and a reminder that all students in his elemental class will meet at the river this session and must leave your class early to ensure their prompt arrival. This means the student Ayve, my good madame." He held his bow till the very end and then stood, hands clasped steadily at his back.

Smoke may as well have puffed from her nose. Madame Gerta glared and whacked her stick on my desk once more. "All passages due tomorrow," she barked. I did my best not to dance out the door.

Master Onan awaited his students down by the docks... as did, surprise again, Master Stevan. So *this* is what had made Stevan so smug. Helping with intermediate magic was one thing, but assisting with an elemental class so early in one's career was unheard of. It was clear the students all knew who he was, and they excitedly whispered together before the class began. As before, we politely ignored one another.

Though I had enjoyed working with Lady Liliane, I was surprised to find I liked working with Master Onan even more. Where Liliane was like Val—bubbly, high-energy, eager—Onan was quiet, calm, and thoughtful. He reminded me of Archer, if Archer could cause the tides to swirl and show visions of the future.

"It's not a very reliable skill," he said modestly as students applauded all around us. "The world is always changing, much like the waters. We can read their currents and make predictions, but a sudden tidal wave or afternoon storm can set off a chain of events that makes the forecast useless. Fortunately, our class will teach far more practical skills," he added to the dismay of many. "This is why Master Stevan has joined me. He's recently spent time studying in Qiameth, and his knowledge will be immensely useful for helping each of you build whatever level of the skill you're at."

We spent the rest of class examining the creatures that lived in the water and learning to check markers that indicated tide height. It had finally stopped raining by the time class ended, and though darkness was creeping in, a few rays glittered on the water's edge. I lingered for a moment, not wanting to miss some of the last warmth of the season.

"What did you think?" Master Onan squinted out at the water. I'd almost think he didn't know I was there if he hadn't spoken to me.

I considered my answer before replying. He didn't seem like the type of teacher who wanted a quick response. "It was interesting," I said slowly. "It's a water class, but at times it felt more like an earth class. And the part where you can use water to divine, that feels almost like air—though I admit I haven't taken a class in that subject yet," I added hastily.

Master Onan seemed pleased by this. "I believe in the philosophy that all magic is intertwined. Dividing it into elements can be useful for studies, but in the real world, it serves no practical purpose. Tell me, where is there earth but not fire? Or water but not air? The elements exist in balance, meaning they need each other. A mage might have a pull towards one particular element, but that doesn't mean they're not capable of knowing the others just as well." He turned to walk back up the hill to the palace and then paused, waiting for me. Stevan had long since gone, so I followed politely at his side.

"Master Stevan agrees with me on this," he noted. "Not many mages do, at least not the ones my age." I snuck a glance at him through my lashes. Though I had thought he was close in age to Zai and Liliane, I was startled to realize he was older, perhaps in his late forties. "The younger mages aren't always right, mind you, but many of them have begun to question the traditional teachings. Stevan is a leader amongst them, and I hope your generation will listen well when he speaks. Perhaps many of you signed up for this class to learn from me, but I look forward to learning from him."

We had reached stairs now, a magicked set cobbled together years ago for classes like this. It was a shortcut back to the palace, though they were steep and made my legs burn. It had started to rain again, and small drops pattered the stones as we climbed.

"How well do you know Stevan?"

The question nearly stumped me. A few months ago, I wouldn't have hesitated. "Not very well, I don't think," I finally said. "We traveled here from Jeren, but he didn't talk about himself much. Or rather he did, but I didn't really understand. I didn't even know he was a full-fledged Master until after he'd left for Qiameth."

Master Onan nodded. "He was one of my favorite students. I used to teach the last level of advanced magic, and I had never seen anyone like him before. He blazed through the coursework in the first fortnight and could have spent the rest of the session doing self-study to pass the test. But he insisted on showing up to every class and helping his classmates. Many weren't pleased with this, of course," he chuckled. "They thought he was trying to make them look bad. But he honestly wanted to help."

"He and Master Elys had us work together in our intermediate class today," I said. I wasn't sure why I felt so comfortable sharing with Onan. I had never spoken to him much before. But he seemed to care what I had to say, and I pressed on. "None of our other teachers have made us do that. The scholars make us compete against each other, and many of the masters have us working *alongside* one another, but never together. I think I liked it. I think."

We reached a landing, and I hoped to pause, but Onan kept climbing, so I soldiered on. "It wasn't long after he finished my class that Stevan demanded to take the final tests," Onan continued. "He said that if anyone had a right to prove himself, it was the mage who had completed his own studies on top of teaching his peers."

"And that argument worked? The panel let him do it?" Perhaps there was hope for me yet.

"The panel?" Onan looked amused. "The panel is always happy to let willing students try. There's a fee, and failed tests just mean more money in their coffers. No, it was Lady Zai he had to convince." There was ever so slightly a shift, I thought. Perhaps it was his tone, or the way his arms swung slightly higher. Still, I could tell that there was nothing more I would get from him on Zai.

"Do you still teach that class?" I asked, hopeful that perhaps he could be my teacher again one day. We were almost at the top, and I puffed a bit as I spoke.

"Not for the past four years, I'm afraid. I gave up most of my classes in favor of assisting the navy shipmasters. I'd thought to return to intermediate magic this year, but Master Elys was offered the role. I bet Stevan is secretly thrilled to find you're in both of the classes he's assisting. I imagine he's curious to work with the young woman who's moving rather quickly through her studies."

"All but etiquette," I grumbled, and then clapped a hand over my mouth. "I'm sorry, Master Onan! I must be tired after such a long day."

He laughed loudly as we summited the steps, arriving at the back of the mages' wing. "Didn't anyone tell you? Madame Gerta believes in the value of time served, not knowledge. There's no leaving her class until you've been there at least two years, and Brother Connol's intermediate class isn't much better. Nothing to do but keep your head down—or up, I'm afraid, depending on whichever obscure curtsey she demands you do."

We had reached the door, and Master Onan saw me inside.

"Thank you for today," I said, hoping he understood I meant more than the class.

He nodded. "And thank *you*. It's not often I find a young person willing to listen to me for that long. You're quite remarkable, Ayve. I'm glad that I'll get to know you."

"And you, sir." I curtsied, eliciting a grin, and headed back to my room. Maybe this session wouldn't be so bad after all.

* * *

The usual group and more turned out at the library for the first night of studying, though very little work seemed to be happening. Everyone was abuzz with what happened on their first day back. Naliah gossiped eagerly with our intermediate magic partners in the corner. Archer sat meekly beside them, overwhelmed by their speed. With Gatlen and Kessa out patrolling, I was finally able to find time with Val.

I knew I would lose my nerve if I stopped, so I didn't, starting at the part where I found Stevan in my room and ending with him at not one but *two* of my classes. I even described Rebekah's kiss.

Val's eyes widened slightly at this part of the story, but she said nothing.

"Well!" was all that came out when I was done. Val smoothed her skirts thoughtfully. "Do you like Rebekah?"

I was taken aback by the question. Stevan was in my life twice a day now, and *that* was where Val wanted to start? "I guess. She's beautiful. But I don't know her. How can I tell if I like her?"

Ordinary Val would have laughed and said looks were half the package, but Problem-Solving Val only nodded seriously. "And Stevan, do you like *him*?"

I thought longer about this question. "When we were traveling, yes, very much. He was the only guy I'd ever had any feelings for besides Rafe. And at the start of Saturday night, I'd have probably said the same. But I can't believe how jealous he got and the way he tried to show off in front of Rebekah. Today he was all about working together and helping each other. Master Onan even said he's big on teamwork. But that wasn't the Stevan I saw at The Crow. If all it takes is a few drinks for him to unravel like that, could I really like him?"

Val considered this, watching the others through the gaps in the shelves. "Choose neither for now," she advised. "If Stevan wants to pretend like nothing happened, that's fine. You can do the same. Maybe he'll bring it up later, but maybe he won't. For now, you can just be friends. And," she added, "since you're not likely to leave the castle again for a while, it's unlikely you'll run into Rebekah any time soon, so you won't need to do anything about her, either. If the time does come where you have to choose, you could always choose both. If you wanted."

"I don't think I could—" I began, feeling unsettled.

"Look. I say this to you as a friend but also as Lady Liliane's apprentice. There are some things about our magemasters that we take to the grave, but I can say I've seen first-hand how messy it can be to love two people. Liliane and Onan are happy, and Liliane and Zai are happy, but Onan and Zai together..." She grimaced. "I like Zai, I really do. I don't know Onan well, but everyone speaks highly of him. And yet somehow, leave those two alone in a room and you're just begging for disaster."

I let out a sound that sounded like a squawk.

Val held up a hand. "I'm not saying it's always a problem. It's not uncommon, having two partners, though rarely tolerated outside city walls. Most small towns don't have enough people around for folks to take on one lover let alone two. *You* know," she said, and I thought of tiny little

Jeren. "But no matter what you do, don't get too mixed up in your feelings, especially since you've never been in love before, and be mindful that people *do* talk," she said, gesturing to the chair where Naliah still chattered happily.

Our serious conversation over, we rejoined the group in an attempt to make something of the night, but it was no use, especially when Naliah insisted on teaching Archer some new tumbling moves. A grouchy scholar kicked us out, and I returned to my room where I stayed up well past midnight trying to finish my extra work.

CHAPTER 21

I HAD THE FEELING I wasn't the only one who had gone to bed late. Gatlen was grumpy, and Kessa was set to patrol again after breakfast. No one was looking forward to the day.

I was scraping the last of my porridge from my bowl when Kessa turned my way. "Ayve, could we have a word? It won't take long, I promise."

I shot a look at Val, who was conveniently busy brushing dust from Gatlen's shirt. I prayed Val hadn't talked to Kessa. I had sworn her to secrecy, but secrets always had a way of escaping her.

I followed Kessa nervously to a busy corridor. "It's harder to be overheard out here," she said. "A trick my sister taught me. Spies learn all sorts of tricks, it seems."

"Tricks?" I tittered. "Like juggling and spitting fire?"

Kessa didn't dance around it. "Like flirting with someone who's clearly spoken for," she said. "Ayve, I love my sister, but don't let her ruin anything good that's happening with Stevan. What she did the other night was absurd. We're not as close as we used to be, but I've heard enough to know she tends to ruin nice things."

I sputtered. "No, she won't. Everything's fine. Really. I'm not spoken for. I mean, I'm not planning to be with either of them. Honest. I just want to get through the term. And Stevan has cooled off a lot since that night. I'm fine. *Really.*"

Kessa nodded solemnly. "Good," she declared, and left me reeling.

* * *

Fall classes were more exhausting, but I wasn't sure if it was the workload, the gloomier weather, or trying to pretend everything was fine with Stevan. In addition to assisting with my classes, he now joined me and Zai once a week on our morning learning walks, though it was the rainiest fall in decades. He and Zai chatted while I tried to find traces around the palace. Sometimes I was successful; usually I was not. Once, I was excited because I found a trace of Val only to find her harvesting turnips on the other side of a bush.

On days when I was particularly tired and my guard was down, I came close to asking Stevan how he convinced Zai to let him take the tests. But Zai was never out of earshot for long, and I always regained my senses before I could venture down that dangerous path.

On the last day of October, it finally stopped raining long enough for the sun to come out, and the air was crisp instead of damp. As I dressed, I smiled, spotting the corner of something small in my drawer. I pulled out my little painting of Freodon. Though the scene was set in the spring, I could imagine what it would be like now: awash in golden leaves, sunlight bouncing off red maples, and the spicy, sweet notes of leaf litter drifting up from the forest floor.

The painting left me in such a good mood that I chattered happily as we began our usual rounds. Zai had taken us on a path through the forest instead of around the walls, and I was delighted to find I could concentrate much better out there. I said as much after finding my third trace of the day.

"It'll be the woods, I expect," Zai said, turning her face up to the sky. "Some clean air and a sparkling sun can work wonders for a mage's abilities. Check again, over there by that stump, and see if you can find another. I'll be back in a moment." She wandered away, waving down a man in cobalt robes who was resting against a tree.

Stevan and I didn't say much at first besides "No, I think she meant *that* one" and "Yes, thank you." I concentrated, and soon enough the stump glowed with the same cobalt blue as the robed mage in the distance.

"The naval mages nearly always have bright blue magic," Stevan noted approvingly as the glow began to fade. "Something to do with their selection process, I think, though I've often wondered if their commander is biased and thinks water shades make for better water skills. They must be surveying for new masts," he said, pointing to the mage who still spoke to Zai. "I imagine they've been hampered by the weather and need to make up for lost time before winter sets in. It's good that we finally have a nice day, even if it *did* take all month to get here."

This was the most we had spoken outside of classes in months. Fortunately, my good mood quieted the anxious voice in my head. "Yes, it's quite lovely. I only wish I could see the city from a distance to take in the full view. I have a little painting of that bluff that overlooks the city, but it's set in spring. I wish I knew what it looked like now. Perhaps I can make it out there next year."

"You have a painting of the palace? From the bluff?" He kept his tone light, but I knew him well enough to understand something was off.

I nodded. "I've had it as long as I can remember. It was one of the only things I kept when I left Jeren."

"I see. Yes, it's probably beautiful right now. My pardons, but I've only just remembered something I need to do. Give my goodbyes to Zai."

He walked back down the path, leaving me utterly perplexed. Zai returned moments later. "Has Stevan gone?" she asked curiously. "I've had interesting news, and I was hoping to tell him."

"He said he had something he needed to do," I apologized.

Zai shrugged. "I suppose he'll hear from someone sooner or later. His loss!" she said, stretching her arms out into the warm air. "Come on, there's more magic to trace, and I bet we can find some in the sun, too."

* * *

If I had hoped to learn anything from Stevan during my classes, I was sorely disappointed. When I told him that Zai had news to share, he merely nodded and said, "Yes, Master Onan told me," before correcting another group's pronunciation.

Even with the clear skies, darkness arrived much earlier, and the sun was already beginning to set as I finished my walk back up to the castle. I called hello to Zai, but there was no response. I assumed she was out talking with other mages about whatever the mysterious news had been. Perhaps, then, with no mage master around to keep an eye on me, I could enjoy a quick nap before dinner. I opened my door, eager to climb into bed...

...only to once again find Stevan sitting there. I hurriedly snapped the door shut. A quick prod with my magic caused the fire to roar back to life.

"What?" I began, but Stevan placed a finger to his lips. His body was much tenser this time, and he crept cat-like to the door, speaking only once he had shoved a towel against the crack and placed several lumpy crystals on it.

"I would have used a silencing spell," he explained, gesturing at the crystals, "but Zai might wonder why there was a fresh trace of my magic on your doorframe when she came home. These crystals are self-contained. I, er, borrowed them from Master Elys's stores." He paced the tiny room until I had no choice but to sit on the bed.

I thought briefly of Rebekah, but I didn't have time to waste. "Why wouldn't you want Zai to know you were here? What could you possibly have to say that she couldn't overhear?" I crossed my arms.

He didn't seem to pick up on my tone. "Where's the painting? The one you mentioned this morning?"

I pointed to my dresser drawer. He lifted it out and gingerly ran a hand above its surface. "It's time to practice your morning lessons," he announced abruptly.

Never had I felt so stubborn before. "I wasn't aware that teaching assistants could barge into students' rooms and demand they do work after hours."

He shook his head. "Be angry later. See if you can find a trace." He thrust the picture at me, and I reluctantly took it.

Several minutes of concentrating left me with nothing to show but a fine mist of sweat on my forehead. "It's like this picture doesn't *want* me to discover its secrets," I complained. "I've never felt such resistance before. But it also doesn't feel magical at *all*. Perhaps it's just an ordinary picture that's tired of people poking at it."

"Dig deeper. If an object ever feels that ordinary, it's probably hiding something."

Still, nothing came from it. "I give up," I sighed. "I've only been working on this skill for a month. Did you come here to rub in my face how I'm not as talented as you?"

He frowned. "What? Of course not. What do you mean?" Without waiting for an answer, he sat on the bed next to me. "Try this." He traced swirling symbols in the air with his hands. "This is more advanced than what Zai is showing you," he explained as he did it again, "but I think you're ready."

I mirrored his motions, feeling silly. "Like this?"

"Sort of. Keep your last two fingers a little more bent, like this." He placed his hands on mine, guiding them into the right shape. *I will not care*, I told myself. *He is nothing more than a friend. And a distant one at that.*

When he was satisfied with the shape, Stevan withdrew his hands. "Try again," he urged. "Remember what Zai taught you about drawing a thread from within. Try to weave the thread through the symbols."

"Sew," I corrected. "This is more like sewing." Years of mending stockings, aprons, feed sacks, and bedsheets came back to me as I imagined green thread trailing a needle in my hand.

Quite suddenly, I could feel it. It was the

faintest of traces, just barely there. And yet it felt so familiar. Who was it that it reminded me of? I tried again, allowing my magic to bind the shapes together, over and over, until, just barely visible in the fading daylight, the painting glowed faintly lilac.

Stevan let out the breath he had been holding. "I knew it."

"Knew what?" I let my hand fall, and the lilac began to fade.

Stevan stood and began pacing again. "Zai had a painting just like this," he said. "The same scene, only in autumn. When we left for Jeren, she held up the painting and said that we had missed the view by a couple of months. But she seemed so sad when she said it. I wouldn't have asked, but it almost felt like she *wanted* me to. And you know how it is with Zai; you get so little with her that whenever you get a chance, you have to take it."

I nodded.

"She said this was one of two paintings from that spot, one made when the artist had arrived, which Zai had lost, and one made right before she left. Well, that was cryptic, wasn't it? 'Who was this artist?' I asked her, not really expecting an answer, and she said her sister had made them."

I stared at the picture and tried to imagine another Zai, only younger. Or maybe older.

Would she be less strict? Or even more of a disciplinarian? Did she have crow's feet lightly stamped around her eyes, too?

Steven was still speaking. "Not once in twelve years had she ever talked about her family. I didn't even know she *had* a sister. I thought the subject was done after that. We kept riding until we reached an inn, and she said nothing all through dinner. But I think she had more wine than she intended. Come to think of it, maybe it was as much as she intended. She took the picture out again and called forth its trace. It was lilac, like this one's was, and just as obstinate about revealing itself." He ran a hand through his hair. "What has Zai taught you about calling forth traces?" he questioned.

I was alarmed to be put so suddenly on the spot. "The stronger the mage, the stronger the trace," I said, racking my brain. "Accomplished mages usually craft dampening spells into their work so they don't blind every magically inclined person who wanders by. Some really advanced sorcerers can hide traces almost entirely, and many can disguise theirs, but a determined person can still find it," I added, remembering the time Zai coaxed forth a rather stubborn blue glow from the stairs that led to the river. "Newer spells leave a clearer trace. Older spells are harder to find. And when their creator dies, they start to fade." I looked at the painting with a sad realization.

"Judging by how hard you had to work, she's been gone many years," Stevan said softly. "Even Zai had some trouble, though it was easier for her. Well, magic recognizes blood. She'd still be able to call forth its trace long after you or I could."

I wasn't sure what to make of everything. "Why do I have Zai's sister's painting?" I wondered aloud.

Stevan let out a whistle. "That is precisely my question. How did it come to be yours?"

I had told Joseth the tale a thousand times, never knowing it might be true. I repeated it for Stevan. "The mysterious woman was Zai's sister," I ventured. "But why was she there? Where was Zai?"

Stevan ran a hand through his hair. "And did Zai know her sister had gone to Jeren?" he said heavily.

"Zai? Know? How could she know?" I knew it was a dumb question the second I asked it. There was so much mystery to Zai. I had only ever seen a fraction of what she could do. What did Zai get up to behind closed doors? What happened in the evenings when I did my work or met with friends? Despite our living together, Zai's life remained elusive.

Stevan waited for me to wrap my mind around these thoughts. "You already know we had planned on visiting Jeren," he said when he seemed to think I'd had enough time. "There was the cave we were looking for, and the crystal, and the vision she had of you when we left. But the thing is, Zai already knew where Jeren was when I brought her the text. No offense meant, but I'm not sure many people have heard of Jeren let alone could place it on a map."

"None taken. Lots of our guests didn't even realize our town had a name. So what, then? Zai's sister ran away and left a painting at my inn? Why?"

He shrugged helplessly. "That's where the trail runs cold. If I had to guess, I'd say she was after the same cave we were, only..."

"It was winter," I filled in, picturing a woman's dark silhouette at the inn's door, framed by heavy snow. "And that trail takes some knowing on a good day. Perhaps she got lost." I imagined the silhouette silently fading away. "But still, why leave a painting?" I argued. "The story says she paid before disappearing, so it's not like she was trying to be forgiven a debt."

We listened to the fire hiss, but no answers sprung to mind.

"Do you think we should return it to her?" I

asked finally.

Stevan hesitated.

"But it's her sister's!" I exclaimed. "If someone had something of my birth parents' and they kept it from me... I'd do anything for even a moment with something of theirs. Surely Zai must feel the same."

He bit his lip. "I'm not so sure. She was sad when she showed me the painting, but also somehow angry? I don't know; that's not the right word for it. But there was something there. Distress, maybe. Not quite hatred, but definitely a passion I'd never seen from her before." He glanced at the silencing crystals. "There are rumors about Zai's early dealings with magic. Some say she found herself down a not-so-innocent path. But then she went off on a spiritual journey, and when she came back, she was more powerful than ever, though humbled. Everyone always wondered what caused her to have a change in heart, but all she ever said was that it was a family matter."

I let this knowledge sink in. "You think Zai and her sister came to Freodon together and got involved in something, so her sister left the city. Why? To pursue something? To escape it? Only to disappear?"

"I know it sounds far-fetched. But I wonder, is

all. Giving her the painting might stir up old memories. And it's not like she doesn't have something of her sister's already. No, I think you should hold onto it for now, at least until we can learn more. It's been yours all this time. It won't hurt to keep it a little longer."

"But *how* will we learn more?" I stood and stretched. I carried the poor little painting to my drawer where it would live in my stockings once again.

"Leave it to me." He collected the crystals from the floor. "Zai should be home soon. Don't tell her I was here." He slid open a shutter. The sun had truly set, and the night air had a wintry bite. He slid from the window and was gone.

CHAPTER 22

STEVAN DIDN'T HAVE AN ANSWER after the first day, nor after the second, fifth, or even tenth. After a while, even though the mystery still intrigued me, it began to fade from my mind, especially as I spent most of my time studying. I was almost starting to agree with Zai that it wouldn't be worth taking the mage tests after all. How Stevan had managed to pass early while maintaining a legendary social life was beyond me.

"Well, he was here for several years!" Zai chuckled when I frustratedly brought that up one morning. We were in the royal forest again, and the first snow of the season dusted bare branches. "You've only been here, what is it, six months? He was barely ten when he started, and you're nearing eighteen. Which reminds me: your birthday is next month, is it not?"

I pushed back my sleeves. Despite the cold, the day's spellwork had me sweating. The protection crystal I was trying to create sat several feet away, glimmering innocently. Already I had split three branches with misspoken words. "Yes, my lady. The first day of the winter solstice festival. Or at least that's what Petyr and Alys always told me." I supposed it should bother me, not knowing my own birthday, but Jeren felt like a lifetime ago.

"It seems only right to keep the date. It's been with you for nearly all your life. Try again." I pointed at the crystal. I raised my hands as I moved my lips, willing my magic to fly from my fingertips, but it was no use. Another branch snapped in the distance, and a crow took flight, cawing angrily.

"Time for a break," Zai suggested.

I brushed snow from a log, and we sat. "Many assistants move into their own rooms when they turn eighteen, you know," Zai suddenly said. "They often long for the freedoms of adulthood."

"What kind of freedoms?" I enjoyed living with Zai, but the word had me intrigued.

"The usual kinds. No curfew. Going out

whenever you want. Having a drink or two at night. Not serving a cranky old lady at the end of each day."

I considered it. "Do they still receive their pay?" I asked. As promised, Zai had given me a monthly purse since arriving in Freodon. I stored most of it in a bag beneath my bed. Besides the festival, I rarely had a chance to spend it. Living on my own would give me significantly more opportunities, though I imagined finding a cheap room in the city would be challenging.

"They do. In fact, many receive more pay as their mentors provide a cost-of-living incentive to ensure they'll stay on."

"Do most choose to move out, then?"

"No."

"Really? Why?"

"Because for non-apprentices, access to schooling only comes with living on palace grounds. Any classes they were taking become their own responsibility should they move out. An assistant's salary, even when adjusted, is rarely enough to pay for both housing and classes."

Another crow cackled somewhere, and sunlight glinted on the snow, making me squint. "It doesn't sound like a very good deal," I admitted. "Who would take it?"

"The few who do are often royally connected.

Wealth doesn't bother them. Sometimes, there are apprentices who decide they don't need school anymore and become lifelong assistants instead." She let out a quick, sharp sigh. "Try to work your crystal again. There's no need to make your decision yet, and it's best we keep going before some poor soul goes out for a morning stroll and accidentally steps in front of a misfired spell." She dusted snow from her trousers and led the way back to the clearing.

* * *

A few weeks later, I had finally finished my protection crystal, and in between my weekend studying, I found time to wrap wire around its base and thread it through a leather cord. It was hardly the prettiest necklace, but I loved it just the same and wore it tucked beside my pregnancy charm.

I was nearly finished studying on Sunday night when Zai noticed it. "Well done," she approved. The rarity of Zai's compliments always made them feel extra important. "I know many mages don't want to be encumbered with a crystal constantly about their necks, but it's a smart move. It's no good packed away in your bags when you need to know if someone means to do you harm *now*. And I have to say, it makes me feel better knowing you've done that, should you choose to live on your own. Which brings me to my question: have you made your choice?"

"I'll stay." I didn't even hesitate. "Even if I never take the exams, I'm learning too much to give up school. And I like living here. You're a good mentor."

I hadn't known Zai could blush. "Thank you. That means a lot. I'm not always..." She cleared her throat. "As of your eighteenth birthday, your curfew will be midnight, and you may leave the castle walls as you please. I expect you to keep up with your schoolwork and duties," she warned, "so be mindful or your new freedoms will be revoked. I still hold the highest standards for those in my service."

"Yes, my lady. I understand." I gestured to the books spread around us. "I promise I'll keep up with everything."

"Good. With that out of the way, we can begin other plans. Which elemental class did you choose for winter session?"

I grimaced. "I haven't. Master Onan thought he would teach another class next session, but he said he's been called away to help the navy. Stevan said he's too junior to run an element class on his own, so now I have to find a new one. I supposed I'd forgotten," I confessed.

"I'll see what other offerings there are. It would be good to have you take a fire class this session. It's damp where we're going, and keeping fires lit when it's wet can be tricky. Perhaps we'll work on adding warming spells to the seams of your clothes, too."

"Where we're going?" I put my book down. My heart raced. "You mean we'll be setting off on an adventure?"

Zai smiled and opened the book she was reading. She unfolded a flap to reveal a large, colorful map of Kreiogny and the surrounding kingdoms. "Here's us," she said, tapping a dot towards the center, "and here's where we're going." She drew a line with her finger to the north along the coast.

"Allerwia," I breathed. I'd heard tales of its beauty from travelers all my life, but I never thought I'd see it.

"I've found several accounts of a cave by the sea with strange etchings on its walls."

"You think the Ole'ad hid more crystals," I charged.

"Perhaps just one, but even so, it would be a tremendous find."

"What are the crystals for?" It occurred to me that I had never thought to ask. "When we found the crystal in the cave, it was all so overwhelming that I didn't even realize they could be used for different purposes. Clearly these must be special if they're hidden. And the Ole'ad are *ancient*. Do they hold some secret magic?"

Zai seemed to be struggling with what she wanted to say. "Power," was all she said at last. "And that's all I'll say for now. The magic is old, and complicated, and it will take several more years of study for you to comprehend it. Even Stevan is only just starting to get there. Don't ask again," she warned, holding up a hand as I began to speak. "I'm not hiding anything from you, and if you keep up your lessons with me, you'll slowly begin to understand. It is for the teacher to know when their pupil is ready, and the answer is not yet."

I nodded, trying to swallow my disappointment.

Zai put the book on the table and stood. "I'm glad you're staying," she said as she rose. "It would have been lonely around here without you." For one wild moment, I almost thought Zai was about to smooth my hair, but the moment passed, and Zai moved on.

* * *

Dawn arrived late on the first day of the solstice, of course. The icy tip of my nose stuck out from my blankets. I had let my fire burn down overnight, wanting to really feel the cold. I couldn't remember a birthday I hadn't been frozen. My room in Jeren had been unheated, and each birthday I would rush into the main room to warm myself by the fire with a cup of tea and warm oats. Birthdays were small in Jeren; celebrations rarely involved more than an extra slice of bread or a new apron. Lying in bed feeling the frigid air on my face now brought a solemn nostalgia.

I sighed and slowly sat up. Traditionally, people gave gifts for the solstice at sundown, but a small package sat just inside my door. Curious, I picked it up and brought it back to bed.

Six tiny crystals clinked into my lap as I unwrapped, each a clear quartz the size of my pinky, with a note from Zai telling me to use them as a blank canvas to create anything I wanted. I whistled. These were certainly expensive, and I hoped I wouldn't ruin them with my attempts.

I held them for a while, dreaming of their potential. It was helpful to have a distraction. My first birthday away from Jeren had dredged up feelings I didn't know were there. Perhaps Zai had known this would happen.

Eventually, the light outside began to grow, and I threw back my shutters. It had snowed overnight, and the courtyard glittered prettily. The first day of the festival meant no morning duties, and I eyed the snow longingly. I laughed suddenly when I spotted Naliah, bundled in too many layers, tromping around in her attempts to build a castle. I might have been eighteen, but I didn't think I was too old to help. I piled on my warmest clothes and headed outside to play with my friend.

* * *

Despite the night's banquet, Zai insisted she didn't need help getting ready for it. I was confused, then suspicious. "I won't need you for this one," Zai offered lamely when I pressed yet again, and I rolled my eyes, knowing my friends had planned a surprise party after all. I had never had a party before in my life, I'd insisted a week ago, and certainly didn't need one now, but Val had been scandalized at the thought, and this smacked of her doing.

With a sigh, I resigned myself to returning to my room until they came to fetch me. The day had been marvelously clear, but it had grown colder, and thick, dark clouds had rolled in as the sun set. I turned the handle to my door, readying my magic to stoke the fire the moment I entered.

To my surprise, the fire was already roaring,

and once again, a figure perched on the edge of my bed. Yet this figure was smaller with a scarf worn loosely about their face.

"Happy birthday, my sweet. And solstice, I suppose, but who could care about that on a day that brought us you?"

"How did you get in?"

Even with the scarf, Rebekah's pretty pout was obvious. "I risk life and limb breaking into a powerful mage's chambers, and you can't even say hello? I suppose I'll try to forgive you. Perhaps you could think of a way to make it up to me."

I eyed the girl suspiciously. Zai *was* a powerful mage, and despite Rebekah's work as a spy, I somehow doubted anyone could break into Zai's chambers without serious repercussions. "Your scarf," I accused. "Zai thought you were Kessa with it wrapped around your face like that and let you in." Just her eyes showed, and they looked so much like Kessa's that only her accent gave her away.

"Maybe," she teased, unwrapping the scarf. Her hair was slicked back in a tight braided bun. "You should be happier to see me. I come bearing gifts."

I felt my cheeks burn. "You shouldn't have," I mumbled.

"Sure I should have. I wanted to, and that is

reason enough. You'd best get over this 'I'm not worthy' act before your surprise party, you know, or you'll break poor little Val's heart. She's been waiting all week to see your face when you walk in. Good thing you have me here to help you practice."

"But I didn't ask for a party!" I wasn't sure where this anger was coming from. I sat beside Rebekah on the bed.

"Of course you didn't. But they love you, and we like to show people that we love them. Isn't that what you did for Naliah all those months ago?"

"That was different," I grumbled, though I knew it wasn't. Somehow, coming of age had made me feel more like a child than ever before. "Oh, I don't know," I groaned, burying my face in my hands. "I suppose I'm grateful. Really."

"Good," Rebekah nodded approvingly. "Then you can start by being grateful for what I've brought you. Go on." She pointed to a paper-wrapped box on the bed. As I unwrapped, Rebekah peeled off her layers, revealing a navy skirt, white shirt, and long, white stockings. She was dressed as a palace servant and could leave Zai's rooms undetected.

The string was stubborn, but I finally pulled off the last piece. Inside the small wooden box was a handful of plump red strawberries.

"They're beautiful!" I gawped. "But they're out of season. How did you find them?" I inhaled deeply.

Rebekah winked. "I have friends in the kitchen."

I wasn't sure if I should be furious with Val or not. Hadn't she been the one to advise me not to act on any of this?

Rebekah seemed to know what was going through my head. She widened her eyes. "I promised I would only drop them off and say goodbye. But that was before I knew you needed to practice your gratitude. Here, let's start now." She held a strawberry by its leaves. "Bite," she instructed.

I hesitated. I couldn't forget who had last sat on my bed. On the other hand... I leaned forward slowly and bit.

"Well?" Rebekah eyed me curiously.

"It's good," I admitted as I swallowed. "Thank you."

"Not bad," Rebekah replied. "But I think you can do better."

We practiced again and again, me uttering my thanks after each, finding it *was* easier to be thankful the more I practiced. Finally, only one berry remained. It was the largest and plumpest of the lot.

"I think you've almost got the hang of it. But perhaps you need a bigger challenge for this last one. Something to really make the lesson stick." Eyes dancing, Rebekah lightly bit the top of the strawberry and motioned me forward. Surely she couldn't mean... But it was clear she did. I wasn't sure what came over me, whether it was the gentle light from the fire, or growing older, or maybe learning to let others care for me after all, but I leaned forward and let my mouth close around the fruit. Our lips touched sweetly.

Rebekah bit gently on the berry, catching the leafy bit and smiling as I chewed. "Yes, I think I'm convinced now." Her voice was a husky purr. It was with great disappointment that I realized she was readying herself to leave.

"You're a quick learner. It's no wonder Lady Zai took you in. Your friends will come to collect you soon, and I think you'll excel at letting them love you. I would stay to let you practice one more time, but we're out of berries, and I have a job to get to. Perhaps another time we can train together. I'm sure I can think of other lessons you need to know."

* * *

Naliah was a terrible actor. Still, I gave my best

yelp of delight and thanked them all for the "surprise." Val's beaming grin told me it had all been worth it.

Liliane's chambers once again served as party headquarters, though this time there were icy blue decorations for my birthday and the solstice. It made me feel like a wintry queen. Zai was there, too, which both surprised and pleased me.

"Won't it cause an upset if you don't attend the banquet?" I asked.

Zai shrugged as she scooped a cup of punch. "Those stodgy old coots could use an upset or two. They've gotten so used to parading me around that I think they've forgotten what I'm actually here for. Besides, who could tell someone that she can't attend her own assistant's birthday party? You will give me an excuse for years to come, so thank you."

Zai slipped away with Liliane sometime later, clearly turning a blind eye as best they could. I was grateful that beyond the initial surprise and a cake, the group kept the party mostly focused on the solstice. I was glad they knew me so well. And to think it had been only a few months ago that I had arrived knowing almost no one! Now, surrounded by friends and warmed by Val's spiced pear cider, I glowed.

At some point it became obvious that Naliah

had snuck a few glasses of the cider, too. When she fell asleep by the fire, Archer and Kessa agreed to help her back to her room. Supporting the yawning girl between them, they led her out.

Val made no mention of Rebekah and the strawberries, though it would have been hard for her to mention anything with how tightly she was wrapped in Gatlen. It was only when I said that it was getting late and I'd best get to bed that Val came back to the land of the living.

"But you'll miss the after-party!" she said, horrified. She tumbled frantically from Gatlen's lap. "Now that your curfew is extended, you can stay out nearly as long as you like, and I promised half our class we would be at The Crow later so they could celebrate you!"

"I don't know," I hesitated. I regretted sharing my curfew news. "They're probably all—"

"They're all exhausted from working for their mentors all year, they'll just be getting released from banquet duty, *and* they'll want to blow off steam, so what better way than by honoring the birth of our friend?"

The door suddenly burst open, and Naliah bounced in, alert and grinning madly. "You'll never guess!" she roared. "I'm drunk, and they took me to bed, but I heard a noise outside my door when they'd left and I need you all to know that Kessa and Archer are *together*!" she whooped. "I opened my door and they were *kissing*! He had his *hands* on her face!"

The duo came running in behind her, panting slightly. "I think she's extra fast when she's been drinking," Kessa groaned. "I've never seen someone take off like that. Well, go on. What did she tell you?"

I grinned wickedly. "She told us enough that we'll all be going to the after-party now, and you two are going to come clean," I goaded.

Archer's face was redder than his hair as he shrugged ruefully. "Ah, well. It was nice to have some privacy while it lasted. Alas," he said, wrapping an arm around Kessa's shoulders. "Let's take Lady Blabbermouth back to bed, and perhaps we can have one last moment alone before the hounds set on us."

* * *

The Crow was full, mostly of apprentices and squires, though a few mages and knights abounded. Many offered to buy me a celebratory drink, but I politely turned them down and slowly nursed another cider. I hadn't forgotten September.

I was reminded of another moment from the harvest festival when Varrick came by our table. "I hear it's your birthday!" he shouted. "Cheers to your health and years!" Varrick said something else, but I squinted at him, unable to hear across the table. He repeated himself, but I frowned and pointed at my ears. Varrick motioned to the back door and to my cloak. I grabbed it and followed him, curious.

There was a courtyard there, buried deep in thick snow. More snow fell softly around us.

"Much better," he sighed. "Being around so much noise almost makes me wish I'd stayed at the banquet. Lady Zai caused quite a stir when she never showed."

I grinned. "That will make her happy. She said they've forgotten what she's actually here for or something like that." I paused. "You know, it occurred to me tonight that I've never asked her what she *is* here for. Most royal mages at her level teach a master class, it's true, but they also do other things, like Lady Liliane with the kitchens, or Master Onan with the navy. Do *you* happen to know what her other job is?" I asked hopefully.

It was hard to make out his face in the dark. "I'm afraid not. Most of the royal mages won't give me the time of day let alone tell me what projects they're working on. I stick to my own world— research and beginner magic. Which, for the record, was much harder without your assistance this past term! I might have earned my degree, but that doesn't necessarily make me good with children, especially not ones so rowdy as this year's crop. Do you know, I think I almost miss Naliah!"

That got a chuckle from me, especially when I remembered the time Naliah accidentally spilled ink on Varrick's favorite book. "I do miss helping," I admitted. "I was always in charge of looking after guests' little ones when they were busy at the inn. And then my brother was born. Joseth. He was more like my own child than my brother sometimes." I was silent, remembering, and looked up at the balcony ringing the courtyard above us.

"Rooms," said Varrick, seeing me look up. He slid gloves onto his hands. "For The Crow."

"There must be three dozen," I marveled. My breath puffed into clouds. "We'd never have been able to fill this many." I felt a pang that I hadn't realized was there again. What was it about this day that was making me miss my childhood so much?

"It must be hard to be away from home on your birthday. Something about big events always makes me miss my home, even though it's been many years since I set foot in Oqira."

"You're from Oqira?" I had never thought to

meet someone from the far-off land. Oqirans rarely ventured beyond their borders.

He may have smiled, but in the dark, it seemed more of a grimace. "Sort of. I was born in Kreiogny—right here in Freodon, in fact—but my family were merchants and traveled most of the year. We were in Oqira when I was two, and the bleeding sickness killed my father and oldest brother. The rest of us were only ill for a few days, but by the time we staggered out of our wagon, raiders had made off with our horses and goods. With no money to our name, we struggled to get by for years after that. No one wanted to marry a widow with so many mouths to feed, not until I started to show signs of magic. An Oqiran married my mother when I was eight and shipped me back to Freodon to study, where I've been ever since."

"Do they still write to you? Your family?" My nose had started to go numb, but I wrapped my cloak tighter and listened. His answer was important.

He paused. "Sometimes. My stepfather... He's not unkind. Just not sentimental. We may have been poor before we met him, but my mother did her best, and I have fond memories of those years. Sometimes I think he only writes to me when they need money. He married my mother thinking he could produce more mages, but none of their children ever survived beyond their first year."

"Did you ever want to go back? To visit?"

"Of course. But Oqira is far. Besides, we could barely afford school. Two trips back and forth across two country's borders were unthinkable. And eventually, when I passed my tests, I wasn't sure what I would find if I returned. I was eight years old a long time ago, Ayve. I'm not who I was when I left. And who's to say they haven't changed, too? It seemed easier for all of us if I never returned."

I finished my cider. It was frosty on my tongue after standing so long in the cold. "I wrote to my family over the summer. To Joseth and Alys. My mother," I added. I thought about adding "adoptive," but something held me back.

"Did they ever write back?" he said abruptly. "Alys and Joseth?"

"No."

"It's just that I—"

The door opened, and Stevan walked through. "Ayve. There you are. Val has been looking all over for you."

The already frozen air nearly iced over when Stevan saw who I was talking to.

"Well, that's my cue," Varrick said hastily, tossing back the rest of his drink. "I wouldn't have wanted to hang out with an old man when I was your age, either. Cheers, Ayve. Master Stevan." He walked back inside, closing the door behind him.

"What were you doing with him?" Stevan's voice was bitter.

I put a hand on my hip. I was not about to play this game again. "We were talking. We have a lot in common. He was my *teacher*, Stevan, like Zai was yours, so I don't want to hear it."

He let out a long, slow breath. "Let me try that again," he said, even taking a few steps backwards. "Happy birthday, Ayve. Happy solstice. You look lovely."

"Thank you."

He came closer, and I could see his brows raise. "What's this? Ayve accepting a compliment rather than brushing it aside? It seems you *have* grown up after all."

I tried not think of who had helped me with that lesson. "Sure have. Eighteen years. A proper adult. Able to do proper adult things." I realized how that must have sounded as soon as it tumbled from my mouth.

"Oh? Like what?"

Feeling emboldened, I decided I was certainly old enough to take charge for once. I looped a hand behind his neck and pulled his mouth down to mine. We kissed for a while, and where Rebekah had been sweet and gentle, Stevan was spicy and wicked.

I was pleased to see he was somewhat flummoxed when we parted. He cleared his throat. "Well," he said. "I *did* ask. I just didn't expect a demonstration."

"Well," I repeated.

Stevan took my hands. Neither of us wore gloves, and our skin was cold where it met. "Ayve, I need to know what this means for you. Because if it means too much... You're still a student. And I'm slowly on my way to becoming a teacher. I never intended to become one, especially not yours, but it happened. I don't mean for it to happen ever again, but..." He shrugged helplessly.

I kissed him again, and he softened. "I don't know," I said at last. "I don't think it *has* to mean anything. Sometimes kissing is just nice. And it's good to see you, and it's my birthday. We have time." Something inside me had shifted that afternoon. "I guess it means I like you, and I don't want you to get mad when you see me talking to other people. I'm *happy* here," I said, voicing aloud for the first time the thing that had been bothering me all day. "I have friends. And I'd like to think I can count on you as one of them, even if we're not ready to go further. At least not yet. Okay?"

He nodded. "Okay." We kissed once more

before he let my hands go. They were warmed where his fingers had touched mine. "Friends. But I'll be waiting."

He went back inside. I let myself sit with my feelings for once. So this is what it was like to be happy.

JANUARY-MARCH 968 CE

CHAPTER 23

"YOU'LL NEVER GUESS what I heard!"

My door opened with a loud bang. Archer and Kessa, who had been sitting awfully close together, flinched at the sound before looking sheepish as Naliah, not Zai, barged in. Val smirked at them as she closed the door. Zai had caught her and Gatlen holding hands once, and we had never let them live it down.

Naliah looked around, breathless. "Well? Aren't you going to ask me what I heard?" she demanded. Several strands of hair had escaped her headband and flew wildly about her face.

"I'm surprised you can hear anything over your own voice," Archer commented.

"Oh, shush," Val scolded. "I want to know. What did you hear, Naliah?" She scooted aside on the bed to make room, but Naliah began pacing up and down.

"I was in the training yards, practicing my wrestling with some of the older squires"—Naliah-code for getting in a fight—"when two students came by to use the archery targets. And they were saying how last night at The Crow, everyone saw Master Varrick chatting up Ayve!"

"What? We were talking!" I sputtered. "He's old! That's gross!"

"He's not *that* old," Val said thoughtfully. "What is he, late twenties? And not hard on the eyes, either." She laughed and rested her head on Gatlen's shoulder as he scowled. "Not as good-looking as one curly-haired knight I know, of course!"

"I'm with Ayve," Archer said, shuddering. "Ten years your senior? That's too old. And he was her teacher, for gods' sakes."

"We were just talking," I stressed again. "How could anyone misread that? He was telling me about his childhood. He grew up in Oqira, did you know? I was just curious if he still talked to his family is all."

"Well obviously I told them they were wrong," Naliah barreled on. "I let Darek go—er, ended our wrestling match—and told them that you and me were in his basics class, and it was nothing like that. They agreed that it sounded too good to be true."

"Thank you!" I was grateful for having such a sensible friend.

"But then!" Naliah continued. "They heard this next part from someone who works in the mews who knows someone who was staying on the upper courtyard floors who heard that Varrick left because a mystery man came out to see her, and when Varrick was gone, Ayve and the mystery man *kissed!*" She plopped onto the floor, finally delivered of her message.

Gatlen's mouth popped open. Even Archer looked surprised. Only Kessa kept her cool, winking once.

"Really? Who?" Gatlen looked curiously at Val. She was feigning innocence, though poorly.

I shrugged, aloof. "Someone. I'm not seeing anyone, don't worry. Let's just say it was a nice birthday present."

Eventually, they let the matter drop, though not before Naliah held a dramatic reenactment for us.

When the sun had finally dipped low enough to require lighting candles, the group began to depart. Val hung back on the pretense of needing the privy and cornered me before leaving.

"I thought we agreed you wouldn't get involved," Val chided.

"I didn't know 'not getting involved' meant my friend could give strawberries to an interested party," I pointed out in return.

Val flushed. "*You* try saying no to Rebekah. She's very persistent."

"I know," I grinned. I described Rebekah's visit and my kisses with Stevan, though I left out some of the juicier details. "I don't think I have to choose yet," I confessed when I was done. "Rebekah is busy with her job, so I doubt I'll see her often. And with Stevan... We agreed it's not time right now. Besides, there's the whole teacher thing," I said glumly.

Val waved that aside. "Master Onan was your teacher. Master Elys was your teacher. Stevan was just an assistant for *one* quarter. It's perfectly normal for someone Stevan's age to court someone your age. If he weren't so dashingly brilliant, he'd never have been assisting to begin with because he'd still be a student himself. It's not the same as someone like, say, Varrick. Although I do think the man is handsome, if a bit boring."

"Gross," I said, sticking out my tongue. "I admire him, but he reminds me of an uncle. Like if I didn't work for Zai, I'd be happy working for Varrick." My stomach flipped. "I hope the rumor doesn't get back to him. You guys are about as close as I have to family out here, and I wouldn't want to ruin that."

Val rubbed my shoulders reassuringly. "I wouldn't worry. He's too smart to let palace gossip get to him. Besides, there was a crazy rumor about Madame Gerta that he must have heard when he was a student here—"

"What? Tell!" I demanded, eyes wide.

* * *

The third day of winter session, Zai plunked an old, dry book on the table in front of me. I lifted the corner gingerly, and the spine crackled.

"You can pretend you haven't seen it before," Zai commented as I inspected the pages. "Technically, you haven't, since this is my copy, not the library's. I can pretend I didn't know you were researching ancient Ole'adan spells in your free time last summer."

I breathed a sigh of relief.

"You'll notice the wording is slightly different," she continued.

"And some of these letters look odd," I added.

"Runes," Zai nodded. "I'm pleased you've picked that up. They're subtle, and not all mages detect them at first glance." She tossed another, slightly newer book my way. "This one contains some translations, though as you know, not all are accurate. We won't always have time for these in our lessons, so I expect you to work on this most nights. Specifically focus on these," she said, tapping the pages flagged with bits of tattered ribbon. "They'll most directly benefit your work with crystals. We've only three months before I hope to set off again, and it's to your benefit that you do most of your learning before we go. Remember how exhausting it was to read each night after walking all day?"

I made a face. "That was in warmer weather, too," I admitted. "And we're headed north."

"Where it's cool, damp, and marshy. Not too many dry places for sitting around a cozy fire at night. I'd suggest studying hard now unless you'd like to do most of your learning cramped beneath a dark, wet cloth."

I shuddered. "I'll learn now," I promised.

Yet it was as if my teachers were conspiring to make that impossible. Each day after lunch began with intermediate reading, and with discussions on texts now taking nearly the full length of the class, I was left with many more passages to peruse each night than I'd care to admit. My brain felt muddled most days by the time I reached intermediate magic. While the spells hadn't gotten more complicated, we were expected to move faster, firing off round after round without error. It was amazing, I reflected one afternoon, how going just a bit faster could have such disastrous results, and I cringed when I pictured the singe marks I had left on Master Elys's sleeve.

Etiquette, of course, sucked whatever remaining soul I had from my body. I couldn't even prop my tired head on a hand without Madame Gerta smacking a ruler on the desk. "No elbows!" she'd bark, which is how I found myself assigned to write about the faux pas of elbows on tables not once, not twice, but five times.

Even fire magic was rough. Master Ysdel was as conceited and arrogant as I'd once expected all mages to be. Only the knowledge that I would need his lessons in a few months kept me going. Fortunately, I was neither the best nor the worst in the class, so I managed to get by unnoticed most of the time.

By the end of the second week, any vision I'd once had of following in Stevan's footsteps and pursuing my own degree had thoroughly, solidly vanished.

* * *

"Whatcha up to?"

I nearly fell off my bed. I eyed Naliah moodily. The girl stood at the edge of my doorframe looking innocent.

"Reading," I said peevishly.

"Looked more like sleeping to me," Naliah said, bouncing on her heels. "Is that what you do after class every day?"

I hastily shifted a large pile of parchments and books as Naliah sat. "I have a lot of work to do," I grumbled. "And if I fall asleep reading about boring wedding traditions, what's it to you?"

Naliah tsk'd. "Sir Rodrick says the best remedy for the afternoon sleepies is a good, hard workout."

"He sounds like a lovely person. I bet he thinks cold baths are good for you, too."

"Actually, they're great for sore muscles. But that's not what you need. *You* need to move. And I am here to make sure that happens."

"Thanks, but I'm busy." I aggressively fluffed a pillow.

"Think about it," Naliah said. "You're doing all this stuff to prepare for your next adventure with Zai. Morning lessons, reading that dumb old book, fire class—but are you ready to walk again, day after day, up and down hills and over sloppy, wet ground?"

She had a point. I remembered how sore I had been the first few days, and that was when I was kept busy at the inn with all sorts of manual labor. When was the last time I had chopped wood? Washed clothes? Chased a toddler?

I stared at Naliah through narrowed eyes. "Zai put you up to this," I said eventually.

"Of course!" the girl grinned. "But you have to admit, it's nice of Zai to find ways for us to spend time together before you're gone for who knows how long. And it's good practice for me before the page exams. They make you show that you know how to do all the basic exercises, and I don't want to flunk because I forgot how to properly stretch or something. Come on," she said cheerfully, slinging an arm around my shoulders. "Get dressed and meet me in the training yards before the next bell. It's better than doing this stuff, anyway."

I groaned and stood stiffly. Perhaps it would do me some good after all.

* * *

Exercise, it turned out, was the perfect way to work off stressful days. A hot bath afterwards, sharing in juicy gossip with Val and Naliah, was also beneficial.

Yet the best way to relax of all, I found, was weekend visits to The Crow with my friends. I was still cautious about how much I drank, but being free of the palace for even a few hours each week felt wonderful.

It was on one of these tavern nights that Rebekah came by. I had known this would happen eventually, but I'd hoped to buy myself a little more time. To my surprise, Rebekah was well-behaved, only nodding a polite hello before engrossing herself in a conversation with Kessa. Even when I excused myself to the privy, no surprise attack awaited on my return.

"Tell us about the mission you're going on," Val was saying as I sank back into my chair.

"Mission?" Rebekah opened her eyes wide. "What mission?"

"For all that you're a spy, you're pretty bad at keeping these things hidden," Val teased. "You always come say goodbye before you go. And you've always done something different to your hair or clothes." True to her point, Rebekah's hair was woven in a simple braid, and beneath her cloak, she wore plain, dark trousers and a woolen coat.

"If I didn't know better, I'd think you were impersonating a sailor... Rebekah!" Kessa sat up, eyes crackling furiously. "You're not off to war, are you?"

Archer spat out his drink. "War? What war? We're at war?"

Gatlen patted Archer on the back. "Not

officially. Not yet. But any knight worth their salt knows we're headed that way. Suuldus has been spying on us for months now."

"And us on them," Kessa pointed out.

"Only because they started first," Gatlen retorted.

"Not defending them, just observing," Kessa replied. "I'm on your side."

"Well, last fall several of our navy ships went missing," he continued. "Just off the coast of Suuldus. Only there were no reports of storms, no dangerous waters. It was suspicious. The palace sent some of their best to investigate, and the waters were eerily devoid of magic."

"You'd expect some to build up," I mused, remembering my class with Master Onan. "Water disperses magic, little by little, and big cities often have accumulations from *centuries* of magic."

"Very good." Stevan took a seat in the last free spot across from me. Small droplets fell from his cloak as he shook it from his shoulders. It must have started raining. "I'm glad to see you remember your lessons. A country like Suuldus, with all those powerful mages? Their waters ought to downright *glow* when tested. But nothing. Not even a shimmer. It would take incredibly powerful magic to wipe out all traces like that. But why? What would they have to hide?"

The group was silent for a moment.

"So that's where you're going," Kessa accused her sister. "Disguised as a sailor, off to wage war against an army of mysterious sorcerers."

"Sailors don't fight armies," Rebekah pointed out dryly. "And spies don't wage wars. We investigate. We learn." She shrugged. "But who's to say I'm not throwing you off my trail? Making a public appearance one way, misleading anyone watching me here, only to sneak off somewhere else when no one's looking?"

My heart raced as I thought about spies around us. I had nearly forgotten about the threats against me. I kept my eyes on the table, but I rested my hand on my protection crystal. It lay unlit against my chest.

Kessa pursed her lips. "Well, I don't like it," she declared. "If anyone should be going off to fight, it's me and Gatlen. We've earned it. Two fully trained warriors, stuck patrolling night after night like the city guard! It isn't right, not when there's real need for fighters out there."

"Oh, I dunno," Gatlen said, and I knew he was holding Val's hand beneath the table. "It grows on you after a time. Besides, our folk need protecting, too, and it's not like the city guard has enough power. Too many thieves' guilds, not to mention corruption in the ranks. A knight's duty is to serve, and Freodon is my home."

"Well, it's not mine," Kessa said bluntly, and she walked off to get another drink.

The table was silent. "I'll need to be going soon," Rebekah finally said. Her chair scooted loudly over the flagstones. "Ayve? A word?" She nodded her head towards the back courtyard and walked off.

I hesitated as I stood and looked at Stevan, though not for the reason I knew he'd hoped. "Master Onan," I said. "Is that where he went? To investigate?"

Stevan nodded. "He's fine," he said quietly. "He's safely quartered in their palace. They wouldn't dare attack him, not when so many of their own mages are here. There are unspoken rules about guests in these situations. He'll come back soon, on the first ship he can get. And if we're lucky, he might even help broker a peace treaty before he goes. I know Kessa thinks we're nearly at war, but you'd be surprised what some of these great mages can do."

I nodded, relieved. I couldn't imagine if Master Onan never returned. I excused myself from the group and headed outside.

It was indeed raining; soft, steady drips plipped from the balcony above. The few lit torches sputtered in the wind.

"February in Qiameth is beautiful," Rebekah said. She leaned against the fence, watching shadows through the mist. "Warm days, cool nights, with all the sweet oranges and lemons a girl could ever want." She sighed. "And here I am about to set off on a cold, wet ship through a cold, wet sea when even the smartest sailors wouldn't attempt it for another month."

"You're really going, then." It hit me, now, how little I knew this woman. She might be Kessa's sister, but we had met, what, three times? I felt funny at the realization.

Rebekah smiled and winked, but there was a sadness behind it. "Perhaps. Perhaps not. A real spy would never give away her secrets, not even to a pretty lady."

It occurred to me that while Rebekah was always free with her compliments, I had never said anything nice back, not even once. "You're pretty, too," I blurted, feeling foolish. "I mean..."

Rebekah shook her head. "No," she said softly. "Thank you. That is good to hear. In my line of work, sometimes I forget I'm allowed to be pretty. But this isn't the time. Not when I asked you outside because I know the last time you were here, it was with Stevan's kiss."

I thought back to what Rebekah had said about being spied on inside. I wondered who had been around that night. "Yes," I admitted. "But we're still just friends. Honest." I struggled with my words and leaned on the fence beside Rebekah, letting our arms touch. "It's the same way it is with you. We're friends, and it would be nice to be more than friends," I said, feeling a blush creep up my face. "But it's just not the right time. And... I don't know that I'm ready. To decide."

"To decide between us?"

"Sort of. To decide..."

"If you love men or women."

I was grateful I wasn't the one who spoke the words. "Yes."

Rebekah was silent for a minute, and we listened to the torches hiss. "Not everyone has to decide, you know," she said finally. "Some of us... it's not so much that we decide as we *know*. Like how Kessa knows she likes men, or Gatlen likes women. Like *I* like women." She paused. "But surely you must know that some people like both. Some women like men *and* women. Some women like men who dress like women. There are all sorts of ways to love. It doesn't always have to look so perfect."

"I know," I said. My heart thumped, and my lips felt dry. "But I grew up in Jeren. This just didn't happen there. Women married men and had their babies. And if anyone messed around on the side, they kept it secret."

"Even if both parties agreed to the relationship?"

I was floored for a moment. "I don't think I realized that was a thing you could do till I got here," I admitted. "Not until I met Lady Liliane. Not until Val told me."

"Have you talked to her much? Lady Liliane?"

I shook my head. "Not really. Hers was the first elemental class I took, but that was before I really understood what... that she and Master Onan and Lady Zai... I think it's hard for her," I said finally. "My lady and Onan are cordial, but I've never seen them act like friends. It's true I've only seen them together at royal events," I added hurriedly, "so there's that element of formality, but..."

"But something tells you it's hard to make it work."

There was a lump in my throat. "Yes."

Rebekah shrugged. "Well, my darling." She leaned forward and gently kissed my lips. "I, for one, don't mind sharing." She threw on her hood, waved goodbye, and slid out beyond the shadows.

CHAPTER 24

"YOU LOOK TIRED."

I blinked blearily. It was late, and Val was snoring softly behind her pile of books. Naliah had called it quits an hour ago, and the library was quiet.

"You'd look tired, too, if a stupid robin woke you every morning at the crack of dawn," I grumbled back as Stevan sat beside me. Val slept on, though her fingers twitched a bit.

"Ah, spring," Stevan sighed. "That magical time of year when animals tell anyone and everyone that's listening that they'd like a mate, and now, please. What a beautiful season."

I stuck out my tongue in reply.

"That's childish," he remarked, and I did it again. I really was tired.

"Perhaps I should leave then, and let you keep working on...?"

"On going mad," I said, thrusting my book at him and digging the heels of my hands into my eyes. "Nothing in this book makes sense! Not that any of these supposed spells work, anyway, so why anyone bothers to translate them thousands of years later..."

Stevan gingerly thumbed Zai's old copy and grinned at a page. "Ah, the joy of Açirin. Every young mage who's ever attempted to translate this book remembers it. Especially that spell. Most folks call it The Godsdamned Spell, though scholars are nicer and call it The Spell. No one has ever gotten it right or we wouldn't still be working on it. And of course you're checking your translations with Zai before testing them, unless you're planning on destroying more trees."

"Ha ha," I replied bitterly. Truth be told, I hadn't checked with Zai yet; I'd hoped to present her with a complete translation at once, and Stevan must have known. I bet he'd probably done the same once. The spells were useless, though, either lost to the ages of time or never really spells at all. "I don't get it. It's like whoever wrote it down was trying to hide its meaning. See, this word here, *erwhusz*," I said, tapping the page with my index finger. "On the page right before this, that word means *force*. But that doesn't make sense here, or else it would be saying something like 'empty crystals are full of force.' The whole point of blank crystals is that, well, they're blank! They don't have any powers on their own. Not unless the stupid Ole'ad knew something we didn't."

"Yes, scholars have posited that," Stevan said, frowning. "But no number of tests have ever amounted to much. Even Zai has poked around at it, to no avail. I translated the word as 'energy,' since..." He flipped back a few pages. "Here," he said, pointing. "In this one, the spell for gentle rains and good harvests, the same word means energy. "'*Çu erwhusz set donnum niey pedt ol'addan.* Let the energy of the rain flow deep into the roots.' My theory was that another word in The Spell was wrongly transcribed. It's not supposed to be about *blank* crystals at all but about *imbued* crystals. Something happened through the ages, and the translation was corrupted."

"And was that right?" I breathed hopefully.

He laughed. "Do you see me sitting on a kingdom of riches? If my translation had been right, every university in the world would have rewarded me a hundred times over. No, this was the only assignment that didn't impress my teachers, I'm afraid," he admitted. "What's your idea?"

I bit my lip. Even knowing I could never get it right, I was reluctant to share. Yet Stevan had trusted me with his theory. "I think you're onto something with a wrong transcription," I blurted. "Because something's not right with a letter." I dug through my pile, knocking over a few thick tomes. Val snorted loudly. I froze, but she merely shifted and went back to sleep. "Here," I whispered, not wanting Val to awaken just yet. It was the library's copy that I had used last summer, almost new and clean next to Zai's battered one. "In this version, it's written one way, but in this version"—I pointed to Zai's—"there's an extra little line drawn in." Stevan frowned, and I traced the symbols on a scrap of parchment:

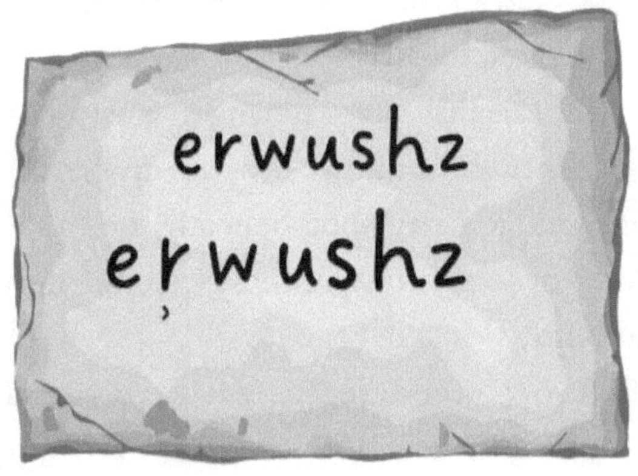

Stevan squinted. "It's hard to say," he said at last. "This is an old book. It could just as easily be a slip of the quill."

"That's what I thought, too. But it happens again, right here, at the end of the page in the *same* word. Why not on any of the other letters? If it's just an inkblot, it seems awfully strange that it shows up on the same letter twice, especially when that word has caused so many people such trouble over the years."

Stevan tugged his dark locks. I tried not to notice.

"It's a good theory," he said at last, "but if that's the case, then what does it translate to?"

I shook my head. It was beginning to throb again, right behind my eye. "That's where I'm stuck," I said, defeated. "I've been combing over the rest of the book, trying to find somewhere else—*anywhere* else—that it appears, but I haven't found it. Not even once. And until I do, I can't move on. I'm just stuck staring at dusty old pages night after night until my eyes get crossed."

He nudged my foot beneath the table. "Still thinking of becoming a full sorceress?" he teased, not unkindly.

Before I could reply, Val gave her loudest snort yet and sat bolt upright. "I'm up!" she shouted. I hastily bid Stevan goodnight and gathered my things before the night scholar could kick us out.

* * *

While the kingdom had been relegated to receiving updates via spell-speak and fire readers in the winter, shipping resumed as soon as the storms began to subside, and it seemed everyone in the city knew that war with Suuldus was imminent.

"It's about time," Naliah said as she slathered butter on her roll one morning. She had grown several more inches since December, and I was fascinated with how much food she could now eat. "Sir Rodrick said he's never seen the king so slow to take action. It doesn't look good for us to just sit here and let threats come our way. If other countries get wind of that happening, they could become Suuldus's allies and put us in even more danger."

"Some say the king is just being cautious," Archer agreed over the clatter of cutlery. "But there are rumors that Suuldus is holding something over us. Something that would prevent us from going to war."

"Something like what?" Val asked.

"Something like a prisoner," Gatlen said glumly as he plunked down at the table. Kessa followed. The dark circles under their eyes indicated another night spent out with the city guard. "Pass the rolls; I'm starving," he groaned.

"It's all the talk down in the lower city," Kessa said as she devoured her meal. "Why the lower city has better gossip than the palace, I couldn't tell you. But rumor has it some of the nobles' children weren't aboard the ship that sank last fall and might still be in Suuldus. And if one of those children were connected to someone high up in the palace, like..."

"Like the prince," Val whispered, pressing a hand to her mouth. "He hasn't been seen in months. They said he went down to Qiameth to learn from university mages, but if that's not true..."

"Wouldn't it be easy to check?" I asked, confused. "If they say he's there, then surely someone would have seen him."

Archer shook his head. "It's customary for coming-of-age royals to go on meditative retreats. Months on end without contact with the outside world, out in the middle of the Qimorathan desert."

"It's important rite of passage," Val agreed. "Noble mages have a duty to learn to commune with the magics of the land. It's important for times of hardship that they can coax the earth back to strength. Otherwise, the kingdom could crumble. Look at what happened to Prince Daimien the Third when he shirked his duties before the earthquake of 694." I looked at her, shocked. "What? I can pay attention in class, too!" Val stuck out her tongue.

"*Anyway*," Gatlen continued, "no one has heard from him since September, and the mages won't confirm his location, so folks in the lower city think that Suuldus has infiltrated Qimorath and is playing puppet master, which is a terrifying thought."

We paused for a moment, each making a sign against evil over our chest.

"The people in the lower city think that means Kreiogny will be invaded soon," Gatlen continued. "Which means the city guard is all the more important. So now not only do we spend our nights breaking up fights and patrolling the walls, but we're also expected to keep an ear to the ground for anything suspicious."

"Are you still happy to do this work?" Naliah was serious, a rare state for her. With a jolt, I realized that if Naliah passed her page tests, she could very well squire for a knight who got sent away to war. The thought made me deeply uneasy.

Gatlen nodded fervently. "A knight's work isn't just shining armor and glory," he explained.

"We take vows to protect the realm. Protection takes a lot of different forms. It's a lesson Sir Rodrick used to try to explain, but it's meant more to me this year than ever before. He's wise, that man. You should listen to everything he has to say while you can."

I snuck a glance at Kessa, who was still gulping down oats hungrily, not saying anything. I had the suspicion she didn't feel the same.

Breakfast was nearly over when Gatlen suddenly slapped his palm to his forehead. "Oh! I almost forgot!" he said, turning to me. "Master Onan is back."

"Master Onan?" I was on my feet before I realized I had stood. "When? Where? How is he?" I demanded.

"Late last night, almost morning. I saw him on our way through the gates. I'm sure he's alright," he called, but I was already halfway out the door.

I had slowed to a jog well before I reached his classroom, suddenly aware that of all the places he might be after a perilous journey home, it was not likely to be at the top of his list. Yet to my surprise, the heavy wooden door opened before I could knock.

"Ayve!" he said, surprised. "What are you doing here?"

"I heard you were back," I stammered. I was

suddenly awkward, wondering what he thought of me showing up at his door unannounced.

Yet to my delight, he gave me a quick hug. His shoulders seemed thinner than normal, and he looked a bit threadbare, but he was alive.

"It's good to see you," he said. I noticed he leaned heavily on a staff, fingers twisted tightly around the knob. "I'm glad you stopped by. I'm afraid our paths wouldn't have crossed if you hadn't. The council plans to hear my testimony and send me off again."

My heart dropped. "You mean the war council."

He nodded grimly. "I won't ask how much you know. Somehow everyone knows more than they should, and yet we still don't know enough. It's why they need me to do research as soon as I've had my say." He waved the books he clutched in his other hand.

"Oh." I tried to swallow my disappointment.

"Master Onan, sir!" barked a voice from the end of the hallway. Two young palace guards marched our way, frowning firmly. "The council is ready."

He nodded. "Stay well," he said somewhat sadly. "Keep up your studies. And tell Lady Zai I say hello." The guards whisked him away, and I was left standing alone.

***

I tried to take Master Onan's message to heart, but it was hard to focus when the Book of Açirin distracted me from my work. A few nights later, I found myself in the library late again. This time I was alone; Val had claimed she was going to bed early, though I had a feeling Gatlen might have had the night off.

"Still working?" Stevan had made no noise as he approached.

"Sort of." At least I was in a better mood this time. "I thought maybe if I stared at it long enough, it would just tell me what secrets it's keeping."

"And?" His eyes danced.

"If it has any, it's not speaking." I sighed, flipping the book shut. "What are you up to?"

"Besides bothering you? Researching Suuldus," he said, growing serious. "I'm sure you heard Master Onan returned?"

I nodded, briefly explaining my visit with him in the hall.

"No one knows what he told the council, but it's clear it wasn't good," he said.

"Archer said that—"

Stevan held up a hand and shook his head. Holding a finger to his lips, he took a small pink crystal from inside his pocket and placed it on the table. He moved his finger to point at it but paused and raised an eyebrow at me curiously. I took the hint and raised my own hand instead. It shimmered before being enveloped in a fine green mist.

"Nice," he said, nodding approvingly. "Your silencing spells have come a long way from what Zai says."

I glowed with pride. "You talk to Zai about me?"

He shrugged. His shoulders moved nicely beneath the fabric. "Sometimes. She tells me about your morning lessons. I'll be joining you again this spring, don't forget," he reminded me. "It's important that I know what you're working on before we get out in the field. Now, what was Archer saying?"

I let my fingers rub the book's leather cover absentmindedly as I explained the missing prince theory. "What do you think?" I asked when I had finished. I had flipped the cover open while I talked, and now my fingers pressed against the worn crease in the spine.

He rubbed a hand over his mouth and chin. "I don't know," he admitted. "I was in Qiameth the night the prince arrived. He disappeared so quickly, who's to say if he went on a retreat or was kidnapped? But if rumors have reached the lower city, something is wrong."

"How do you know?" I asked. "I'd think those rumors would be less credible, given that most city dwellers have never ventured too far from home."

He shook his head. "The city is more complicated than that. The average person doesn't go far, sure. But like the palace, the city has its own inner workings. There are underground sources, what with the thieves' guild everywhere. They have their ways of getting information, and most of it is better than what the palace finds. If our monarchs weren't so uptight, they'd find a way to work together, at least in times like these," he said bitterly. I was glad for the silencing spell; I had never heard someone so openly critique the kingdom before. "Your friend Kessa's sister is the closest link we have to this underground knowledge."

"Rebekah?" I was so startled I nearly fell from my chair. "Rebekah works for thieves?"

He laughed, and it sounded like a bark. "Kessa would never admit it, of course. She's ashamed. Well, you rise from nothing to become a knight and your sister runs around with questionable folk like that, and *you* might be ashamed, too."

"But I thought Rebekah was with the *palace*

spies." My head reeled. How come everyone knew more about everything than I did?

"She is. It's the worst-kept secret in their ranks. Everyone knows the palace has a spy in the thieves' guild, and everyone knows it's Rebekah, but she's so good at hiding in plain sight that she can get away with it. The girl you've seen—" He tried to keep his voice casual, but his face looked strained. "The girl you've seen is just one side of her. Some say she can change her appearance at will, even looking different ways to different people in the same group."

"What is she, a shapeshifter?" I joked. Even the youngest children knew shapeshifters were a myth.

"Maybe," he replied seriously, and I wasn't sure if he was kidding. "Oh, probably not," he conceded. "I might mistrust her is all. Point is we don't have enough knowledge about what's going on, and unless someone finds out soon, we're in a dangerous position."

I let my fingers stroll along the inside cover as I thought. The leather was soft and dark from years of wear. The top inner corner of the first page was smudged with grime. I squinted at it. "Hang on," I said slowly.

"Hm?" Stevan's hand was over the crystal as if he were about to pocket it, but he paused.

I grabbed my quill, scratching it across my parchment several times before remembering it had no ink. I dipped it carefully and then wrote, attempting to recreate the smudges:

We stared at my work when I was done. "What was Lady Zai's sister's name?" I asked, though I was sure I knew the answer.

"Aila," he said finally.

The writing stared back at us. I felt rather than knew what to do next. I stood, raising my hands and repeating the motion Stevan had taught me not long ago. He linked one of his hands into my free one, and I felt his magic join mine. I strained, heat growing in my face, until the edges of the book slowly glowed lilac.

The light began to subside when Stevan let go of my hand just like it had with the painting. We sank into our chairs, shaking slightly.

"So it's Aila's book," Stevan said finally, talking us through it. "She writes her name in the front, only over time the writing smudges, so it naturally would look like that."

I shook my head, hair loosening in its pins. "You're wrong," I said. "And you know you're wrong. That's the same symbol that's in the spell. I told you, it looked like someone hand-inked those markings. But why add them? And why change a letter in your own name to match?"

Stevan shook his head, too. "There's a lot we don't know about the Ole'ad," he admitted. "Theirs was a mostly oral tradition. Anything that's written was transcribed long after the fact. There's bound to be letters or whole words that got lost in translation. Maybe Aila knew something no one else did."

"But *what*?" I asked.

The book lay innocently on the table, leaving the question unanswered.

CHAPTER 25

I ASSUMED THE ANSWER would take its time in finding me, but it happened faster than I could have hoped for, and in the least expected of places.

"Pay attention!" Madame Gerta yelled for the fourth time. I struggled to lift my heavy lids. Even the threat of sore knuckles couldn't budge me from my stupor. The sky was clear, and the sun warmed the courtyard for the first time since fall. Yet Madame Gerta insisted on keeping the fire burning, and it was all I could do not to fall asleep sitting up.

"My apologies, Madame Gerta," I droned, reopening my scroll. "I was studying late last night."

Madame Gerta sniffed, a clear sign of how she felt about young ladies who stayed awake late studying. She probably would have gone on a tirade about morals these days when I first saw it.

"Queen Aila was originally Princess Aiṛa of Oqira, daughter of King Isfan and Queen Esztes, a descendant of an ancient Ole'adan line," the text began. *"She married Prince Eltoneth the Second in 25 CE. Having no Kreiognan letter equivalent, court scribes changed her written name to Aira before eventually converting to the modern Kreiognan spelling of Aila, an antiquated word loosely meaning 'essence' or 'light.' King Eltoneth and Queen Aila began their reign in the summer of 37 CE upon the passing of King Isfan. They bore nine children: Princess Taiy, Prince Thom..."*

My heart raced. I grabbed my bag in one hand and the scroll in the other. "I've got to go!" I shouted over my shoulder as I ran. "Moonblood troubles!" I had bought myself hours of punishment, but it was bound to be worth it.

I sat on the first empty bench I could find and dug through my bag frantically, finally grasping the leather cover with my fingertips. I flipped through the pages with ease. And there it was. The one, little letter that made all the difference.

Without thinking, I ran again, eager to catch Stevan before my next class began. My soft leather shoes pattered down the hallway, and I lifted my skirts with frustration. I would have to remember to wear trousers again for our adventures, I chided myself.

I skidded to a stop just outside what I thought was his office before bursting through. "I've found it!" I shouted.

Several very young children stared back at me with blank faces. A few giggled.

"Ayve?" Master Varrick stood at the front of the room, glittering fire in the jar before him.

"S—sorry," I stammered. "I thought I was—this is children's magic—I was looking for Stevan—"

"Ayve?" said another voice, and a warm hand found my shoulder.

"Sorry!" I called again, and I let the door fall softly closed.

I buried my face in my hands as Stevan led me to a stone bench down the hall. "Gods, I embarrassed myself," I groaned through my fingers. "I must have turned one hall too early. I didn't mean to interrupt like that!"

"Yes, well, they're little. They'll get over it," Stevan said. "Now, what was it you're so eager to show me when I have a divining circle to set up?"

I pulled out the scroll and book, explaining what I had found. "The crystals aren't full of power but *essence*," I clarified. "You were right;

someone probably wrote the wrong word when they transcribed it. It shouldn't be *erwuszh* but *aiŗa*. She wrote the symbol from the original spelling of Aira to keep it secret so no one else would know. That *has* to be it. Why else would Aila write her name that way?"

"Maybe she descended from the Ole'ad and wanted to honor her heritage in her name," Stevan suggested, though he didn't sound convinced. "Or maybe she just liked how it looked. There are a dozen reasons she could have written like that. You can't know just from one scroll." His tone was uneasy, and he rubbed his knees slowly.

"I'm right," I argued. "And you know it. Maybe this isn't a spell. Maybe it's a page of history documenting how there's a special type of crystal that has some kind of essence or power in them that we don't know about. That would explain why Zai wants to find the crystals you've been hunting so badly. They're some kind of unique magic that's been lost to time."

Stevan let me ramble for a while longer before finally standing. "I have to finish setting up. You should stay here," he cautioned as I tried to follow. He looked around furtively. "I should have remembered to use a silencing crystal."

"There's no one around; everyone's in class," I said impatiently, flapping my hands. "Surely you don't think someone spied on us in an empty hallway!" I gestured to the vacant corridor around us.

Still, he looked troubled. "Just wait here till the bell rings," he instructed. "And speak to no one. There's more we need to know first," he breathed, and I suddenly wondered if he understood more than he was letting on. My fear passed when he smiled. How could I ever be worried when he had that smile?

"Alright," I agreed. I listened until his footsteps faded. I had the answer. Now I had to figure out what to do with it.

* * *

Trying to keep something from Zai was torturous. I did my best to feign ignorance whenever she asked if something was wrong, but her pursed lips and furrowed brows made it clear she wasn't convinced.

Fortunately, I had a built-in distraction: page tests were beginning, and the whole palace was aflutter with preparations. While the practical tests wouldn't occur until closer to midsummer, the written exams were held in the early spring, and every page was tight with tension. More than one scuffle broke out in the halls, and not always just between pages. Even the mage students were on high alert.

"It's because the page tests signal the beginning of the end for us," Val said gloomily at dinner the night before exams began. "We only have so much time left to study now. Plus some of the panel members will sit on the mages' panel, too, so it's a preview into your own future. Some years they're dreadful."

"There was that one duke from Trask," Archer pointed out helpfully. "The one who smelled like goats and failed nearly every candidate he saw. The king had to persuade him to let at least some of the mages pass, or else we would have been looking at a year with no university candidates at all."

"Thanks," Val replied dryly. The bell chimed, and she sighed. "I better get going. We leave at dawn, and I still haven't finished packing. At least I don't have to finish my homework." She hugged the group goodbye sadly. She and Lady Liliane would be leaving for a month to aide a neighboring village. Some of their fields hadn't sprouted, and with a looming war, they couldn't afford to risk their food supply. Several mages hypothesized that the ground had grown weary from years of constant planting, so Lady Liliane was taking Val to repair the soil before they completely missed the growing season.

Val hugged Naliah tightly, wishing her luck, before turning to me. "Don't do anything stupid," she murmured in my ear when we hugged, and though I knew she meant about Stevan, my mind couldn't help but wander to the book.

"I won't," I promised. I hadn't meant for it to be a lie.

* * *

The library was the quietest I had ever heard it. The eighth bell had only just rung, but no one was around. Even the evening scholar on duty was missing, probably off in the dusty shelves somewhere enjoying the silence. Legend had it any pages who studied the night before the exams would fail, so naturally everyone did their last-minute preparations in their rooms where no one could tell them they were cursed. Mage students used this as an excuse to skive off their own work for the night.

Researching the Ole'ad wasn't *really* studying, I bargained with myself, so I dragged some old books to a table and began flipping through their pages. The texts were ancient, and I lifted their corners gingerly. Some of the illustrations surprised me: delicately inked depictions of ancient people woven into the forests like vines through trees. Oddly enough, some of the people seemed to have light purple skin.

"Yes, it's a peculiarity of that particular book."

I jumped. "Good evening, Master Varrick," I greeted him as he sat. "Do you know why? The purple, I mean."

He slid the book towards him and lifted a hand, almost as if to run it over the page. "There are lots of theories. Least credited is the idea that the Ole'ad were actually purple. There are enough explorers' journals from the end of their time that we know the Ole'ad looked ordinary enough. A bit peculiar in their habits and primitive in their fashion, but their skin tones were much like ours. The most convincing theory I've heard is that all Ole'ad had purple magic, though no one can explain why that would be. Magic reflects an individual's essence, and it's unlikely that all Ole'ad had similar essences. More than likely, some explorer stumbled upon a purple-magick'd Ole'ad, and some poor artist was tasked with recreating this encounter, forever dooming them to a single-hued history."

Each time Varrick had said the word "essence," my heart had jumped a bit.

"Ayve?" Varrick was frowning at me. "Forgive me if I'm intruding. You seem distracted. If now's not a good time?"

"No, no!" I rushed. "I'm sorry. I was thinking.

You were asking?"

"I was asking if you remembered our conversation from a few months ago, at the tavern. When I told you I was from Oqira."

I nodded. "Of course. Did something happen? Are you going back there?"

He shook his head. He was nervous, I realized. "Ayve, I...." He hesitated. "I almost didn't want to show you. I don't want to destroy... It didn't seem fair. But I thought about how I would have felt when I first arrived here, if my letters..."

"Letters?"

Varrick pulled a bundle from beneath his robes. Neatly tied together were many of the letters I had tried to send: to Joseth, to Rafe and Martha, even the one to Stevan when he was in Qiameth. "How did you get these?" My voice sounded far away. "Did Zai give these to you?" The truth was glaring, but I didn't want to see it.

"I'm sorry, Ayve." Varrick's voice was soft. "I stopped by to visit Zai one night and found her burning some things in the fire. It's not uncommon, you know, for mages to burn letters, especially important mages like her. But there was something about it, like she knew she shouldn't be doing it. When she wasn't looking, I grabbed what I could." He spread his hands wide. "I tried to rationalize it, to think of a reason she would burn your words. But the more I've thought it over, the more I've thought about how I would have felt if my letters home had never made it."

I felt like the air had been pulled from my lungs. "I don't understand," I said finally. "Why would Zai burn my letters? Why would she tell me to write to them if she didn't intend to send them?"

Varrick looked around nervously, rubbing his fingers together. "There's something you ought to see," he whispered. "Can you meet me tomorrow near sundown, by the markets?"

I frowned. "The page exams," I began.

"End well before then," he assured me softly. "You'll have plenty of time to celebrate with friends. The palace will be quiet again tomorrow night," he said, gesturing to the library around us, "with everyone readying for the second day of exams. It'll be that much easier to sneak away. Please."

I couldn't say no. Not when I could see Joseth's name on the envelope before me. "Alright," I agreed.

He nodded and looked around before he stood. "You'll understand soon. I promise."

I wished I understood *now*.

* * *

At sundown the next day, I stood shivering in the brisk March wind outside the markets. The weather had turned early in the morning, and all day, dark clouds had brooded over the palace. It left everyone in a foul mood, especially the pages. Naliah was convinced she had failed an exam, and without Val there to cheer her up, she had skulked off to her room before even eating dessert.

"Come on," I muttered to myself, bouncing my knees to get warm. I watched the sky warily. Any minute, the rain that had threatened all day might start. Rain was good news for the fields, but if it stormed like it was threatening to do, Val and Liliane's work could be destroyed by floods washing away unsprouted seeds.

The market was winding down for the night, and few people were out. Shops were closing, and yet still Varrick didn't appear. An old man lurched down the street, mumbling to himself and pointing wildly. I shrank back as he came closer. The man didn't look well. His little remaining hair was stark white, and his bones jutted out of his body at sharp angles.

"They've no right, no right!" he seethed as he passed by where I stood. "Fools, all, and damn 'em all to hell." He paused and, without warning, looked directly at me. I froze, pinned down by his icy, wild blue eyes.

"Traitor!" he roared suddenly. "You stole from me, with your magics! Thief! Witch!" He lunged, reaching for me.

Without thinking, I raised a shield as I had done so many times in practice before, and the man went flying backwards, repelled by the power of the spell. He sat dazed on the cobblestones, spittle dripping from his mouth.

"I'm sorry," I choked, but my feet wouldn't seem to move toward him.

Two members of the city guard rushed towards the man. They were surprisingly gentle, and I suspected the woman touching his shoulder must have worked a soothing magic on him as the man's breathing slowed.

Her partner, a man about Gatlen's age, turned to me, stern-faced and square-shouldered. "Did he attack you?" he asked briskly.

"No, he tried to, but—I have magic," I said carefully. Was I about to be arrested?

But the man simply tsk'd and nodded. "You're alright then. His family has been looking for him. He's not well. Thank you. Up now," he instructed the man, and they helped him walk away. The old man didn't look back.

It was nearly dark, and I was shaking from fear and cold. I sat on the edge of the fountain for a moment, struggling to take deep breaths.

"I'm sorry that this had to be the way you learned." Varrick's sudden appearance was hardly shocking after such an event. I wondered if he'd been there the whole time, masked behind a cloaking spell. "But I needed you to see what they do before I can explain."

"What *what* do?" I croaked. Fingers shaking, I uncorked the water flask in my satchel and took a deep swig.

Varrick sat next to me. He fiddled with a jewel on his bracelet. The cold from the fountain stone seeped through my clothes, and I wished he would hurry. I was in no mood for suspense.

"That man," he said at last, "was Zai's first apprentice."

I didn't follow. "I thought Stevan was her one and only apprentice. You mean to tell me she took on an old man first?"

"That man wasn't old. That was Lord Andors of Ivansso."

I knew the name was supposed to have a bigger effect on me. "Is that someone I should know?" I asked. I tried to smile politely, but it felt strained.

He sighed. "I should have remembered. You haven't been here long enough to know the lore. Andors went to Qiameth as a young boy to pursue magic. Stories say he didn't have much aptitude, but his family was wealthy, and at that time, Qiamethan mages had... looser morals about accepting non-magical students for money in their schools. He met someone when he was there, a woman, and fell in love, but she didn't love him back. He followed her for years until one day his family learned he had grown mad, just like that," he said, snapping his fingers. His bracelet jangled loudly. "Overnight from young to old, from sane to dangerous. He claimed a sorceress had stolen his soul.

"Most agreed that was nonsense, especially after the beautiful young woman who brought him back explained that *she* was the supposed sorceress in question, and she had done nothing besides spurn his love. She was powerful, and charming, so his family never held ill wishes against her. She paid for him to have attendants for the rest of his life and then left him in the city while she went galivanting around the world on marvelous adventures. I'm sure you know by now who she is."

"Zai," I said, though I didn't want to admit it. "But her story sounds true. How could anyone steal someone's soul?"

"What about their essence?" Varrick asked quietly, and I thought suddenly, horribly, of The Spell.

"Have you ever seen Zai with any special crystals?" he asked. The wind snapped the market flags sharply in the night. "Something small, unassuming perhaps. Something that Zai has asked you to touch, or to test?"

Without meaning to, something inside me dissolved. The story poured from my mouth, from the cave in the woods to probing the grubby crystal in Zai's rooms, and the groggy feeling it always left me with.

It was truly dark now, and few torches had been lit with the coming storm. My bones ached with cold. "And now we're supposed to go to Allerwia to find more," I finished. "Zai thinks they're hidden all throughout the kingdom, and she thinks she knows where to find the next one. I'm supposed to join her and help her find them."

"There's another part to the story," Varrick said. "About her sister."

"Aila."

Varrick looked startled. "Yes. How did you know her name?" He shook his head before he could get an answer. "Never mind. There will be time to talk later. It's getting dark, and anyone could be listening." He looked around, though the square seemed deserted. I supposed it had seemed empty when Varrick was cloaked earlier, too. "I'd hoped we'd have more time, but if Zai gets wind of what I know... Ayve, we must go away."

"What do you mean? Like leave the square?" I knew what he meant, but I didn't want to consider it.

"In part, yes. But then we need to get away from the city, and far, until we know how to destroy these crystals. Zai is far more powerful than nearly any other mage, and I'm sure she's been hiding her true strength. I shudder to think what she could do if she found more sinister ways to fuel her powers."

"But how could we destroy them? It took me long enough to learn what The Spell is truly about. And," I said suddenly, rising and pointing a finger accusingly, "how on Earth did you know its true meaning? No one has ever worked it out, and you come rushing down here knowing something I hadn't told you!"

Two members of the guard were strolling by. Varrick stood, hands raised before him, and approached me cautiously. "I will explain, I promise, but walk with me," he said in a low voice. "They may be spies. Please."

Reluctantly, I took the arm he offered and fell into step beside him. I hoped this wasn't a mistake.

"I left my classroom to listen to you and Stevan the other day," he said as we walked. Our footsteps echoed on cobblestones. The guards' boots clattered not too far behind. "I admit it wasn't my finest teaching moment, but from the look on your face, it was clear you knew something important. I'm a master of disguise, as you may have noticed, so I cloaked myself and—"

"Snooped," I finished bluntly.

"Yes," he agreed. "Forgive me. But I've had my suspicions about Zai for years. With Lord Andors on the loose, Zai's history was fresh in my mind, and when you described empty crystals that contain essences, I knew it was important not only to save you from Zai but from Stevan, too."

"Stevan? What does he have to do with it?" My hackles were raised.

In the passing light of a torch, I could just make out Varrick's face. Perhaps it was concern that crossed his face as he spoke, but I almost mistook it for contempt. "He knows more than he's letting on. Why else would a young boy—an ordinary young boy, from common country folk—become so powerful at such a young age? Become one of the youngest to pass his mage tests in over a century? I'm certain he didn't do that on his own. Surely his powers were aided."

"I don't know." I was doubtful. I had seen Stevan, and I knew there was a special something about him. There had always been something elusive about Zai, something I just couldn't put my finger on, but Stevan?

"You don't have to believe me yet," Varrick said as we reached the palace gates. I unhooked my arm from his. "There is more to say. But now is not the time, and there is no time to lose. You must pack quickly, before Zai sees you. Meet me at The Crow at midnight. I'll explain more there, and if you believe me, we can depart before morning. Now go. And speak to no one."

If I had been feeling in a funny mood, I would have laughed at how he was repeating Stevan's words exactly. But trouble clouded my thoughts instead, and I hurried inside as the rain finally began to fall.

CHAPTER 26

MY BAG WAS NEARLY PACKED when I heard the front door close. I held my breath as I stuffed stockings into my bag, hoping I was misreading the quiet footsteps in the other room. Zai was only quiet when she was mad.

"Are you going somewhere?"

I nearly leaped out of my skin. Zai was leaning against my door frame, arms crossed, scowl on her face. I hadn't even heard my bedroom door open.

"I've decided it's time to move out," I said lightly, though my whole body shook. I tried to keep the tremor from my voice. "Val convinced me. She said we should move in together. We found rooms in the city, and I had to move fast or we would lose the place. I'm sorry I didn't say something sooner."

Zai still leaned against the door, sucking her teeth. "Val, who's currently out of the city for a month? *That* Val?" she growled.

"We talked before she left," I lied, feeling sweat gather on my collarbone. I was wearing my warmest clothes, and the room was already hot without being grilled by a furious mage. "She said I should act quickly if I found anything while she was gone. So she'll come home to a new place; isn't that nice?" I put a fake smile on my face and began to tighten my knapsack. There was no time to check if I had everything; I'd have to look later once I had escaped. Because that was what it had become: an escape.

I braced myself as I passed Zai, expecting to be thrown back by physical or magical force, but Zai didn't move, and I slipped through the door with ease.

"What about the rest of this?" Zai gestured to the remaining belongings inside my room and to the books scattered around the common area. "Or did they tell you that you could only move in with your trekking gear?"

I flushed and hesitated, reaching for a new lie.

"Stop it. You know I know. At least have the

decency to tell the truth," Zai ordered.

"So you can lock me up?" I shot back. A fire glowed in my chest, and I realized I really *was* glowing, my fingertips sparking green in fury.

"I hope I have never given you reason to think I would hurt you," Zai said quietly. Her voice sounded strange. Were those tears in her eyes? "And if I haven't stopped you from leaving yet, you must know that I won't stop you at all. So at least give me a chance to explain. Sit. Please." She pointed at a couch. If I hadn't known better, I'd have thought Zai was pleading.

"You had spies in the market," I muttered darkly as I finally sat, throwing my bag beside me.

"Of course." Zai's voice was crisp again. She swept her black skirt back and sat on the couch across from me. "I've kept eyes on you your entire time here. For your *safety*," she insisted when I began to protest. "I wasn't lying when I said someone was watching you. Two times I had mercenaries intercepted. I believe one had planned a kidnapping. Had I not had you followed, we wouldn't be sitting here having this conversation right now."

"You've still never said *why*!" I nearly shouted. "Who could want to do me harm? They certainly couldn't be worse than the person with the soul-stealing crystals," I sneered.

Zai ignored the insult. "I didn't say why because I wasn't sure," she explained. "I didn't want to let my prejudice cloud my judgment. But after the market... It's Varrick. I'm sure of it."

I scoffed. "Varrick? He's never done anything but help me," I laughed coldly. "How convenient to blame the one person who's trying to get me away from you." Lord Andors' wild eyes were still fresh in my mind, and I shuddered.

Zai was angry, yet her expression was troubled. "I know how it seems," she began before giving an exasperated sigh and throwing up her hands. "I don't even know where to start! You tell me. What do you want to know?"

I asked the first question that came to my mind. "Who was that man? Lord Andors? And why is he like that?"

Zai took a deep breath. "You want to start at the beginning, then. Yes, let's. That will make this easier. Andors was a dear... friend," she said, struggling to find the right word. "No, that's not right. He was Aila's friend. Aila was my—"

"Sister," I filled in flatly.

A pained look shot across Zai's face. "Yes, sister," she repeated. "Aila was six years younger than me. You have to understand, that was a massive difference for most of our lives. I was more like her mother. And we were sent away to school so *young*. I was ten, but Aila was only four! It was different back then," she explained. "If you had the money, the Qiamethan academy didn't care. Our parents traveled often, and they couldn't supervise a four-year-old while they worked, not without my help. You remember what that was like, caring for Joseth," she noted.

"Don't mention his name," I hissed. I didn't want Zai's fake sympathy, not when I knew she hadn't mailed my letters. "And you still haven't explained Andors."

"He was right between us, Andors," Zai continued. "Three years my junior, three years Aila's senior. He came from a noble family that had been disgraced. Three generations had been banned from gaining status or training as knights. Andors was the last generation to suffer this punishment; his children would be able to freely do what they liked. But his family was angry, and they wanted *something* for the boy. It's like I said: Qiameth was much more indiscriminate in who they took," she said with a hollow laugh, "even if the student they accepted wouldn't have been allowed anywhere else. The king was furious that his family found a workaround, so he spread the rumor that Andors had no magic at all."

"And did he?" I couldn't help but ask.

Zai shrugged. "Some. He wasn't powerful, but

he could handle basic spells. He followed me around from day one. I think he sensed in me a mother figure, the same way Aila did, and he was lonely. He was just a little boy," she said sadly. "To Aila, he was the big brave prince of bedtime stories, there to rescue her from the scary and confusing world. But to me, he was just another responsibility." She sighed heavily. "I regret it now. But at the time, being so far from home and in charge of Aila already, when all I wanted to do was learn magic...!

"I wasn't unkind," she clarified. Her fingers plucked absently at the side seam on her skirt. "I just wasn't as gentle as I could have been. Yet still he followed me everywhere, wanting to learn what I learned, trying and failing at so many spells. I should have stopped him," she admitted. "He was unprepared for so much of what he attempted. It could have been disastrous had my magic not been as strong as it was. I was just so desperate to get rid of him sometimes."

"Desperate enough to kill him?" My eyes darted to the door. Perhaps I could make a run for it.

"Kill him? Gods, no!" Zai's fierce eyes met mine, and I felt pinned to the spot. "Did I want him to learn to leave us alone? Certainly. But to kill him..." She shook her head. "I know you want to paint me as a monster, Ayve, but I'm not. Not even back then." She looked away, and I could move again.

"You have to understand that I was powerful. I'm not bragging, Ayve. I *did* brag back then, a lot. I was top in all my classes, and I could have finished my studies before I turned thirteen if I'd wanted. Only Aila stopped me, begging me to stay on long enough that she could study hard and pass her tests early so we could go off adventuring together."

I remembered with a lurch how I had felt the first time I'd heard that word. If I'd had any compassion left, I would have been able to imagine teenaged Zai turning down a journey for a sister. As it was, I could barely look at her without flinching.

"We did just that. I passed at eighteen, like Stevan, and spent the next year helping her study. She passed at thirteen, just as I had wanted to. I was a fool, Ayve." She shook her head, gray shadows dancing across her face. "Mages are supposed to be of age for a reason. But it was me and Aila, Aila and me... and Andors. Desperate not to be left behind, he had his family pay the academy to falsify his degree."

"Liar." I tossed my hair over my shoulder and loosened my scarf. A cool sweep of air brushed against my neck. "You can't falsify test results. Everyone knows that. There are systems built into place to prevent it from happening."

"Systems that didn't exist over twenty years ago, especially not in a time and place where money could buy anything," Zai noted gently. "Andors was part of the reason they put those systems into effect. After he..." She cleared her throat. "But we're not to that part of the story yet.

"Andors 'passed' at the same time as Aila. He begged to accompany us. Pleaded. Cried. Ultimately confessed his love to Aila and said he couldn't bear to live without her. He was lying, of course. He was in love with me."

I snorted. "Of course he was. Because everyone *loves* the great and powerful Zai." For a brief moment, I thought Zai would snap back at me, but Zai simply took another breath and continued.

"That's not true, and you know it. I'm a hard person to love. But remember, I had been a mother figure to Andors. He trusted me in ways he couldn't trust others. And as he grew older, that love became complicated." She was blushing, I was surprised to see, her cheeks tinged with pink. "But as you know, I was not interested in men," she continued, and her face turned an even deeper red. "I was barely interested in love in the first place, but I knew by then I did not love men. But Aila loved him more than anything. He joined us under the guise of her suitor, and we set off on our journey. You know for what, I assume?"

"The Ole'adan crystals. You said yourself that you were proud of your power. You wanted more." I felt brave, speaking so openly, but I thought Zai was right. If she hadn't attacked yet, she wasn't going to.

"Yes." For the first time, there was something Zai seemed to be holding back. She struggled with herself before the moment passed. "I didn't tell Andors what we were after. Aila loved the boy, but I wasn't dumb. I knew the risks. The magic was dangerous, and we couldn't endanger his life by letting him get involved. We snuck away after we found the first crystal, hoping to test it out." Her voice had changed again, and a faraway look took over her face. "But he found us. Aila told him. She had been expecting her world to change after he claimed to love her, but he fawned after me the whole time instead. I think she'd hoped she could *make* him love her if she shared what we were doing.

"I still remember the way the moon shone on his unconscious face when he—after he—" She took a hurried sip from the mug on the table. The tea must have been ice cold, but she didn't flinch.

"He shouldn't have touched it," she grieved when she put the mug down. "The crystals were once used to defeat powerful enemies by trapping their essences inside. When Andors touched it mid-spell, it was like he *bled* into it. He just lay there, pale and unmoving. I can still remember Aila's wails as she bent over him, begging him to move."

The hairs on my arms prickled. I swore I could hear a wail in the distance.

"He awoke the next morning, but the Andors we knew was gone. He was wild and shouting nonsense. Spells erupted from him without warning. We were left with no choice but to place him in a stupor and return him home. I told his family it was an accident, which it was, but if they had known... Ayve, I was a fool. I was only twenty. I know that may seem old and wise to you," she said, holding up a hand as I began to protest, "but that is so gods-damned *young*. I grew up so much that day. I vowed it would never happen again. I worked hard as an academy mage, earning enough to send money to Andors's family each month for his care. And I made Aila stay home. Yes, made," she said grimly. "I set a spell on our rooms and wouldn't let her leave. I had proven to myself that I never should have let her take her tests early. I was convinced that if I could just keep her inside until she was of age, she would grow up and thank me."

"Hm, keeping someone under a curfew." I was bitter. "I can only imagine how that felt."

Zai didn't even seem to hear me. "We still studied the crystal together, working over its true powers. But something had happened that night. When Andors touched the crystal, it was like he became part of us," she said slowly. "His magic only served to enhance ours. And while the thought frightened me, it seemed to energize Aila. She was adamant that we find the rest and become the most powerful mages of our time. I understand now that she was frustrated with being held captive. She saw power as her way out of her prison. But I was still naïve, and I thought she wanted to be powerful with *me*, her sister. Our parents had long since died, and we were all the other had. So when she turned fifteen, we set off again, taking on new people to help us." She fell silent, giving me the opportunity I needed.

"You found people and stole from them with your crystal," I snarled. "You used your magic to destroy others, which is *evil*, so how could you ask me to stay here with you instead of trusting someone like Master Varrick, who's always told the truth?" I snatched my bag as I rose from the couch.

"Ayve, *no*." Zai stood, too, and she towered

over me menacingly. "It wasn't like that. We only took people on to assist us, not to steal from. There were tests, don't you see," she insisted, and I flinched as Zai walked by, but she was only pacing the floor frantically. "We had to make sure the right people helped us, people strong enough to survive if they made a mistake. We couldn't work with just anyone or what happened to Andors would happen all over again. There was more to the crystal than what the book said, and we tried to learn, tried to understand what other powers it could hold." She leaned against the door to the hall, exhausted. "But it happened again. Whether it was a mistake, or if Aila did it on purpose..." She was troubled. "The next mage didn't survive for long. I wasn't there, and she didn't tell me until days later. By the time I found him, it was like his magic had run dry."

I was shaking again. "Is that what will happen to me?" I stared Zai down, urging myself not to cry. "You've made me probe that crystal we found together. Why? Are you stealing my magic, too?"

A small sob escaped Zai. "Ayve, I would die a thousand times for you," she choked. "You have to understand—I need more time!" she cried, pounding her fists against her thighs. "How can I make you understand when there isn't time? I've researched," she hurried as I picked up my bag again, "over and over for years, and you're the only other one who can do it safely, Ayve, I'm sure of it!"

I glared as I opened the door. "Likely story. Seems to me that you've just gotten better at hiding your crimes. I bet you've been bleeding me into it over and over, just waiting for me to die." I hurled the insult at Zai, hoping my final words would cut and sting in ways my exit couldn't.

"Ayve, I could never do that to my niece. To my sister. To your mother."

I paused, hand on the knob. The world had suddenly flipped upside down, and my heart was in my belly. Zai was doubled over, crying.

"Please," she croaked, pointing at the couch again.

I closed the door but remained standing. I wasn't sure my legs even worked. "Talk," I commanded flatly.

Zai took a deep, shaky breath. "I think it all started with Andors," she began, and I nearly opened the door again. "No, please!" Zai cried. "I promise it will make sense!" She wiped her eyes with her sleeves. Black streaks ran down her cheeks. "Andors's magic fed ours, yes, but it seemed to make Aila reckless. She might have passed her tests, but I don't think her essence was ready for so much extra power to be thrown at her.

I was able to absorb the energy, but Aila's essence was still moldable. It changed who she was. Even the color of her magic changed. We used to have the same purple, but hers lightened a few shades after everything happened. And her personality... Some days she was sweet as pie, and other days she was cruel and vicious, ranting and raving at shadows of shadows. Part of why I kept her locked away was for her own safety. I was afraid of losing her.

"I worked for the academy by day, and by night I learned everything I could about Ole'adan history. I dug deep into scrolls trying to cure her. I visited Andors often, trying to understand what had happened to him, and yet even though I found ways to soothe his ailing, nothing worked for Aila.

"After the second mage was destroyed, I lost all control over her. She wouldn't stay inside, and I couldn't hold her. For several weeks, she came and went as she pleased. When she did show, I never knew which Aila I would get. More often than not, it was the terrifying Aila, the one who schemed and plotted ways to grow her powers.

"A few months later, right before she turned sixteen, I came home to find Aila sitting in my chair and laughing, holding her belly. She was pregnant, she said, and she just kept laughing, and laughing, and laughing. Something about her had changed, and I was finally able to hold her within our walls again.

"I needn't have bothered. Once you were born, the old Aila was back. She was quiet, and kind, and she loved you so very much." Zai's eyes were red, and tears leaked from them nonstop. "She wouldn't tell me who your father was, but he wasn't a mage. You didn't have any trace of him on you when you were born. But you looked just like her," she said wistfully. "Big eyes, soft brown hair, delicate nose."

I ran a finger along my face before realizing what I was doing. I lowered my hand angrily, clenching it into a fist.

"That first year of your life was wonderful. We came to Freodon, and she cared for you so deeply. I would rush home each night to join you for your walk in the gardens. You took your first steps there." She sniffed and dabbed at her eyes again.

"So why am I standing here with you instead of with her?" The suspicion I had felt for months finally erupted to the surface. "What happened to my mother? Where is she?"

Zai hugged herself tightly. "I don't know," she whispered. "By October, I began to lose her again. Only this time it wasn't to anger but fear. She became deeply paranoid, terrified that someone was trying to get you. She was convinced…" Her voice cracked. "She was convinced I was going to hurt you. I tried to save her. I quietly sought advice from even the seediest underbelly of magic that I knew, but it was no use. She took you and fled."

"And you didn't try to find her?" I asked bitterly. "You just let your half-crazed sister disappear?"

"Of course not. The second I knew you were gone, I tried to follow. I had taken a prestigious job at the palace, and I left it in a heartbeat to find you two. I knew it meant I might never be allowed to return, that I could be dishonored for abandoning my post, but that never would have stopped me.

"Aila was powerful, though, even in her madness. She had always been better at star magic," she granted somewhat begrudgingly, and I flashed back to our conversation around the fire nearly a year ago. "She used star spells to make the two of you untraceable. It's a tricky magic even for modest practitioners, and I was nothing close. Grasping at straws, I wrongly assumed she would go to the next place we had thought might have a crystal, a grassy meadow on the outskirts of Trask, but I found no trace of her there.

"By this point I had been gone half a year, and when I returned, I was defeated. It was only through the kindness of my friends that the monarchs kept me on, though not without much groveling on my part. I continued my research in secret, using every excursion and holiday to seek out the suspected locations of crystals in the hopes of finding some trace of you two."

She fumbled blindly for her mug through her tears. It would have been easy for me to pass it to her. I let Zai struggle instead. Something was bothering me. "But you found me," I said. "In Jeren. You knew I was there. You said that Stevan found the cave, and that you had a vision, but you knew I'd be there, didn't you." It wasn't really a question.

The tea had steadied Zai's nerves. "Yes." She was calmer now, and though her eyes were still red, she had stopped crying. "The cave in Jeren had never caught my eye as a possible location, not until Stevan found it in that book. But when he did, I knew for certain that was where Aila had gone. One of the last travels with our parents before we left for Qiameth took us through Jeren. Our mother was fond of the village. It was much smaller back then, hardly a blip on the map. My mother was not a family woman," Zai admitted. "But she told us that her grandmother had grown up not far from the town, over the hills towards Hendassa. She still had relatives there, though we never met them. She was too proud of how far her family had come to go back.

"So I knew: Aila hadn't gone after the crystals after all. She had gone looking for family. Ayve, Stevan may have found a cave with a crystal, but I wasn't in Jeren because I was seeking *it*. I was seeking *you*."

It sounded believable, yet how could I trust Zai? Everything sounded too good to be true. Varrick had warned me to speak to no one. Had he suspected that Zai would try to trick me?

I didn't know my own question until I heard myself ask, "How did you know it was me? I could have been anyone. I could still be anyone," I challenged. "I might not be related to you at all."

I thought Zai might start crying again. "There was a man at the inn who knew you weren't Petyr and Alys's. A man who knew all sorts of things."

"Rooster," I whispered automatically.

"He told me that years ago, there was a woman who left her child behind. No one had heard from her since, but her child was still there, none the wiser. And when I saw you," Zai said helplessly, "Ayve... you could be her twin." Her lip trembled.

I was sick of seeing Zai like this. She was

supposed to be a powerful and mighty mage, not a pathetic, whimpering mess. If anyone should be upset, I fumed, it should be me, not Zai. "You still haven't answered my other question. If I'm here, where's my mother? Why did she...?" I quickly changed my words. "Why is she still missing?"

"It was winter, Ayve," she said softly. "It was dark, and snowing. She was probably hungry and tired. She was half mad at the best of times. If she had gotten lost, if she hadn't known the way..."

"But she left me at the inn," I argued. "If she set out for Hendassa, why would she leave me behind? It doesn't make sense!" I roared, stomping my boot on the floor.

"Oh, child," Zai said, and she moved as if to hug me but stopped, hands grasping her skirts. "I wish I knew. I can only guess that Aila knew she wasn't right, and she was worried she might not make it through the storm. I believe she thought she was protecting you from me by hiding you with Alys. She loved you, Ayve. I'm sure she planned to find our family and return for you."

"But she didn't!" Now I was the one who was crying, and my face burned in shame. "If she made it to Hendassa, why didn't she ever come back?" I tried not to listen to the answer and brushed tears from my cheeks.

"I tried tracing her," Zai said after a long pause.

"Using the last few items of hers I had. But her essence is so faint. I'm sorry, Ayve. It's unlikely that she still lives."

Rain lashed the dark windows. The fire was bright, but the room felt cold.

"I can't make you stay," Zai said at last. "I've said that from the start. But I hope you will. We're family, Ayve. The only family we have left." She gave me one last look before stepping into her rooms and quietly closing the door.

CHAPTER 27

I KNEW I SHOULD get to The Crow. Varrick was waiting. But my world had turned inside out in the blink of an eye, and I didn't know what to do about it. I started towards the palace doors only to turn back the other way when they opened, afraid to make any decisions.

"Ayve?"

"Oh. It's you." I had never been so glad to see a friend.

Stevan looked at my knapsack before gently steering me into an empty classroom, closing the door softly behind us.

"What happened?" he asked as we sat at a table. He pulled the heavy bag from my shoulders.

I had thought it would be impossible to describe anything, but once I began, the words poured from my mouth like the rain beyond the windows. I told him everything I had learned about the crystals and Lord Andors, though the part about Aila being my mother got stuck in my mouth. Stevan kept silent, letting me talk, until I felt my rambling die off.

"I'm glad I caught you," he said when I finished. Water dripped from his hair, and he pushed a wet lock away impatiently. "This is awful. I'm sorry that you had to find out like this."

"Yes, it is," I began again in a rush, "and... What do you mean, 'find out?'"

The look on his face told me everything.

"You knew," I accused, eyes widening in horror. "You knew about Aila, about Andors, about the true purpose of the crystals. Gods, and here I was babbling on about understanding The Spell, and you sat there playing along, when you knew!" I felt like an idiot.

"Ayve, no." He clutched my hands in his. "Parts of it, yes. I knew what happened to Andors, and I knew Aila was involved, but believe me that I didn't fully grasp the big picture of the crystals until a few days ago. I've always theorized, but it was your work that made it clear. Please don't go," he begged as I frantically reached for my pack.

"There's more you need to understand! Zai said you might—"

I stopped cold. I turned to Stevan, lip curled. "You told her what I learned, didn't you? You told me not to talk to anyone, yet you went behind my back and told her what I discovered. You're on her side," I growled. "It doesn't matter what I say now. She's poisoned you. You're working with her. It's not a coincidence you're here tonight," I realized aloud. "She told you I was leaving. Didn't she?"

He hesitated. "Yes, but—"

"But what? But you think it's okay to steal people's essences? Or rob them of their strength until they slowly, painfully die?"

"Of course not," he said quietly. "Ayve, I know you're upset, and you have every right to be. I was too. But there's more to this spell than you understand—"

I snorted. "You sound just like her." My words reminded me of something else. "Did she tell you that Aila's my mother, too? How good old Aunt Zai wants to steal magic from her niece?"

"What? No, I—what? Your mother? Gods, Ayve, I..." He grasped at his face, running his fingers over his chin. I didn't buy it.

"You could at least tell me the truth. I'd expect lies from her. But not from you." I slung the bag over my back again.

"Honest, Ayve, I didn't have any idea. Your mother!" He stood as I strode angrily towards the door. "Please," he begged again, dashing in front of me. "Stay. I can explain. We both can."

But I had finally had enough. I slammed him sideways with a blast of green. Off guard, he stumbled, and I slipped through the door and ran out into the night.

* * *

My heart was a mess, but my feet were sure. A look of relief came over Varrick's face when I crossed The Crow's threshold.

"I was worried," he said, helping me remove my outer layers and hanging them on a hook to dry. "Was there trouble?"

We slunk to a table by the back. I opened my mouth to speak, and a crack came out instead. Varrick flagged a waitress for a pitcher of water. I downed a full tankard before I tried to speak again.

"Gods help us," he swore after I shared Zai's version about Andors. "I knew she would try to sway you. I wouldn't buy her story that Aila was crazy. There is little known about their time together since Aila was kept hidden for so long, but the few stories I've heard say that Zai was the mad one who refused to let anyone see her sister. I wouldn't doubt if Aila fled in an attempt to free herself and her daughter. That poor child. I wonder what became of the two of them."

I hesitated. I hadn't told Varrick that part of the story yet. Some part of me whispered that it was just a careless omission, but another, quieter part warned me not to share it. "Mm," I said when he looked at me, making a decision in the moment. "Dead, perhaps."

"Most likely." He fiddled with his bracelet. Its blue jewel reflected the light from the fire. I felt like my soul had been battered. It was nice to drink another tankard and admire the jewel's gleam. "Well, she won't come after you tonight. Not when her spies think you've left the city."

"Left the city?" I yawned, jaw cracking.

Varrick smiled. "There are some magics you haven't learned yet," he said in a low voice, "like illusions and deceptions. My specialty." Something gleamed in his eyes. It was almost frightening. *I'm exhausted is all*, I reassured myself, and the feeling passed as soon as it had arrived. "Zai will think you're on your way to Allerwia. After all, that was your next intended location, was it not? She'll convince herself that you want to find the remaining crystals before she can, and she'll visit every possible location before you can thwart her. But that's not where we're going."

"We're not?" My eyes were beginning to sag. "Where are we go-o-oing?" I slapped a hand over my mouth. "Sorry," I apologized. "I'm tired. I shouldn't talk too loud, or someone might hear—"

"We're disguised in a spell, don't worry," he reassured me. "Anyone who looks at us would see nothing more than a road-weary merchant and his wife. But," he said, almost whispering, and this time it was I who leaned in, "we're not going to Allerwia. Think, Ayve—where are the Ole'ad originally from? Where could we find answers to all we want to know?"

My mind felt sluggish. I could almost hear it creaking as I thought. "Oqira," I realized at last. A rush of excitement briefly woke me up. "Master Varrick, will you get to see your family?"

"Perhaps," he said, blinking. "But we will need to move quickly, and quietly. If my theories are correct, there are only a few remaining crystals out there. Once she has them all, she'll continue trying to find you, and we can't let any word get back to her. Which means..." He hesitated. "Ayve, you won't be able to use your magic for a time. Not until we're far enough away. One trace of your spells and Zai will know where we've gone. I know it's asking a lot for you to come with me to a far-off land without any magic to protect yourself, but I promise I mean you no harm," he implored.

"I will protect you if only you'll trust me. Do you? Trust me? Will you leave with me, to stop a great evil from setting root in our kingdom? In our home?"

Home. I thought about home. It had changed a lot in the past year, from sweeping floors and watching Joseth to tumbling with Naliah and laughing with Val. Home was eating strawberries with Rebekah, drinking ale with Kessa, and even, I remembered, kissing Stevan.

Was I willing to risk saying goodbye to it all in the hopes of saving it? If I wasn't, what would become of my friends if Zai's powers continued to grow? What would become of me? I thought of how many times I had touched the crystal and shuddered as I envisioned my mother's descent into madness.

"Ayve?" Varrick looked at me expectantly.

My heart began to pound. I knew which choice I had to make.

Acknowledgments

For a story I started in 8th grade, it sure took a long time to get here. The list of gratitudes could go on forever, but for starters:

To Elyse, Catherine, and Amy, the drafts I made you read weren't good, but you generously gave gracious feedback anyway (even if I didn't remember and had to ask you before writing the acknowledgements page... sorry, Amy!). Thank you for not laughing at my dreams.

To my family, oops, sorry, I wrote a trilogy and forgot to tell you that I was doing a Big Thing again. Thanks for going with the flow?

To my partner, thank you for letting me steal your last name. Hey, how do you feel about two cats?

About the Author

Erin Dawn Allen has lived in Pennsylvania, New York, Arizona, and Washington state. Now a New Hampshire resident, she is a middle school teacher in eastern Vermont. When not convincing preteens that reading and writing is fun, Erin enjoys gardening, sewing, running, and CrossFit. She and her partner are happily childfree and cater to the every whim of their very spoiled cats, Pippin and Merry. You can find her on Instagram @erindawnallen.

Thanks for reading! Please add a short review on Amazon to let me know what you think.

DON'T MISS
THE SORCERESS OF
STARS TRILOGY
BOOK 2:
THE CRYSTAL IN
THE FOREST

THE DREAM STARTED the same way it always did: Long corridors stretched out in never-ending rows as she raced wildly through the palace. Door after door slipped by in a dark blur. It was late, and the few torches that were still lit sent up plumes of dingy soot. Some part of her knew this must be a memory. The palace had long since switched over to spelled lightglobes to reduce the choking smoke. But that meant she knew what was coming, and the woman ran forward with panicked urgency Maybe this time she could change the outcome. If she was lucky...